Secret Santa

Sophie Jomain

Illustrated by Manon Bucciarelli

AUZOU
CANADA

Welcome!

Open **a sealed chapter** every day to discover the next instalment in a love story that will take you right to Christmas Day. Make sure you have a letter opener and some hot chocolate by your side!

Happy reading!

1
December

"The sociologist breaks the enchanted circle by trying to make known what the world of knowledge does not want to know, especially about itself."

If there's any circle to be broken, it's the one where I go to classes so boring they make me wish I was still in bed. I fight to hold back an enormous, jaw-dislocating yawn.

"Can anyone tell me what this sentence means?" asks our sociology professor.

Not one student in the lecture hall ventures a reply. But then the professor's probably struggling to take us seriously anyway. There are about a hundred and eighty students, and over half are wearing a Santa hat or a Christmas sweater or headband. It starts every year on December 1st. And on the last day before the vacation, some even dress up as Santa (or Mrs.) Claus.

"Anyone?" he says again.

Nope, it doesn't look like it…

I lean towards Ines. Out of the two of us, she's the one with brains. "Go on!"

"Oh, sure!" Ines whispers. "As we all know, I've memorized every single book this guy's ever written!"

We both snicker.

It's eleven o'clock, and the lecture is over. There's no mistaking it; everyone is putting away their stuff. But the professor stops us in our tracks with a screech of the microphone. I should have guessed – until we leave the lecture hall, anything is possible.

"Because you all seem so fascinated by him, I want you to get into pairs and write a complete biography of Pierre Bourdieu, as well as an essay on the critical import of his research. You have until next Thursday to hand it in; that gives you seven days. Good luck."

A collective sigh goes up. There are only ten days until our end-of-semester exams; we're screwed.

I close my notebook, put it in my bag and turn to look at Ines. Pigs may be about to start sprouting wings with what I'm going to say.

"Do you want us to get working on it now?"

Even Ines is surprised. "You're kidding, right?"

"Nope. Why don't we grab a quick sandwich and go to the library? I bet we won't be the only ones there," I say. "Come on, it'll be fun. But more importantly, the sooner we get it done, the sooner we'll be free to have fun!"

"Annette Reynaud, you're a poet…"

"And don't you forget it!" I laugh.

I look up to see a guy weaving through the seats with a determined look on his face, aiming right for Ines. It's almost funny; he's actually pushing people out of the way.

"Red alert! Sleazeball at three o'clock!"

Ines doesn't look around, but I can feel her tense up. "A guy with brown hair and glasses?"

"That's the one."

"Oh, shit, not him. Hurry up, let's go."

Unfortunately, he's quicker than we are.

"Hi," he says to Ines hesitantly. "We've never spoken before, but since last year we've been in all the same classes."

She just nods.

"Um… are you doing anything right now?"

Bam, he just comes straight out with it. I mean, why bother wasting time? But you don't need a degree to see that my friend is annoyed.

Ines is the kind of girl that turns heads. Medium height, sporty, dark skin from her dad's Berber ancestors, light green eyes from her French-Irish mom and long, brown hair that falls into gorgeous soft curls. Every time I look at her, it bums me out. I'm the total opposite – too tall, too skinny, with straight blond hair and skin as white as a sheet of paper. Oh, and don't forget the freckles.

"Yeah, I'm just off to start the assignment with my partner," Ines replies distantly to the guy, who can't stop gawking. "Sorry, I have to go."

She doesn't say bye, just grabs her stuff and gestures to me to follow her. This is the thirty-seventh time since the start of the year that someone's tried to hook up with her. I think she's sick of it.

I give the would-be admirer an embarrassed smile and join my friend. "Are you all right?"

"Yeah. I noticed him staring at me during the lecture. It really gets on my nerves. Do I have a sign on my forehead saying: 'Give it a go, she might say yes'?"

"Why don't you try and be a bit uglier?" I joke.

"Sure, I'll do my best!" she grins. "Hey, speaking of ugly, look who's here..."

I raise my head and see a guy walking in my direction, a movie-star smile on his lips. It's Gavin, my boyfriend. He walks with a laid-back air, running a hand through his thick blond hair as he stops in front of me with a look that would charm the pants off anyone.

"How're you doing, angelface?" he asks as he takes me in his arms and kisses me on the neck.

As he lets go, I see Ines making a face. She hates that nickname.

So do I, but it was either that or 'babydoll,' so...

"What are you doing here?" I ask him.

"Someone told me they saw the prettiest girl on campus in this hall, and I had a free moment, so I came to see if it was true."

"And?"

"They weren't lying, so I've come to invite you to lunch."

I turn to Ines who remains unmoved, totally immune to Gavin's charm offensive.

"Go if you want, I'm going to the library to start the assignment," she says. "You can come and join me afterwards."

"You're sure you don't mind? You don't want to come with us?"

"No, no, I'm working this afternoon at the school, so I want to try and get ahead with the Bourdieu thing now. Go on, we'll catch up once you're done."

"Are you still teaching those little kids at the after-school centre?" interrupts Gavin in a disparaging tone. "Are you not done with that yet?"

"Yes, but you know how it is, we can't all rely on Mommy and Daddy to pay for everything. Some of us have to make our own way through life. See ya," she finishes curtly.

Gavin raises an eyebrow as he watches her leave. "Is she mad at you?"

"At me? No, she was speaking to you."

And she was brusque for a reason: Gavin dropped out of university six months ago after his second year ended. Since then, he's just been playing around. He goes on trips to Belgium, the Netherlands or England, he goes out on the town whenever he wants, and his parents pay for everything. He has it so easy, and he doesn't even realize it.

Gavin starts laughing.

"You think she was talking about me, angelface, but your parents have money too. Way more than mine!"

"That might be true, but I'm not the one who's always so cocky."

His smile grows. "I know, that's why you love me!"

Yeah, whatever…

He narrows his eyes and looks at Ines, who's disappearing around the corner of the street. "She's a real killjoy that one. She's always such a drag."

I frown. "No, she's just being honest. Her parents can't afford to pay for everything, and so she has to work part-time."

"You love to play the good Samaritan, don't you."

"Are you serious? No, I don't!"

Which makes him laugh. "You want to know what I think? You shouldn't be a sociologist, you should be a social worker. If you're so worried about her, why don't you just send her some money."

Which would be a sure-fire way to get into a fight with Ines. She would hate it.

"Come on, let's get something to eat," he says to close the discussion. "And then you can go and join her afterwards, since you seem to really want to."

"Actually, I think I'm going to *play* the good Samaritan and not leave my friend in the lurch."

"Ohhh, did I offend you?"

I pout, so he pulls me in and kisses me on the neck.

"It was just a joke, angelface! OK, let's compromise. There's a snack bar over there. We can get a sub and then you can go?"

"That's not being a good friend, Gavin."

"But you wanted to come, and she said it didn't bother her."

"She only said that because she was being nice."

He pulls away with a sigh. "I'll never understand…"

"Understand what? Me?" I ask with a wink.

"Yeah. And also why you bother going to university when you don't even like it. You have tonnes of money. You don't have to."

We've had this conversation a hundred times already. If only I knew the answer…

Gavin and I come from the same world, and when he was still a student, we led exactly the same life. We went out all the time or went away for the weekend wherever we wanted, and money was never a problem. But now, somehow, we've gotten out of sync, and I can't seem to keep up. Nothing seems to interest me these days.

I'm still silent, so he smiles. "Fine, you win. I'll leave you in Grumpy's capable hands."

He leans over and gives me a kiss. "But I'll see you tonight, OK? At your place?"

"Yes, of course!"

I give him a final peck on the cheek before we go our separate ways. I hoist my bag onto my shoulder and go join Ines at the library. I must really be a glutton for punishment…

When I get there, Ines is sitting at a two-person desk, and she has her computer out. I look around and can't see anyone from our year. We truly are the only ones to have thought of this. Ouch.

Ines looks up in surprise. "Already?"

I put my stuff on the table and settle in opposite her. "I felt a bit guilty for leaving you on your own."

"Gavin is so irresistible, I totally would have understood."

Her edge of sarcasm doesn't go unnoticed.

"You really don't like him, do you?"

"The main thing is that you like him."

I don't say a thing. She frowns. "You do love him, right?"

"Yes, of course," I reply. "So, what have you found? Did Bourdieu lead a fascinating life?"

Ines sighs. "In one hour, I'll know all his deepest secrets, just wait and see."

"Shhh!" says a voice next to us.

We turn around to discover a guy with brown, curly hair that is so messy it looks like he slept here overnight. And that's nothing compared to his beard! In front of him there are open books with lots of formulas, tables and DNA sequences. I lean towards Ines and whisper, "Another med student. Those guys take sleep as an optional course."

She giggles. "Did you know that when I started applying to universities, my parents wanted me to do Health Sciences?"

"Really? So you could go on to med school?"

"I know! Even the thought of a needle makes me want to faint!"

"Shhh!" says the student, a bit louder this time.

Ines lifts a hand in apology.

A total wet blanket. I almost roll my eyes at him.

Ines pushes a huge, open book over to me. "Come on, lazybones, don't think I'll be doing it all."

I sigh and give in.

The med student looks up and our gazes cross.

He has the bluest eyes I've ever seen.

When I leave the university at 5 pm, the metro is jam-packed, but the ride to Lille-Flandres only takes ten minutes. On the way, the atmosphere changes completely. The austere campus gives way to the kind of city centre I'd never seen before coming here. Houses with gables, red-brick buildings, and modern Baroque monuments and neoclassical architecture. The first time I visited, my eyes didn't know where to settle. There's something interesting no matter where you turn.

Lille is a beautiful city. It's so welcoming.

It's absolutely freezing, and it's getting dark, but the streets are alive with people. It's always like that here, in summer and winter; and in December, every street corner just screams Christmas. There's a fifty-metre-high Ferris wheel on the Grand-Place decked in lights, cozy blankets are waiting for those who want to sit outside, the Christmas tree is all lit up opposite the La Voix du Nord building, the headquarters of our local newspaper, and the wooden chalets for the Christmas market on the Place Rihour are a constant reminder to start your Christmas shopping list.

As always, I am incapable of going home with empty hands. I start off just wandering through the streets, but inevitably I end up buying something. Yesterday it was a giant Christmas bauble and today a paper garland to put in my bedroom. Tomorrow? No idea, but I'm sure I'll find something.

I get home at 6 pm. The apartment I share with Ines isn't far from the Notre-Dame-de-la-Treille Cathedral; it's on the fourth floor of a brick building.

Our apartment is cool, with its hardwood floors, decorative ceiling mouldings and large windows. We each have our own bedroom, and we share a small kitchen and a big living room. My parents bought it when we knew I'd be studying in Lille, but because I didn't want to live on my own, we put out an ad for a housemate. Ines answered, and she turned out to be the best housemate ever.

When she first moved in, I didn't want her to pay rent – my parents and I really don't need it, but hers insisted, and so did she. The Abads don't want to owe anything to anyone. That's also why she has a part-time job, so she doesn't have to justify her purchases or outings to her parents. On that count, I have to admit I live in a different world. I've never had to think about things the way she does because I've never had to worry about money. It's as simple as that.

My parents aren't just rich… they have mountains of money. They could buy a super yacht if they wanted, but they've always hated showing off their wealth.

Their generosity towards me is unlimited, as is my bank account. That's one advantage of being an only child.

People often imagine that this kind of life is incredible – and it is, there's no denying it – but being an ultra-rich student has its own price. Unlike Gavin's parents, who inherited their fortune, mine earned theirs on their own, bit by bit. So they expect me to get the best grades at the best school, to have an amazing career and follow the same path as them, the whole shebang.

The pressure is intense.

My parents would never leave me hanging high and dry, but I always have to prove to them that I'm on solid ground. And I have to admit that right now I'm not standing on much at all. My only companions are unanswerable questions.

I frown and look at my watch. There's not much time left until Gavin arrives. I decide to take a long bath to get rid of the little grey cloud above my head.

The bathroom here is huge. There are shelves and mirrors on each of the four walls, candles everywhere and a Bluetooth speaker that I had installed as soon as I moved in. Gavin complains every time he has a shower in here, saying that if he stays in for too long, he'll turn into a Disney princess.

I'm about to get in the bathtub when I get a message from him.

Sorry angelface I can't come over tonight, Dad needs me. Is it OK if we catch up tomorrow instead?

Ah… OK.

Are you upset babe?

It's fine, don't worry.

OK, cool! Sorry, I'd better go. See you tomorrow. 😘

😘

I slide into the water feeling kind of indifferent. Tonight won't be the right time for relaxing anyway. Knowing my luck, Ines is going to want to work on the Bourdieu assignment or, even worse, study for our end-of-semester exams that are only ten days away.

Living with Ines means that studying is the one thing I can't avoid.

Apart from two electives, we're taking exactly the same classes. Except that unlike me, she didn't choose to major in sociology because she didn't know what else to do. I chose it by default, and now I feel like I'm drifting somehow.

The reason I wanted to go to university is that I've spent my whole life travelling around the world with my parents, and we never stayed more than two years in one place. Up until last year we were in Canada, so the deal was that when I finished secondary school and we came back to France, we wouldn't move while I was studying. I want to feel settled, to start a new life, to be a bit more normal, I guess. My parents understood. They moved to a place just out of Aix-en-Provence, where I was born, and I've ended up in Lille, studying sociology, propelled into the life of your average student.

But as time goes by, I'm wondering if I might have messed up. And I'm not even sure that it's because of the classes I chose. I'm starting to feel totally lost, and I don't know what to do with my life. That's how I feel all the time, adrift without any sense of direction.

Not one day goes by without me thinking about it, not one evening without going to bed feeling like I've taken the wrong path, but without knowing which direction to choose instead. Should I speak to my parents? I know they'll be disappointed, and I just can't bear the thought of that.

But what about me?

I stare up at the ceiling and sigh. No point imagining I'll find the answer up there. But the more I look at it, the more I think.

What if I just threw it all away?

No.

Yes.

Argh!

I pinch my nose and sink my head under the water, trying to turn my thoughts off.

Blurp.

2
December

“Annette Reynaud?”

I put my hand up, but I don’t like the tone of my professor’s voice…

“Seven out of twenty. Your research wasn’t sufficiently in-depth, the introduction is unimaginative, the arguments are unclear and disorganised, and the conclusion is lacklustre. At this rate, your end-of-semester exams are not looking good.”

The economics professor puts my essay down in front of me with a dismayed look and moves on to the next person.

What a great start to the day.

“It’ll be fine,” Ines whispers to me. “I’ll help you.”

She didn’t get a perfect score, but almost. Obviously.

I’m just going to tell her I didn’t study at all. It’s easier.

“Not at all?” she replies.

I shake my head.

The professor looks at us out of the corner of his eye, so we fall silent.

Ines puts her hand on my arm. She’s trying to be reassuring, but all I want to do is scream. I just don’t want to be here.

The rest of the lecture is torture. I know I should be paying attention and trying to catch up, but all I can think about is how I'm failing.

I need to get out of here.

"Annie, are you all right?" asks Ines when we leave the room.

It's midday. We have barely an hour for lunch, but what I really need is a whole year to work out where I'm at and what I want to do with myself.

"I guess so."

"Hey," says Ines. "It was just a practice essay, it's not serious."

"A practice essay I failed, just like I'll fail the real thing."

She stops in the middle of the corridor and looks me straight in the eye. "Why would you say that? I know you don't like some of your classes and that it's not all easy, but I also know that you're super brainy."

"I'm so unmotivated."

She smiles at me, for want of a better alternative. "That happens to everyone. But I'm here for you, OK?"

Ines is a great friend. I know she's trying to reassure me, but this time she's on the wrong track: the last thing I care about is failing my exams. The problem is way more complicated… What I really want is to feel good again. And at this point, I couldn't feel worse. I just don't know what to do to change things.

I smile at Ines. "Thanks, friend. Look, it's the weekend tomorrow, so I'm not going to force things. If I skip today's classes, would you mind lending me your notes? I really need some time off."

"No, of course not. Take a break. I'm going out with some of the other tutors tonight, so I might get back late, but how about we talk things through tomorrow?"

I nod.

"And don't worry, Annie, we'll study together, and it'll be fine. There's plenty in there!" she adds with a grin, pointing to my head. "You just need to believe in yourself a bit more. Anyway, I'd better go, I'm going to be late for my next class. Mwah!"

I watch her disappear down the corridor, as elegant as a ballerina going on stage.

Believe in myself… But what am I meant to believe in?

If only I knew.

I leave the campus with my heels dragging. What's happening to me? I was the one who wanted to come here. I had imagined my new life, free to do whatever I wanted. I had never been sure if I had chosen the right major, but I had thought I'd get into it. At the beginning I was so happy to be settled in one place and have at least five years ahead of me to build something. Last year, everything was new, and I convinced myself it would be fine. But the more time has gone by, the more I realize that nothing is turning out like I thought it would. Nothing in my life feels familiar.

But I can't even identify what's missing.

It's like I can't seem to set myself an objective.

It starts to rain, so I run to the metro, only to discover that it's out of service and they don't know how long for.

Fantastic.

It's too far to walk home, there are no cafés nearby, and the last thing I want to do is wait around in the cold. All I'm craving is a bit of peace and quiet. I don't really want to go, but the library is right next door, and at least I'll be able to keep warm until it stops raining.

Just as I arrive, the skies open up, and I walk in half drenched. There's a librarian hanging up Christmas decorations in the hall. You should see the way he's looking at me, just because of a few raindrops on the floor.

Does he think that I'm doing it on purpose?

I give a forced smile and head to a desk; the same one Ines and I were at yesterday.

I get out my books so at least it looks as if I'm studying, then raise my eyes. The med student is still there. Now that's what you call single-minded.

Our eyes meet, and again, I can't get over how blue they are.

And look at his skin. I bet you he goes to a tanning salon! Shiny, curly hair, dark eyebrows and… oh! He has a tiny scar on his cheek. I'm staring so he gives me a strange look. I reply with a polite smile.

He runs a hand through his hair and nods before returning to his books. Woah! He is dedicated, but hot! I can almost hear myself sigh.

I can't help it; while he's concentrating on his DNA sequences, I realize I'm studying him just as intently.

He has a worry wrinkle across his forehead. He's reading, taking notes, crossing things out on his pad, looking for information in his books. Everything I should be doing, instead of running things over and over in my mind.

What must I look like? A girl who's completely lost? Yup.

Elbows on the desk, I close my eyes and sigh, squeezing the bridge of my nose. I feel so apathetic and upset by the situation that I almost want to cry.

"Are you OK?"

I look up with slightly damp eyes: the med student has gotten up and is quietly walking towards me. I can't help eyeing him up. The sleeves of his sweater are a bit short for him and his jeans are fraying at the pockets. This guy is a giant!

"Are you all right?" he says again.

"Um… yeah, sorry. I'm just a bit tired."

"Have you tried sleeping? I've heard it can help."

A sense of humour!

"I bet that's something you know all about, you're looking super fresh yourself," I say weakly.

He gives me a lopsided smile and looks at my bag sitting on the desk.

"What are you studying?"

"Second-year sociology. And you're doing medicine?"

"Second year."

The med school campus is about ten kilometres away, and its library specializes in health sciences. I wonder what he's doing here.

"Are you lost? This place doesn't really deal in your subject matter."

He gives me a bigger smile.

Wow. I didn't know that teeth that white even existed.

"There's a snack bar not far away where I work during lunchtime. When I have time, I come and do a bit of studying here."

"Do you have exams soon?"

"In ten days."

I give him a grim smile that probably shows just how tense I am.

"Same. And I haven't even started studying yet."

"Oh, right."

Another tight smile.

"I was just going to get a coffee at the machine, do you want to come?"

An opportunity to avoid more studying? I take it eagerly.

"OK!"

I practically leap up from my chair. And yes, I can confirm he is huge! He's a good head taller than me, even though I'm 5'9 myself.

"I'm Romeo," he says, introducing himself.

"And I'm Ann…"

I come to a stop as I realize what my name sounds like. I've never met someone with a name as unique as mine. All my life people have been amused by the classical undertones of my name, and I guess Romeo must have faced the same thing.

"Yes?"

"Um… Annette, but everyone calls me Annie."

He looks at me, taken aback, and I give a snort of laughter, making a nearby librarian who is shelving books look over at me with a scowl.

"Shhh!"

Oops.

"Romeo and Annette," he says with a laugh.

"This is the first time I've ever met a Romeo."

"I've never met a Annette either."

I smile at him as we reach the coffee machine and pull out a euro coin from my pocket, one that miraculously made it through the wash. I never usually have a cent on me.

But Romeo is quicker; he already has his finger on the button.

"Coffee, hot chocolate, tea? Sugar? Milk?"

"A latte with no sugar."

He pushes the buttons, the paper cup falls with a thud, and the liquid starts to flow.

"Annette. Where does that name come from?"

"It's French, but to me it sounds like such an old person's name."

"I like it!" he says. "It's original."

"Hmm… And what about you, Romeo! Wherefore art thou called Romeo?"

He raises an eyebrow.

"Ha, ha. First time I've heard that one."

"Sorry…"

"But wait, you haven't even heard my last name yet."

"Which is?"

"Payet."

I blink.

"Pay it, like pay it forward?"

He rolls his eyes.

"No, like the football player."

Ah ha.

"You don't know him?"

I shake my head.

We look at each other – me, wondering whether his name is totally fake, and him, thinking I'm totally uneducated.

He gets himself a coffee and motions for me to follow him into the foyer, where we sit down on a couple of imitation leather armchairs.

In just thirty minutes, Christmas has suddenly come to life around us. There's a Christmas tree with cute little flashing lights. A tiny Santa Claus is sitting on the reception desk, with a few velvet reindeer to keep him company. There's even a sparkly mushroom amongst them, which I don't get at all.

"People get in the spirit of things early here," says Romeo.

"For the Christmas decorations, you mean?"

"Yeah. On Réunion Island, where I come from, we don't start so soon."

"Oh! I went there once with my parents, I loved it! It wasn't Christmas, but it was just so beautiful! The Indian Ocean, the tamarind forests, the mountains… I'm sure you know all that already, but I have such great memories of it."

"For me, it's the North of France that's going to leave me with great memories. Even the rain has a certain charm!"

he says, pointing out the glass door. “And where do you come from?”

“From all over the place! I was born in Aix-en-Provence, but my parents and I moved around a lot. I’ve lived in a quite a few places.”

“Was Lille your first choice?”

I nod in assent.

“And you?”

“I applied for Paris, but it’s quieter here.”

He gets up and throws his empty cup in the trash.

“I’d better get back to it. I start work in the snack bar at half past noon, and then I have class straight after. But it was cool to have a break.”

“Totally!”

Just so he doesn’t think I’m following him, I let him go back into the library and quietly finish my coffee. He actually ended up being quite nice!

It’s 11:00. The metro should be working again now. I’m about to return to my desk and get my stuff when my telephone vibrates. It’s a message from Gavin.

Hi angelface!
I’m trying again for another lunch date. Are you free?

Hey, yup nothing planned for this afternoon. I’m at the HSS library.

OK! I'll come and get you in
an hour, OK?

Perfect XX

So, that works out well!

I have an hour to kill. There are two options: either I grab a manga, or I start work on the assignment so Ines has less to do. Even though I really don't want to.

Ines wins the day. It'll just be for an hour, then I can have fun with Gavin and try not to think about anything serious.

I throw away my empty cup and return to my desk, sneaking a glance at Romeo as I go past. He's deep in concentration and doesn't even notice me walk past him.

Gavin sends me a message at 11:30 to tell me he's double-parked in a street not far from the library. I quickly gather my stuff together. Romeo is no longer at his desk, but his bag and coat are there, so I guess he's gone to the bathroom. I'm tempted to write him a note to say goodbye, but that might be a bit weird. I wrap my scarf around my neck and head off to find Gavin.

He's waiting for me in his car, a black Audi e-tron. He's so proud of it; it's ultramodern and fully electric. But E-tron is a terrible name for the French market, all the more so if you don't pronounce it with an English accent.* I once told Gavin he had a shitty car, but he didn't seem to find it funny. I didn't keep the joke going, especially as I don't even have my driver's license.

"Hi! Phew, that was lucky, it's stopped raining."

I lean over and give him a kiss. He smells nice, and he looks like he's just been to the hairdresser. Gavin could easily have been a fashion model. He cultivates a certain style, and although it might be a bit superficial, it sure looks good.

"What do you feel like eating?"

"A hamburger! With loads of fries and no salad!"

He cracks up.

"My girlfriend is a guy!"

"Hmm, you never know!"

"I do, actually," he says with a mischievous wink.

He kisses me again without realizing that the car is rolling backwards, until we hear a bang.

"Hey!" yells a guy behind us.

I get out at the same time as Gavin to see if everything is all right, only to discover Romeo, who, hit by the car and unbalanced by the weight of his backpack, has fallen backwards onto the sidewalk. Bundled up in a navy-blue duffel coat and a beanie, he's finding it hard to get up.

"Are you OK?" I ask, as I give him a hand.

"Yes, I'm fine," he says, standing up, "Scared the crap out of me, but no harm done."

---

* TN: 'Étron' in French means turd.

Instead of making sure no one was injured, Gavin rushes to check his car bumper.

"Shit, I hope it's not scratched."

I frown.

"Your car is perfectly fine. But you could have hurt him."

Gavin turns to Romeo and looks at him as if he were a bug.

"Well, I didn't. Next time look where you're going, dude," he says, with that condescending tone that he's so good at.

I can't believe it. "Gavin, he was on the crosswalk!"

"OK, fine. Sorry. Are you OK?"

Romeo's jaw is clenched. I don't even know him, but he looks angry. Which is fair enough.

"I'm fine," he says in a voice that is quiet but sounds like a ticking bomb.

"Sorry," I say, trying to calm things down. "He didn't mean to. Are you sure you're fine?"

"Totally. Bye."

He walks over the crosswalk without a backwards look, but with the air of someone who might just rip out a tree or two on the way to calm himself down. When we get back in the car, I'm upset too, and I turn to Gavin.

"Why are you like that?"

"Like what?"

"Like… that! The poor guy was minding his own business, and you acted like it was his fault. You barely even apologized."

Gavin takes a breath, runs his tongue over his lips and tries to smile. His whole attitude shows he's doing all he can to stay calm.

"It's OK, Annie. It just stressed me out, that's all."

"Because of your car."

"Yes, because of my car. Right, why don't we go to Mouscron* to get your burger and fries?" he asks, as if nothing had happened. "It'll only take us half an hour."

I nod without saying a word. I keep thinking of Romeo and the look on his face as he left.

I don't smile the whole way there.

I hate what just happened.

* TN: Mouscron is a town in Belgium, just thirty minutes' drive north of Lille.

3
December

For a typical student, the weekend involves studying or chilling out. Ines is planning to study, but I'm thinking more about chilling.

Between the two of us, you'd think we strike the perfect balance, but things are actually getting out of hand. There are fewer than ten days until exams, and the little motivation I had seems to have disappeared. After breakfast, I tried opening a couple of books, reading over my notes and listening to a YouTube podcast recorded by one of my professors. I lasted for twenty minutes then found all sorts of excuses to distract me: housework, tidying, even trying to make cinnamon Christmas cookies.

Big fail.

I'm not what you'd call skilled at manual labour, and cooking is perhaps the worst of my talents. For all the years I spent with my parents, we mostly ate out in restaurants rather than at home. I can even burn pasta in its cooking water, if that gives you an idea…

In the end, I end up doing what I've lately become best at: absolutely nothing. I curl up on the couch with my phone and start scrolling through moronic TikTok videos.

"You're not studying?" asks Ines as she joins me in the living room with an empty mug.

"No… Hey, it's stopped raining, you want to go into town for a bit?"

She frowns. "I can't, I really have to study."

I pout.

She heaves a great sigh.

"Come on," she says, sitting down next to me. "Are you going to tell me what's really wrong?"

I shrug. "Nothing new. I'm just sick of it all."

"It's that bad?"

"Yup…"

She looks at me, and I can tell she really does feel sorry for me. "What can I do?"

I don't even know how to reply to that.

"Are things OK with Gavin?" she asks carefully.

"Yeah, totally. It's just… I don't know. I can't seem to find meaning in what I'm doing."

"You want to change your major?"

"I'm not even sure. Mom started out from nowhere and has built a multinational business, and Dad worked his butt off to open his lawyer's office, and now it's one of the most respected in Europe. They're so successful at whatever they do. But I don't have a single project or even a general goal. At least when we were travelling around the world, all I had to do was follow. Now I feel so lost. It's like I'm the black sheep in the family."

"Hey… you don't think you're just a bit worn out?"

I shrug my shoulders; I'm not even capable of holding a discussion. But I know this is more than just tiredness.

Ines suddenly gets up, a big smile on her face.
"You know what? I have a foolproof idea."
"Foolproof?"
"Yup. Come on, it's time to move your ass!"

Ines leads me to the ice-skating rink. And not the big one at Wasquehal where the Lille ice-hockey team trains. Instead, she takes me to the one for little kids, the one they've set up in the Palais de la Bourse while the Christmas market is on. And obviously, since it's Saturday afternoon, we're not the only ones there. We're surrounded by dozens of moms and dads, with what seems like hundreds of little kids zooming round like they were born on skates. And here I am, desperately hanging on to the guardrail. In my defence, I'm about as talented with my feet as I am with my hands.

"Come on!" yells Ines as she slides gracefully towards me.

"My legs were made for walking, not for waddling on the ice like a penguin! I bet you I'm going to break one of them!"

"You didn't go skating when you were in Canada with your parents?"

"Nope, I'm not crazy! And have you seen what you're sliding around on? It's not even ice! It's like cooking oil. What do you think I am, a French fry? Hey! I can see you rolling your eyes!"

She giggles. "Come on!"

"No, I'd rather admire the surroundings."

Because at least that's worth the effort: above our heads there's a huge glass dome. And all around we're surrounded by beautiful woodwork, and frescoes, and arches, and to top it all off, a gigantic disco ball reflecting flashes of light onto the walls. It looks gorgeous, but I have zero trust in those things. I've heard about them suddenly crashing down and squashing whoever's underneath.

Well, it's not going to be me!

Ines joins me again, digs her hand into her coat and pulls out a Santa hat that she squashes onto my head.

"Where did you get that?"

"Over there," she says, pointing to one of the stands at the edge of the rink. "Alright, enough of this. This time you're coming with me."

And without warning, she pulls me by the arm, making me cry out in surprise. Even going backwards she's far better than me. And then she lets go.

Jeez.

"Where did you learn to skate?"

"The biggest rink in France is in Cergy. My brother and I used to go all the time. Come on, just copy me!"

There she is, breaking down all her movements and looking around, while I can't tear my gaze away from my feet. I'm terrified one of these little sprogs is going to cut me off. And… sure enough, it happens!

I lose my balance, my arms swinging like windmills to try and keep me upright, but in the end, I fall over spectacularly and land on my butt, my legs splayed out.

"Ha ha ha!" laughs Ines. "You're about as elegant as a football player!"

A football player. Not them again...

And suddenly, a hand stretches out in front of me. I look up before grabbing it and see my economics professor. The two kids next to him are looking at me pityingly.

Shame!

"So, Miss Reynaud, I see your studying's going well?"

I accept his help and get up as best I can. "Thank you, sir."

"I guess you needed some fresh air to keep your brain from losing all that hard-earned information?"

Honestly, how am I meant to reply to that?

I glance at Ines, but she's looking away, the traitor.

Cue the embarrassed smile...

"Um... yes, that's it!"

"Well, don't spend too long here," he says. "Exams aren't far away."

I nod. Could he be any more demoralizing?

"No peace and quiet anywhere," laughs Ines. "Come on, cheer up. Let's go and have a Christmas beer."

"Yeah, better that than cooking oil. Shall we get a waffle as well?" I suggest.

"How about two?"

We rush outside and line up at one of the stands in the Christmas market, then, with beer and waffle in hand, we decide to go and sit down at the edge of the fountain, just under thc brightly lit Ferris wheel.

Christmas is such a big deal here! It's kind of like being in Disneyland. There are twinkling lights everywhere, chalets covered in artificial snow, music in the streets, the smell of roasted chestnuts, a fake Santa Claus under the giant Christmas tree and a tonne of children lining up to get their photo taken with him. And the amazing Ferris wheel. I haven't been on it yet, but I bet there's an incredible view of the city from the top.

As we reach the fountain, we see Julie, Djamel and Ben, three students in our year. We don't know each other all that well, but we've already been out for a few drinks together. Because we're not totally uncivilized, we sit down next to them for a chat.

In the beginning it's fun. They're in the Christmas spirit and talk about all sorts of different things, but eventually they can't help themselves, they start talking about their classes and exams. They go over the whole semester, compare different ways of studying, discuss their fear of failing…

I look at my nearly empty glass and wonder whether I shouldn't go and get another. Gavin always says that if you want to switch off, you shouldn't hang out with your classmates.

He is so right.

"And what about you?" Julie asks Ines.

"Um, I have lots of things on the go. This morning, I sat through economic anthropology.

Mancur Olson, Polanyi…"

"And Godelier!" adds one of the guys.

Oh man, kill me now. This is not what I went out for. I clear my throat.

"Hey guys, do you want to go play pool or get a beer somewhere and some tapas? My treat! I'm starving!"

They all look at me as if I just said the stupidest thing they ever heard.

"That's a nice offer," says Julie, "but I'd better get back to my studying."

"Same," add the two others.

Are they for real?

"Oh, come on, relax. It'll just be for an hour."

"Yeah, nah. It's not really the right moment," says one of the guys.

And the others all copy him, of course. It's like I'm scaring them away.

Ines gets a strained look on her face; she almost feels sorry for me.

But actually, they're totally right, and I'm the one who's deluded. So I resign myself to the fact there won't be any tapas and look at them as they head off.

Sucks to be me. Really sucks.

"So, now you're going to do some studying too, right?" says Ines, grabbing my arm. "Because our little break is over. And you know, you can't always pay for everyone, especially if it's just to avoid studying!"

"Why not, if I can afford to?"

"That's not an excuse! And we're not on vacation yet. Got it?"

"Yes, Mom!"

She laughs and pulls me along with her, through the square packed with people.

Given the state of my motivation, I really need to give myself a kick up the ass. Ines has shut herself in her room, and I'm in mine, but after barely thirty minutes there are notes scattered all over my bed, surrounding me as I lie there, staring up at the ceiling. I read out loud, in my head, but can't seem to retain anything. It's pathetic. There's no point in bothering. I try to study, but it's as if the lines blur in front of my eyes and turn into incomprehensible gibberish.

Finally, I get up to make myself a mug of tea and walk past the closed door to Ines's bedroom. I sigh. She'll be fine, that's for sure. She's doing everything she can to make sure of it. But I don't believe in miracles. I'm definitely going to fail. Without a shadow of a doubt.

I'm about to return to my room with a mug in one hand and a packet of cookies in the other, when my phone starts ringing.

It's Mom. Time for the video call we have every Saturday.

I take a deep breath before picking up and get ready to put on a strong, bright voice. I quickly do my hair and sit cross-legged on my bed.

The screen lights up and I see my mother, with her blue eyes, long blond hair and gorgeous smile. She's in her office, dressed to the nines. She doesn't have a hair out of place, and her collar is starched and perfectly ironed. I bet she spends all day on video calls.

"Hi, Mom."

"Hi, darling. How're you?"

"Fine. Studying hard," I say, showing her my bed covered in notes. "And you?"

"I'm just giving you a quick call between two meetings. No rest for the wicked, even on the weekend! Is everything OK?"

I hate lying to my parents, but if I want to avoid any tricky questions, there's nothing else I can do.

"Yeah, great! I've got lots of work to do, but it'll be fine. We don't have classes next week, so I'll be able to study hard then."

Mom's eyes crinkle as she smiles.

"You're looking well."

"Thanks! How's Dad?"

"He'll call you later, right now he's in a meeting with a client."

I smile at her. My parents work non-stop. When we were abroad, they never took more than one day off a week. They would work from home and never really switched off. I know they would be so disappointed to hear that I'm not following in their footsteps.

"Everything still going well with Ines?"

"Yup, no worries on that front."

Mom frowns. She's sharp, really sharp. "And on the other fronts?"

"No, no, Mom, everything's fine."

"I'm glad to hear it!"

I give her the brightest smile I can.

"You know, your father and I are really proud of you," she says suddenly.

"Oh, really?"

"Yes! After all these years following us far and wide, we wondered whether you'd be able to leave the nest and be truly independent. And just look at you! You're managing so well. You're really getting into your classes, and you're working hard. We are so proud of you."

I swallow. It feels like I've got a huge ball stuck in my throat.

"Thank you."

"Oh, and we haven't talked about the Christmas vacation. You'll come home straight after your exams, I suppose? We were wondering about going to New York for New Year's, or even a few days before! Maybe for Christmas. Wouldn't that be fun! We could stay until the 1st. What do you think?"

I smile. My parents and their last-minute ideas. They never change. Two years ago, they whisked my four grandparents away to the Maldives with us for ten days. This year my father, mother and I will be on our own for once. I think Mom's worried we'll get bored.

"Why not?" I answer.

"Well, there's no hurry! Worst case scenario, we can just meet up at Paris-Charles-de-Gaulle.* You have plenty more important things to think about. Speaking of which, I'd better let you go. I don't want to keep you from your studying! I love you loads, darling."

"Me too, Mom. I love you."

Keep me from my studying…

I hang up, my stomach in knots. How can I keep lying like this?

My parents are convinced I'm living my best life, but they're wrong. I suddenly realize how remorseful I feel, but

* TN: This is the name of the main international airport for the city of Paris.

also how paralysed I am by the idea of disappointing them, especially since they have always supported me in everything I've done. What are they going to think if I fail my exams? They won't understand, because I haven't told them how I'm feeling. I've been pretending this whole time, and they'll never see it coming. That would be worse than telling them the truth now.

I press the bridge of my nose and close my eyes.

My heart has never beat so fast.

I pick up my phone again and call Mom. But not with the video this time.

She picks up straight away with a laugh.

"You already miss me?"

"Mom, I… I haven't been entirely honest with you."

There's a small pause.

"What do you mean?"

"Things aren't going so well."

"Are you sick?"

"No…"

"Is it your boyfriend? Did you have a fight?"

"No… Mom, it's that I really don't know where I'm at with my studies."

"Oh, that's normal," she breaks in enthusiastically, before I can say any more. "You're tired. Second year is a big deal, you know. There's way more pressure, and so many changes, too. You have to work much harder, and sometimes we don't always have enough energy to give."

"Mom, it's more than just being tired, I think."

I can hear her sigh, but is she truly listening to me?

"You know what. Why don't you take Sunday off and just do whatever you want? Run a hot bath, watch a film, eat all the candy or ice cream you want – anything that makes you feel good. Don't let yourself brood over things and on Monday you'll feel so much better, you'll see. And anyway, it's almost time for your vacations!"

"Mom…"

"You know, I went through periods like that too, when I was your age. I would get so fed up, and whenever exams came round, I always wanted everything to stop, so I could curl up in a ball and hibernate for a year. What you're going through is perfectly normal."

I hold my breath.

"Annette, are you still there?"

"Yes, Mom."

"So, what do you think?"

Everything feels so muddled, so I try and calm my racing heart. I open my mouth.

"Mom…"

"Yes?"

"I'm dropping out."

Just then, I turn my head and see Ines, standing stock-still in front of my door. She can't believe it.

Me neither.

4
December

Well, that was a horrible night. Never-ending explanations to my mother, and then my father. Doomsday scenarios from Ines, my own doubts. Not to mention Gavin's totally predictable support. He thinks I just made the best decision of my life. Out of all my friends and family, he's the only one to think that.

I went to bed both anxious and relieved. Anxious because my parents are panicking, and I hate that it's because of me. And relieved because it's so good to get everything off my chest.

Now for the million-dollar question: what am I going to do with my life?

If anyone has any ideas, I'm all ears.

As soon as I get up, my feet start to drag. It's like I've got a ball and chain attached to my ankles.

Ugh! I'm not looking forward to today.

Ines is up and she's already been to the bakery to get some croissants. That's not like her. She's busy in the kitchen; I suspect she might already have a cake in the oven. To celebrate my self-proclaimed death warrant? Is that it? Humph.

"I didn't sleep a wink all night because of you," she says, wiping her hands on a dish towel. "You really scared the hell out of me."

Oh, no, not again. I can't handle it.

"Sorry..." I think the tone of my voice lets her know how I'm feeling.

"Hey... I'm not trying to make you feel guilty. I'm just wondering if I've been a good friend to you. I mean, I knew things weren't great, but I didn't think they were that bad."

I give a sigh.

"It's not your fault. I don't even know myself what's happening. Well, actually I do. It's like I have no purpose. I can't seem to think about tomorrow, it feels like it's a million miles away. But the worst thing is I'm so conscious of how easy it's been for me up until now. Not like you. I mean, I don't need to work to get by, I'm not struggling, and I..."

Ines puts up her hand to stop me.

"I'm not judging you, and honestly, I don't like it when you justify yourself because of that. You didn't choose to have all that money, and you don't need to feel bad about it. Rich people have their own struggles too!"

As I sit down, Ines serves me a big cup of milky coffee without sugar. She knows what I like to drink on those mornings when things aren't going so well. She knows me really well.

Then she gives me a butter croissant. Five hundred calories a mouthful.

"How did your parents take it?"

"They're worried, but they're also saying that everyone is allowed to change their mind. But they think I should at least finish this semester."

"You know what? They're right. You'll have the credits and it'll be easier if later on you decide you want to pick it up again."

"Ines, I get that, I do, but I just don't know if I can go through with it."

"But do you at least agree in principle?"

I breathe out and nod. "Yes, but everything seems so…"

"Complicated?"

"Annoying! I can't see where this will take me. I just don't get the point."

"But there is one."

"You're just saying that because you know what you want to do in life." I rip off a piece of croissant and swallow it practically without chewing. I feel so apathetic.

"How did you choose sociology?" asks Ines. "And don't say 'randomly.' It never is."

I think about it for a few seconds, taking my time.

"While we were travelling, I was always fascinated by people in one country compared to another, their different lifestyles, their different expectations, but then how they all ended up wanting the same thing: to feel useful and fulfilled."

"And do you feel useful?"

"Meh. And I definitely *don't* feel fulfilled either. I rest my case."

"So right now, do you want to feel useful?"

I nod. That might make me feel better, yes. Because my classes are definitely not doing it for me.

I need a change of scenery.

"I'll be back in a minute," says Ines as she gets up from the table.

Surprised, I watch her leave. She disappears and reappears with her laptop, a look of excitement in her eyes.

"Here," she says, turning the screen towards me. "I got an email from the Maison des Associations.* The ASEL is looking for volunteers for the month of December to help at the community food market."

I lean closer in interest. "The what?"

Ines reads aloud from her screen. "Association Solidaire Estudiantine Lilloise.** You want to feel useful? Here's your chance! And you know what, history and social psychology are your favourite classes. Maybe you'll find out what you really want to do?"

"But I don't even know what kind of help they're looking for."

"So? I know this is crazy, but they have a telephone number. How about you call them and find out?" she teases me.

"OK…"

"So are you going to call them?"

"Yeah," I concede. "I'm going to go mental if I don't do something."

Ines gives a huge smile. "Great decision!"

---

* TN: The Maison des Associations is a kind of hub that has information on all the different organizations and charities that can be found in the city.

** TN: Stands for 'The Lille Solidarity for Students Association' in French.

The ASEL is on Rue du Chaufour, in the Wazemmes neighbourhood, not far from the Gambetta metro stop. It's bitterly cold today, and the sky is so grey and threatening, you'd swear it was going to snow. I tug my woollen hat down over my ears, pull up the collar of my jacket and walk past the square where people are dismantling their farmer's market stands.

It's Sunday afternoon, but the president of the association wanted to meet me as soon as possible. I think they urgently need extra people to help.

I walk along the paved street and stop in front of an old red-brick building. A big green metal shutter is blocking access to a garage, and on the left, a holly wreath, looking a bit the worse for wear, is hanging above the entrance door. Above me I can see a large bay window covered in Christmas stickers and draped in Christmas lights. I look for some kind of sign, but there's nothing. There is an intercom, however, so I press the button and wait.

"This is Annette Reynaud. I have an appointment."

A woman who looks about forty opens the door. She's blond, petite and very slim, with a beautiful smile.

"Hi! I'm Elise Presle. Come in before you catch a cold! I'll start with a tour, shall I?"

I nod timidly.

"This is our community food market!" she announces proudly as she opens a door. "Everything we sell comes from donations, wholesale markets or leftover stock, with a reduction in cost of up to 90% compared to supermarket prices."

There are wooden shelves everywhere, like in a supermarket, with cleaning products, pasta, biscuits and anything else you might need on a daily basis. And right at the back is an old-style counter with a cash register.

Woah… This place is unreal, and from the outside you'd never guess it was here.

"We open the market twice a week, but we also have an office to support and help students find organizations that can help them in other ways. In addition, we organize various activities for our customers and offer them a safe space, where they know they'll be listened to."

It's all going too fast for me; I can't keep up.

"Um… It seems like you do a bit of everything?"

"Just the basics," she answers, without losing her cheerful manner. "Come on, I'll show you our common room, it's on the second floor."

We go up some stairs that open out into a big room that is full of light, thanks to the bay window that you can see from outside. It has oak floors, exposed beams, and wood panelling everywhere: it's really nice.

"Seventy-five square metres!" she tells me proudly. "This is where we meet up to chat, play cards, do baking workshops, or for theme nights. We want this space to be as welcoming as possible!"

There are couches, armchairs, a flat-screen TV, bookshelves and a big table that can seat at least twenty people. I'm starting to get the idea.

I'm tempted to say it's like a summer camp for university students, but I'm not sure she'd appreciate the joke. I imagine the people who come here have been through tough times, so I decide not to say anything.

"We haven't put up the Christmas decorations yet, but that should happen any day now," she adds. "Shall I show you the third floor? That's where my office is. Watch out, it's an old staircase, the steps get narrow as they go round the corner."

So this is where the serious stuff happens.

We arrive in an open space where two desks are set up opposite one another. She sits down behind one that is barely visible underneath all the papers and files covering it.

"There are two of us who run the association: me and Anthony. We are looking for someone to help us on Monday and Thursday evenings in the market for the month of December. The tasks are simple: stack the shelves, work the cash register, fill the weekly food bags. Usually, our volunteers are often students themselves, and they don't stay long since they have a busy timetable. We always need new people. Have you ever done anything like this?"

Is this where I say that I grew up in exactly the opposite circumstances? No, that might scare her off.

I need to stay natural and not let her see how nervous I am.

"No, never, but I think I can do it. Except that I'm going home for the Christmas vacation."

"Oh course! No problem. A bit longer would have been good, but ten days is a great start. We're open from 5:30 to 7:30 pm, is that OK for you?"

I hear myself answer without even having thought about it. Also known as 'How to Leap Off a Cliff Without Knowing What's at the Bottom.'

Annie, you're discovering your hidden adventurous side…

"Um, yes. My classes finish at 5 pm at the latest, so that leaves me enough time to get here from Villeneuve-d'Ascq on the metro."

"Perfect! You're studying sociology, right?"

I nod. But for how much longer? No one knows. Maybe I should open up the bets. One week, two weeks, a month, a day?

I wouldn't bet on anything. I have no idea.

"Well, there's nothing like a bit of first-hand experience to get an idea of the real world," she says.

An awkward titter slips out of me before I quickly stop it. She doesn't realize how right she is, even though I don't yet know where all this is going to take me.

"Yes, I can imagine," I reply, just so she's not talking to herself.

"I do hope you'll enjoy the experience, Annette. Do you have any questions?"

No. Yes. I'm not really sure, so I come up with one just so she doesn't think I'm crazy.

"Yes, I was wondering if there were as many men as women among your customers."

"Ah ha! The analyst in you is coming out!" she says enthusiastically. "Social and economic vulnerability has no gender preference. Both men and women are affected. You should know that some of our customers start the month with only 5 euros. Life is very hard for them."

I look at her in disbelief.

Is that even possible?

"Our most vulnerable students need this kind of facility more than ever," she goes on. "Everything has become more difficult since Covid. We decided not to set up our market too close to the university, for greater privacy, but there are at least a dozen organizations like ours around the various campuses."

I feel a bit shaken. Not that I didn't know these places existed, it's just that I didn't know there were so many of them.

She leans over to open a drawer and pulls out a file. She pushes aside some of the paperwork on her desk and hands me a piece of paper and a pen.

"Can you fill out this form, please?"

I cast my eye over it; it asks for my marital status, my intentions, when I'm available, my contact details.

"I'll also need a copy of your ID. Is that OK?"

"Yes, of course."

I rummage through my bag straight away, and, as I hand her my documents, I catch sight of her happy smile.

But the burning question is: what have I gotten myself into?

I walk to the metro just as dusk is falling. The interview didn't even take forty minutes.

I didn't think it was a good idea to tell her that I was there because I'm totally lost. But I don't think that Elise Presle would care even a little bit. I said I wanted to help, and that was enough for her.

I'm chilled to the bone, and I forgot to take my gloves, so I speed up before I freeze to death. But just as I start down the stairs to the metro station, I see Romeo coming up. I stand rooted to the spot like an idiot. The last time we saw each other, he almost got crushed by Gavin's car.

He eventually notices me and comes over. "Hi there!"

He doesn't seem to be holding a grudge, which is a relief. That would have made me really nervous.

"Hey! Do you live around here?" I ask, for want of anything better to say.

"No, not at all. You?"

"Me neither!"

Tick… tick… tick…

There's a moment of awkward silence. How horrible. I feel obliged to say something, anything to end the uncomfortable moment.

"Sorry for the other day."

Romeo shrugs. "You're not the one who backed into me with your car."

"I know, but still, it wasn't cool. Gavin didn't seem to realize that he could have hurt you."

"Typical," he replies a bit scathingly. "Are you going out with him?"

"Um… yes."

"Then next time, you take the steering wheel."

"I'm not sure you'd be any safer if it was me driving. I don't even have my driver's license yet!"

Not to mention that Gavin is so protective of his precious car that he would never let anyone else drive it, license or no license.

Romeo smiles.

"I'll let you in on a secret: me neither. Which means that if one day I come and pick you up somewhere, it'll be on my bike."

I blink. Huh? What? Where? How?

"Pick me up to go where?"

He's looking at me as if I have said something funny.

"It was just a figure of speech."

When I'm feeling a bit flustered, I get this weird laugh, and Mom always says I sound like a donkey. I bet if it hadn't started snowing right then and there, I would have started braying and made a fool of myself for life. Because honestly, the donkey sound I make is utterly mortifying. It has to be heard to be believed.

As the first snowflakes drift down around us, Romeo lifts his head and looks up towards the sky. It's as if he's completely changed tack.

"Snow is the craziest thing I've ever seen."

"You think?"

"In Réunion, pretty much all you see in the sky is the sun. Or a cyclone."

I laugh. "Yeah, I can imagine! When I was a kid, I used to eat the snow. Hey, don't look at me like that, that's what all the kids do here!"

"OK, OK!" He smiles, brushing a hand over his hair, which is covered in snowflakes.

"It was nice seeing you, Annie, but I'd better go now. I've got to be somewhere in ten minutes."

"Oh, yeah, sure. See you next time!"

He winks at me and replies in the same tone of voice: "See you next time."

As I walk down the stairs, I feel like I'm floating. University, Ines, my parents, the association, the snow… it really was a bizarre day. But what disturbs me the most is the idea of being on a bike with Romeo.

Romeo on a bike.

Now there's a mental image.

Oh man, stop it.

5
December

"You have got to be kidding me."

Before answering, I grab a snowflake sticker and position it on the living room window.

"Nope. I start tonight."

Gavin looks at me, then at Ines, who is decorating the Christmas tree in perfect silence. He is outraged. My latest news about working for the association has pushed him over the edge.

"This is crazy. You do realize it's totally wrong?"

"Why?"

"Because you have nothing in common with those people! Imagine how they'll react when they realize you're using them just to get in your parents' good books."

"I'm not using anyone! And my parents haven't asked me to do anything."

"Yeah, whatever. Let me paint you a picture: 'The sad little rich girl doesn't know what to do with her life, so she visits the poor people to help her work it out!' But it doesn't matter whether she does or not, 'cause her parents have her back."

I immediately feel angry. He is so arrogant!

"May I remind you that you're taking a year off without having to worry about money?"

"Yeah, but I'm not mixing with the plebs just to make myself feel better!"

"That's how you see it, Gavin, but I just want to feel useful. And if it helps me find out what I want to do, then so much the better. There's nothing wrong with that. And anyway, I haven't told them about my financial position."

Gavin shakes his head. "And you think they won't work it out?"

"There's no reason they should. It's not like I'm going to hand out copies of my bank statements."

"And what do you think?" Gavin asks Ines.

"That I don't want to get involved in your conversation," she says as she hangs an angel on a branch.

Gavin clicks his tongue in annoyance. "Damn it, Annie. You're not from the same world as them! You're going to go and hang with a bunch of hobos and then come home and sleep in your silk sheets? I can't believe it."

I recoil from him in outrage. "They're not hobos!"

He shrugs. "You can justify it however you want, but I know exactly how this is going to end: you're going to be bored out of your brain, and you'll realize it was a complete waste of time. Honestly, I thought you made the right decision when you told your parents you wanted to quit school. I just don't get why you're doing this, unless it's just to put you off university even more."

"She might actually be in for a pleasant surprise," Ines eventually says.

"I thought you didn't want to stick your nose in," replies Gavin sharply.

Ines pretends to zip her mouth shut and returns to her box of decorations.

"And what are you even going to be doing? Shelving stuff? A check-out chick? A social worker, maybe? You deserve better than that."

"They also deserve better than what they have."

"Mother Teresa, pray for us!" he says mockingly. "Still wanting to play at being a good Samaritan."

"You've already pulled that line. Listen, I know I'm privileged, and I can imagine what it must look like, but I'm not as sure about quitting school as you seem to think I am. I just don't know what's best for me yet, you know? Mom and Dad are right. I have to do everything I can to find out."

"And you think this is going to help you find the answer?"

"I don't know."

He throws his arms in the air and heaves a sigh. "Well, do what you want, but don't come crying to me when you realize it's been a waste of time!"

As if I would.

He glances at his watch then hands me the sheet of stickers he's holding. "I've got to go. What time is your thing tonight?"

"5:30."

"OK. Shall we catch up tomorrow?"

"If you want."

I reply noncommittally, but I'm not even sure he noticed.

He leans over to kiss me. "Of course I want to. Just so I can hear you say it was the worst two hours of your life!"

His comment doesn't merit an answer.

I accompany him to the door and watch him leave without saying a word.

When I return to the living room, Ines is just finishing putting up the lights on the Christmas tree.

"Sorry about that."

"Don't worry about it."

I flop onto the couch, wracked with doubt. "Ines, do you think I'm being a hypocrite and I'm just in it for myself?"

"What? No way!"

"Do you think I should tell the president that my parents are loaded?"

She puts down the lights and comes and sits next to me.

"Honestly? I'm not sure. It might not be the best thing to say. Why don't you do your trial week, and if you like it, you can let them know that you're a 'poor little rich girl'?" she says, mimicking Gavin's voice.

"You're right."

Then I frown. "I'm sorry about Gavin, he's so…"

"Cocky? Arrogant? Full of himself?"

I sigh. Ines doesn't even try and pretend she likes him. And I get it, I have to admit that today he really annoyed me too. Just like I hated his behaviour towards Romeo when he nearly knocked him over.

"You know, he's not all bad. Most of the time he's really nice, and he's funny too."

"If you want my opinion, it's been ages since I've seen you laugh at something he's said. Maybe you want to think about it a bit. All he does is disagree with the choices you've made!"

I have to acknowledge that since Gavin dropped out of school, our relationship hasn't been the same. We used to have fun all the time. We went out, we made the most of each moment together, and all we thought about was the next time we'd see each other. Now it feels like we're not on the same wavelength anymore. He's annoyed all the time. It's like he can't stand it when I don't make the same decisions as him. For months he was the only constant in my life, the only person who came from the same world as me, and that was so reassuring. What's happening? Why does everything feel so uncertain all of a sudden?

"Well, the main thing is you have this amazing friend, and at least she's funny!" says Ines.

She leans forward, grabs a packet of fake snow and throws a handful right in my face.

Taken by surprise, I spit out pieces of glitter and rub my eyes.

"Hey! Now it's your turn!"

She tries to dodge me, but I manage to grab the bag out of her hands and boom! Revenge! The two of us are throwing the snow around and in zero seconds flat our hair and the whole living room is covered in white snow powder.

Thank god for the vacuum!

To the sound of Frank Sinatra and that great anthem 'Let It Snow!', we spend the next hour finishing our Christmas decorations, putting the stickers on all the windows, hanging a wreath on the front door and another on my bedroom door, laying out lots of little tree-shaped candles in the living room and hanging two big woollen stockings above the couch, for want of a mantelpiece. And for the final touch, I place on the couch two blankets with reindeer on them and the snowman cushion covers I bought last week. That, plus the two Santa Clauses who sing a Jingle Bells duet when you turn them on, and everything is ready for a session of Christmas films on Netflix!

"Right. I'm going to go and study for a bit," says Ines at half-past three. "What about you?"

"That's the last thing I want to do, but I'm going to give it a try too."

"Wise decision, my friend! See you later."

I try and play the game, I do. I attempt to memorize rules about work and family sociology, definitions, quotes… But my brain is about as effective at retaining information as a colander, so – and I can't believe I'm going to say this – I actually can't wait for my appointment at the community food market.

I arrive twenty minutes early. The door is open, and there are already about fifteen people waiting on the sidewalk.

Elise is running everywhere; it's like she's connected to electricity sockets. I can see other volunteers here too. They're easy to recognize: they're all wearing Santa hats. Elise sees me and comes over with a big smile.

"Ah, I've been waiting for you to arrive! Yeah, I know," she says, pointing to her red dress and green-and-white striped tights, "but we always dress to theme in December! I won't put you on checkout on the first day, but would you mind giving a hand in filling the bags?"

"Sure!"

"Great! Eddie, Mathilde and Hassan are busy preparing them, they'll show you what to do. Oh, and sorry, there are no more hats left."

Instead, she hands me one of those headbands with red, sparkly reindeer antlers on it.

Oh, man.

It sounds like I'm complaining, but I always think it looks great when I see them on other people.

Come on, Annette Reynaud, don't be a snob! Relax! This is cool!

"Oh, and while I think of it, the bathroom on the second floor is out of order. If you need to go, there's one on the third floor."

"OK!"

"Hassan, can you show her the ropes?"

"Yes, boss!"

He introduces me to the others who are all just a bit older than me.

Hassan has a shaved head, Mathilde has piercings everywhere, and with his shirt and V-neck sweater, Eddie looks like a bit of a study geek.

"We come every Monday," explains Hassan. "Is this your first time?"

I nod.

"Not too intimidated?"

"No, it's all right. Are you guys all studying in Lille?"

"Yup, and we're all born and bred here. If we weren't living with our parents, maybe we'd be in the same situation as the people we're trying to help, you know? And you?"

His remark almost prevents me from replying. I feel uncomfortable because even though I'm not from here, I'm not struggling at all.

"I come from Aix-en-Provence."

I don't plan on adding anything else.

"Oh, OK. So anyway, these food bags have fruit and veggies in them. Eddie and Mathilde are preparing individual portions with bananas, carrots, potatoes, lettuce and mandarins. I put them all in one big bag, and you can add six *papillotes** when the person comes to pick up their bag. But no more than six; we want to make sure there are enough to go round. Every last item counts here."

"No problem."

"Elise manages the list of those who have signed up for a food bag, and all we do is fill the bags. Those are the ones we've already done," he says, pointing to a shelf full of them.

"How many people are on the list?"

"Today there are thirty-two, but there are often people who join the queue at the last minute. Elise never turns anyone away. You'll see. Some grab their bag and leave as quickly as possible, others browse through the shelves or go upstairs, because at least it's warm here. There are all sorts."

"OK, team, the doors are opening!" cries Elise.

* TN: A papillote is a chocolate wrapped in a piece of paper with a message on the inside. They are usually eaten at Christmastime.

No more time for questions: the first wave of people is about to arrive. There are girls, boys, short and tall, dressed up or wearing casual clothes: people of all ages and sizes. I don't want anyone to see that I'm a bit shaken, but I've got such a lump in my throat.

When you're on campus, you have no idea; no one looks closely at anyone else, and no one really talks to anyone else properly, but here it's real. I arm myself with a smile; they're not here to be pitied, I know that much.

But still, it's super hard.

"I'm not a fan of carrots," says one guy as he takes his bag.

I look at him, unsure.

"Is that some kind of euphemism?"

"No, not at all. I just don't like them."

"Oh… Hassan, is there anything other than carrots?"

He shakes his head.

"No, not this time, sorry."

I look up at the student and don't know what to say.

"We can swap if you want?" suggests the girl right behind him. "I don't really like potatoes."

"Oh, you wouldn't mind?" asks the guy.

"Definitely not!"

They swap the bags of veggies, thank me and move on. The food bags disappear faster than we can fill them.

Hassan, Mathilde and Eddie are working hard. The stock of fruit and vegetables is getting dangerously low. I get that there is the exact number of food bags for the people who signed up for them, but what about the ones that Hassan mentioned, who turn up unexpectedly?

It's stupid, I know, but I'm starting to panic on their behalf.

I take a deep breath, turn around to get a bag, and when I turn back again, I almost drop it.

Romeo is right there, standing in front of me.

We look at each other in shock.

Shit. That's why I bumped into him the other day not far from here. He clenches his jaw.

OK. Just act as if nothing was out of the ordinary.

I pull myself together and smile at him. "Hi there!"

"Hey," he answers as he takes his bag.

"There's some papillotes too!" I take six and give them to him.

"Thanks," he says with a nod.

He makes way for the next student and heads towards the shelves to continue shopping.

I can't help watching him to see what he buys. Pasta, shower gel, shaving cream, a bag of coffee. Nothing extravagant. I picture him buying me a coffee at the library and my stomach turns. I never would have imagined this.

He heads to the check-out and instead of leaving the store, I see him go upstairs. I feel relieved. I didn't want him to disappear right away. I need to talk to him, to let him know, without saying it outright, that the fact he comes to the food market is not an issue for me and that I would never judge him.

We come to the end of the bags. There are no more fruit and veggies, but there are a few students who have missed out.

"We'll find something for you," promises Elise with a smile. "We've got some unsold items from the farmer's market. Would that be all right?"

They all nod in agreement.

Then the volunteer team starts to tidy up. We pick up the stray lettuce leaves that fell on the ground and pack away the crates for next time. It's already 7:15 pm. I totally lost track of time.

"Did everything go smoothly?" Elise asks me once we're done.

"Yes. Were you able to find something for the extra students?"

"Yes, don't worry, we always manage somehow. So how was your first day?"

"Intense."

She nods. She knows what it's like.

But this was a first for me, and my head is spinning.

Physically I kept up, but when I think about how Ines and others like Romeo have to work every day, I wonder how they manage to keep up with their studies.

There are lots of people in that situation, I know, but for me it seems incredible.

Emotionally, I feel like I've been through the wringer. All these students that live like this. I knew it, but I wasn't ready to be aware of it. It's awful that there are so many who need to come here.

"So do you think you'll come back?" asks Elise.

"Of course. But I saw a student I know, and he's gone upstairs. Do you mind if I go and see him before he leaves?"

"No, of course not. And thanks for your help today. Everyone appreciates it."

"Don't mention it. And anyway, I should be thanking you, Ms. Presle."

"Annette, call me Elise, please!"

"OK, I will, and please, call me Annie! See you on Thursday!"

I put my reindeer headband on the counter and leave the store, going into the corridor and up the stairs. I sigh as I look around at the few students in the common room, laughing as they read the jokes from inside the papillote wrappers. Romeo isn't there. I didn't even see him leave.

Damn it. But I'm sure I'll bump into him again. Another time.

I hope.

I leave the building and there he is, leaning against the wall, bags at his feet. I get the feeling he's waiting for me. My heart starts to race.

"Hey!"

"I didn't expect to see you here," he says in a slightly hoarse voice. "I was going to leave as soon as I finished my shopping and then…"

"Hey, don't worry, you don't need to justify yourself."

He digs into the pocket of his jeans and pulls out a piece of paper that he hands me.

"I wrote down my phone number."

He bends his knees, picks up his bags and lowers his head a little so he can look me straight in the eye.

"Call me."

And he walks away.

Without looking back.

I'm not sure how I'm feeling right now, nor what he must be thinking.

Why does he want me to call him? And if I do, what would that mean? We'd definitely get closer, wouldn't we?

Is that reasonable?

The truth is, I don't care.

I already know I'm going to call him.

6
December

The good thing about getting up early is that you can do lots of things. Like bake Christmas cookies. Even if, like me, you're not great in the kitchen. But I don't care about the inevitable carnage and head off to the Monoprix* to get the ingredients I need.

I know Dad'll be up, so I give him a call on the way to let him know I've decided to do some volunteering.

When I tell him, he's quite surprised. "Oh? Was this something you were planning? I can't remember you talking about it."

"No, it wasn't, but an opportunity came up and… I took it."

"So, how's it going? Did you like it?"

"'Like' isn't really the term I'd use to describe my first day. It's more that I felt useful."

I tell him about how it went yesterday and how affected I was by the students' situation.

"I wasn't really aware of it, you know. I mean, I was, but it's not the same when it's right there in front of you."

---

* Monoprix is a supermarket that also sells clothes, housewares, books and other products.

"No one realizes until they're truly confronted with it. Are you going to do it for long?"

"At least until the Christmas vacation."

I hear Dad grumble. "I know you're not too sure of your plans, darling, but don't do anything that might distract you from your studying."

I smile. Dad was really understanding when I told him I wanted to quit school, but I know what he's like: he's hoping it's just a rough patch and that I'll realize I actually enjoy my classes.

"Don't worry, Dad, it's only four hours a week, and I'm glad to be involved in it."

What I don't tell him is that food market or not, I'm sure I'm going bomb my exams. Because to succeed I'd need a tiny bit of motivation. And that's just not the case. It's more like any excuse to avoid studying is good one.

We chat for another five minutes, then I hang up. I'm right in front of the Monop'. It's time to clear the shelves.

I start shopping, and obviously I get ten times more than I need. Typical.

Then, at one point, as I'm slowly making my way through the aisles, I can't help comparing my activity with what goes on at the food market. Here I am, taking whatever I need, as well as stuff I don't need, without checking the price or worrying about anything, while hundreds of students struggle to make ends meet.

After yesterday, I'm not sure if I feel guilty or just a bit more aware of things. But I suspect I'm not going to be able to keep my head buried in the sand any longer.

I'm not too sure where to start. I've never been faced with this kind of situation before, but there's one thing I do have: the money in my account and… this supermarket.

The food market has needs, and I have the means. For now, it's as simple as that.

There are carts for sale at the entrance to the supermarket. I go and get two and fill them with anything I think might be useful or that might make someone happy. Food, personal care products, candy and… some Christmas decorations. I just can't resist!

I know that if I want people at the store to think I'm just your average student, I shouldn't be doing this, but for now it's the only thing I can do. I'm sure I'll think of an explanation.

I've got a smile on my face as I leave the supermarket and have just one thing on my mind – bake my cookies, go back to the Wazemmes neighbourhood and give all this to the association.

I go back to the apartment laden like a pack mule, and my phone buzzes just as I head through the door.

It's Gavin.

It's only 9 am, he must have fallen out of bed.

Hi angelface!
So how was it hanging with the rabble?

Gavin, that's not funny.

Chill out, I was just kidding!
So are you going to keep doing it?

Yes, I think so. I liked feeling useful. There was such a good atmosphere!

See, I told you! You're going to turn into a do-gooder.

Whatever...

His comments are really starting to annoy me. And I don't think he even realizes.

Guess where I am!

Yup, I knew it. He has no idea. I give a random answer.

I dunno. In your car on the way to the Netherlands?

Nope! Dad and I are on the Croix-en-Ternois racing circuit! We thought we'd give it a go. We're doing a race car driving course. It's amazing!

So I know I said I'd come round today, but I don't think I'll make it. How about tomorrow?

OK, no problem. We'll catch up tomorrow.

Cool, I'd better go, we're going to try a Maserati. See ya babe!

And the conversation stops there.

Did he notice my total lack of enthusiasm? No. Gavin is true to himself – completely self-absorbed. So why is this bugging me now? He's always been like that.

It's bugging me because I need to feel connected, and it's like Gavin and I no longer really are. Neither of us seems interested in what the other is doing. Which isn't great…

Time to think about something else, quick!

There's a mug in the sink. Ines must have gotten up, had a coffee and, I'm betting, has already gone straight back to her room to study.

But not me! I get out my Betty Bossi* recipe book that my grandmother gave me when I moved here and decide on two recipes: jam-filled cookies and lemon shortbread. The book claims they're failsafe recipes, but we'll just see about that.

I grab my floral apron that I only bought because I thought it was pretty. Butter, sugar, eggs, flour… Here goes!

---

* TN: Betty Bossi is a fictional cook created in the 1950s. The brand now publishes cookbooks and magazines.

Just as I'm rolling out the dough for the first lot of cookies, Ines bursts into the kitchen grumbling. "I'm sick of him, so damn sick of him!"

She throws her phone on the counter, leans against it and folds her arms across her chest. "What does he think? That I'm at his beck and call 24/7? I can't believe it!"

I frown and dry my hands on the dish towel. "What are you talking about?"

"My boss! He knows that this week I'm busy studying and that I need to be left alone, but he's determined to make me go to his office instead of just talking on the phone. He's so freaking annoying."

"What does he want?"

"To sort out the schedule."

"So what are you going to do?"

"I'll go and see him tomorrow before work. Which means one hour less studying."

She opens the fridge, grabs a can of Coke and drinks half in one go, before noticing what I'm up to. "Are you baking?"

"I'm trying to make Christmas cookies."

She looks around at the cookie cutters I took out, the flour scattered everywhere, the egg I broke before it got into the bowl, making a puddle in the middle of the table, and raises her eyebrows. Ines knows that cooking is not my forte, unlike herself. Everything she cooks and bakes is perfect.

"All of a sudden you just got the urge?"

"Yup…"

I try and roll out the dough, but it rips everywhere. It's a wreck.

Ines looks at the six kilos of flour on the table and pulls a face.

"Are you thinking of baking enough cookies for a football team plus the reserve players?"

"No, but I thought I might take some to the food market for the students."

She gives me a questioning look.

"Aren't you meant to be going on Thursday?"

"Yes, but I want to help Elise with the common room too. No, I mean ask her if there's anything else I can do to help."

Ines observes me closely for a moment. "What?"

"You've got a crush on someone."

"No, I don't!"

"Yes, you do. You've got a crush on Romeo!"

"What are you talking about? I so don't! Look, you were the one who encouraged me to work there. And it makes me feel useful. That's all."

That'll teach me not to tell her everything! She doesn't seem convinced but then throws her hands in the air. "OK, OK… Romeo Diamante has nothing to do with it!"

"What? His last name is Payet!"

"Pay it, money, diamonds, whatever. You always get the hots for annoying guys."

"Hey, he's not annoying! You've only seen him that once at the library, and we were disturbing him while he was studying."

"Whatever you say."

I poke my tongue out at her.

"Um, one last thing… I think you mixed up the sugar and the salt," she says as she leaves the kitchen. "The sugar is in the other container!"

"Huh?"

I look at the container on the table, poke my finger inside to taste it, and grimace.

Oh no!

I didn't know if I'd bump into him or not, but I still feel disappointed when I don't see Romeo in the common room. There aren't many people here, just five or six who are studying, playing cards or reading quietly in an armchair. Elise is in her office. With the cookie tin in my hands, I walk up the stairs. I can see her working at her desk, but to be polite, I give a little knock on the wall. She's not alone; there's a man in his forties sitting with her.

"Oh, Annette, come in! This is Anthony, our treasurer. Annie has just joined our team of volunteers."

He greets me with a nod of his head. He has kind eyes.

"Hello," I greet them both. "I hope I'm not bothering you?"

"Not at all!" Elise smiles. "I wasn't expecting to see you today!"

"I've left a shopping cart downstairs, in front of the store. I live in an apartment building in the centre of town, and all my neighbours donated something."

The lie comes to my lips with surprising ease, and even though it's for a good cause, I don't add anything else.

"Oh, how nice of them! And you for having organized it!"

"And I made some Christmas cookies. There aren't that many, and I don't think they're very good…"

"This one's a gem, isn't she?" says Anthony. "I'll give one a go."

As I open the tin, I can feel my cheeks getting pink.

He tastes it and doesn't choke; that's a good start. Even though the one he took was way overcooked. To be fair, the others are hardly less burnt.

"Not great, right?"

"No, they are," he says politely. "They'll go perfectly with a cup of coffee!"

I smile and turn to Elise.

"Elise, I was thinking, I'd like to come a bit more often than just Monday and Thursday. This week I'm studying and next week I have exams, but after that I'll have more free time leading up to Christmas. I'm not going home until the 21st of December. I wondered if there was something I could help you with?"

Elise and Anthony look at each other, and then back at me.

"That is very generous of you. It's always difficult finding volunteers towards the end of the year, so I accept gratefully. How are you at creating Christmas spirit?"

"Um… what do you mean?"

"Quite a few students don't go home for Christmas because their parents are overseas or because they can't afford to. So every year we organize a Christmas party here. We cook a meal together, with a Christmas yule log for dessert, music, sometimes karaoke. If you have any other ideas, I'm all ears."

"Secret Santa!" I suggest spontaneously.

"Pardon?"

"Where each person draws a piece of paper out of a hat and gets a gift, is that it?" asks Anthony.

"Almost, yes!"

Elise purses her lips.

"It's a cool idea, Annie, but I'm not sure the students here can afford to buy a gift for anyone."

I think for a moment. Often the gifts are less than 5 euros; it's just something to mark the occasion. But even that would be too much for the people here.

No problem. I've thought of an idea!

"No one needs to buy anything. All they need to do is make something with whatever they can find – an old match-box, bits of glass, mandarin peel, whatever they want. They're allowed to use anything at all."

"Great idea!" says Anthony. "We could even get together some bits and pieces if needed."

I'm so excited I clap my hands.

"OK, let's do it!" says Elise in agreement. "How shall we organize it? How about I get everyone together and you explain how it works?"

"Sounds perfect!"

"OK, I'll send a group email to find out who will be here on the 24th and who wants to come. This is really going to liven things up, I'm so glad you came back and spoke to us!"

I smile at her, totally over the moon.

"Right, now that that's been sorted!" Elise continues. "I didn't have time to introduce you to the students on Monday.

There aren't many here today, and I don't think they'll be here on the 24th, but it's the perfect opportunity for you to introduce yourself and hand out some of your delicious cookies!"

Delicious? I wouldn't bet on it!

I go home totally worn out, but happy. I push open the door to my room and flop onto my bed.

Given my background, I didn't think it would be easy to fit in so naturally. My mother with her professional approach would call it 'supply and demand.' My father, who has a poetic streak, would say that the pieces of the puzzle 'fit together' perfectly. And somewhere between the two of them is me and my practical side: the association needs more people and here I am! It feels good to be useful, to get out of that spiral of negative thoughts: *Annie, what are your skills? What direction do you want to go in? What does the future hold for you? Don't let anyone down, OK? Blah, blah, blah…* The couple of hours I spent at the food market might have been exhausting, but paradoxically, I feel more relaxed than I have in the past few months.

I grab my phone and hesitate a little, but not for too long, before looking for a number. I should be calling Gavin to tell him about all my experiences today, but he wouldn't understand. And mostly, there's something resolute and uncontrollable that whispers to me that it's Romeo I should be contacting.

Why?
I don't really know, but here goes.

Sorry I didn't call. I didn't want to disturb your studying.

I brought cookies round to the ASEL today, I thought I might see you. Did you work all day?
Annie

I'm just getting my head above water!
Can't believe I missed your cookies.
Were they good?

Totally inedible, but no one had the heart to tell me. I'm a terrible cook!

Any left for me to test?

So you're a risk-taker?

Yup!

OK, next time I'll make you some, but you're going to regret it!

Challenge accepted!

And sorry for yesterday. I left in a bit of a rush.

Don't worry.

Are you free tomorrow?

You want a break from your studying?

If you're up for it.

I'm up for it!

5 pm in front of the Black?

Cool, see you tomorrow!

I say yes without even asking what the Black is.
Oh well, I'll see it tomorrow.
And I didn't even ask him what we were going to do.
Oh well, I'll find that out tomorrow as well.
For now, I'm only excited to see him again.

7
December

"No way, you're going on a date!"

I roll my eyes. Ines is still doing her crazy talk.

"Nope. You're way off the mark."

"Well, what is it then? You're meeting up for a game of Scrabble?"

"And what if I said we were?"

She puts her mug of coffee on the table and smiles. "I wouldn't believe you."

I sigh and bite into my toast. I'm not a morning person, so if Ines starts asking questions and imagining things, that's going to make me even more grumpy.

"Look, he suggested we catch up, what else do you want me to say? I'm not interested in him. I already told you that."

"Maybe he's interested in you?"

I shrug.

Have I considered it?

Yes.

Would that bother me?

Yes, no, maybe... But who cares, that's not the issue right now.

I'm going out with Gavin, period.

"And what about you? Instead of poking your nose into my love life, how's yours getting on?

"At a standstill. And I prefer it that way."

"You haven't heard from Mehdi?"

Mehdi is a childhood friend. Ines told me that they ended up being more than just friends and that they really clicked. Except she went to Lille to study and he's in Nantes. Not ideal for having a relationship. They had a massive fight over the summer and decided to have a break, give themselves time to think about what they really want out of the relationship. But since they got back to school, they've hardly been in contact. I don't even know if this upsets her, she almost never talks about it.

"No," she replies tersely to my question.

"And how do you feel about that?"

"I just take it as it comes. I actually think I've let it go somehow."

"You don't love him anymore?"

"No."

I watch her, waiting for her to add something, but soon realize I'm not going to find out anything further. Ines is so self-contained. She loves to listen but hates opening up. Getting information out of her is like pulling teeth, which I am not going to do this morning. I didn't sleep well, and my brain is barely functioning. But Ines hasn't finished yet. Interrogating me, that is.

"Are you really going to go and meet up with someone else, even though you're going out with Gavin?"

I frown. Is that a criticism or just an observation?

She's definitely touched a sensitive point though; I can feel it.

"What's the problem? If you're with someone, does that mean you have to lock yourself up in a convent and not speak to anyone of the opposite sex?"

She looks into my eyes with her deep green gaze.

"It's just that since you've been with Gavin, which is ever since I've known you, you've never done this. Not once. In fact, you only ever go out with him."

"And?"

"It just seems like you and Gavin aren't really in sync anymore. Well, that's my conclusion anyway. But you do you."

I look down at my mug.

"Look. Gavin's out there having a great time, and I still don't know what I want to do with my life, so obviously we're on different wavelengths. But it's no big deal. Our outlooks are a bit different at the moment, that's all."

"If you want my opinion, it's not just your outlooks that are different, you guys are in total opposition, and you always have been."

"We share the same background, Ines."

"Background, yes, but you're not the same type of person," she clarifies. "Hey, I know it sounds like I'm judging you, but when you think about quitting school, it makes you worry about your future. Whereas Gavin thinks there's no need to worry about the future because he's rich. For me that's the fundamental difference between you."

I make a face.

"Do you think I'm being unfair?" she asks in a gentler voice.

"No. I don't know."

Ines gives a rueful smile. "But you know what's cool about all this?"

"No…"

"You can go to your date, oh, I mean, your appointment with Romeo Swarovski without feeling guilty!"

I end up smiling too.

I am definitely OK with the not feeling guilty thing!

I get to the Black ten minutes early. I'd never noticed it before, even though it's only a few blocks away from my apartment. And for good reason: the bar is just a bit removed from the heart of the old town, and there aren't many passers-by. It's in a large, brick building that used to be a factory.

The façade is made of dark smoked glass, with a kind of big, stylized sun painted on the double automatic doors. At first glance it looks like an esoteric kind of place. If Romeo asked me to come so we could get our cards read, I'm out of here! Well, maybe not, because I spent the whole day studying – I know, that's not like me – and now all I want is a Christmas beer or whatever else will make me forget the fact that most of what I read has already disappeared out of my brain.

"So, you're a punctual type?" I hear a voice behind me say. I turn and see Romeo looking at his watch.

"See, it's not necessarily women who are always late!" I reply as I look at my own.

"I'm not late!"

"Yes, you are! One minute late!"

He walks up to me but doesn't give me a hug. He just looks down at me. He really is very, very tall. I can't help it, I really want to know…

"Exactly how tall are you?"

He cracks up.

"You really do jump from one topic to another. I bet you invented the expression 'off-on-a-tangent'"

"You never know!"

"I'm 6'5."

I can't help but whistle. "Are you parents tall?"

"Not particularly. Are yours?"

"Not particularly, either! Must have been something in the water!"

He makes a face. "You mean the rum! Shall we go in? If there's one thing here I really can't get used to, it's the temperature. It's freezing!"

Ah, yup, it sure must change from the weather in Réunion! I don't tell him that in Quebec the temperature sometimes dropped to around –20°C. He'd be bound to ask me if I've travelled much, and I'd have to tell him about my parents. I'd rather avoid that for now.

As we enter the bar, my jaw drops. It's huge. The hardwood floor stretches back almost twenty metres. There are exposed wooden beams on the ceiling and tables everywhere, separated by a metal railing that leads down to the basement. And in the middle of all that, there's a massive ceiling light made of empty beer bottles.

And that's not to mention the Christmas decorations! I don't think I've ever seen so many in one place. There are dozens of Christmas lights with big, coloured lightbulbs, red Santa hats are hanging off all the coat hooks, and blankets with snowflake designs are folded over the backs of the chairs. There's a Christmas tree that's at least two metres tall in one corner, and other teeny-tiny ones on the tables. I also see numerous Christmas baubles, wreaths and, sitting on a rocking chair, there's a huge gingerbread cuddly toy so big it makes you want to hug it.

And… no way, I don't believe it! Right at the back of the room, along the entire wall, I spot piles of board games!

You're meeting up for a game of Scrabble?

Ha ha, Ines, if only you knew how right you were.

"A bar with board games?" I ask, completely dumbstruck.

He pulls that face again. His trademark?

"Yes, but a bar with board games at Christmastime. What's the deal in mainland France with all the Christmas decorations? Why are there always so many?"

I burst out laughing.

"Because we don't have the sun and white-sand beaches to make us forget about winter?"

The bar has just opened and as we walk into the room, all the tables are free.

"Do we sit wherever we want?"

"No," answers Romeo, "I booked us a table. You'll see, in an hour it'll be packed."

"OK, so, here we drink and… play games?"

"And we get fries too! Which is perfect timing, I'm starving."

I smile and follow him to a table just in front of the bar.

"They brew their own beer here. Shall we get one?"

"Sure, why not!"

He grabs the menu and hands it to me. "Are you hungry? Order whatever you want."

My eyes widen when I understand that he wants to pay.

"Why are you making that face? You think you're going to bankrupt me? It's too late for that," he adds, deadpan.

I don't know what to say. I don't want to make him feel uncomfortable. I really don't. What can I say that won't be awkward or misread?

But he continues: "Go on, pick something, it's fine."

I think quickly. "No way, we're going halves! It's the 21st century, in case you hadn't noticed."

He shakes his head with a smile and admits defeat.

"Are you ready to order?" asks the waiter.

I choose something randomly – fries with cheese and fried onions on the side. Romeo gets the same thing as me, as well as a mustard and ketchup hotdog. He's clearly not worried about his cholesterol levels.

"You don't have any money worries," he says, point blank.

His comment comes out of the blue. I can't avoid the subject, so I give a half-hearted answer. "No, my parents pay for most things."

"Do you live on your own?"

"I have a housemate. And you?"

"I rent a furnished studio in Fives. It's small and simple, but it's quiet and easy to keep tidy."

He stops speaking and looks hard at me. It feels like I'm being consumed by his gaze. My hands under the table are clenched, fingers interwoven.

"Right, I'm going to cut to the chase and answer the question you've been dying to ask – why I go to the food market."

I don't say anything, feeling embarrassed to have been so obvious.

"I have two brothers who are ten and twelve. My parents own a bar on Réunion and in order to buy it, they had to get a loan. They're not able to help me out much. The rent in Lille is expensive, even in a neighbourhood like Fives, and the few hours work I do here and there isn't always enough to pay the bills at the end of the month. The food market is my lifeline. Without it I wouldn't be able to buy food. But I'm not complaining. There are people who are far worse off than me, you have no idea."

"I'm sorry. We're not all in the same boat financially, and that's not fair."

"That's life."

"Are you doing OK with your studies?"

"I'm lucky to even be at university, so I'm doing everything I can to stay. All I know is that if I have to stop, it won't be of my own free will."

He can't imagine the effect his last sentence has on me. This guy is giving his all to keep studying, and I'm flippantly giving it all up. Honestly, some days I feel like such a loser.

"Are you OK?" he asks, noticing that I've slumped down in my chair a little.

"Yeah, fine!" I pretend.

"OK. Right, enough with the sob story. Things are about to get serious!"

Romeo stands up and comes back with a wooden object. The base has a T-shaped pole sticking out of it, with two rings attached by strings hanging off each end of the cross-bar. At the bottom of the pole there are two hooks, opposite each other.

"What on earth is that?"

He smiles and places another base on the table; this one has five circular indentations in it. There's a little wooden cup sitting in the middle one.

"This is the hook and ring game!" he answers. "It's really common in the *estaminets** around here. It's simple and super addictive: you pull the string towards you, let it go, and every time you manage to get the ring on the hook, you move the cup in your direction. The first one to get the cup to the last hole wins. You get three attempts and then it's the other person's turn."

"Um… OK."

To be honest, I've never done anything like this before, but Romeo seems to be totally in his element, unlike me.

Come on… I'm not afraid of anything!

By the time he's explained the rules to me, the place has filled up, and we can barely hear each other speak.

* TN: An estaminet is a traditional café found in the North of France and southern Belgium.

I go first. Obviously with my legendary agility, I manage to make the ring go way too far.

"Hey! Are you trying to get me in the eye?" laughs Romeo.

Oh no, definitely not those eyes!

He has a go and… boom! He gets it right at the first try. It's infuriating.

I try and concentrate, and don't even notice the waiter bringing us our beers. I fight an internal battle not to stick my tongue out the side of my mouth, an old children habit; I don't want to look stupid. And to the sound of people behind us laughing, playing and telling jokes, after the tenth go, I finally manage to hook the ring.

"Yes!" I yell, jumping up from my chair.

Romeo gives me a wink and shifts the cup one space towards me.

"Well done!"

Our fries and his hotdog arrive while we're playing. It only takes him five minutes to gulp everything down. It's quite impressive.

"I'm a total glutton," he says in explanation.

"A what?"

"A glutton. I'm super greedy and eat too quickly!"

"Your stomach must be rock solid. If I ate like that, I'd get sick."

"The glutton and the princess. What a cliché – it almost sounds Shakespearean!"

Except that we're not in love… Is what I almost reply, before managing to bite it back. Because I really don't want to say that.

We play another couple of rounds of this diabolical game, then Romeo goes and puts it back on the counter. He comes back with an apologetic look on his face.

"I can't stay much longer. I've to get up early to study. Do you live far from here?"

"No, only about ten minutes away."

"OK, I'll walk you home then."

We wander through the streets lit up with Christmas lights in almost perfect silence. It's cold, and it feels like snow is on the way. It might even settle this time. When we arrive at my apartment building, I don't even notice Gavin's car parked on the sidewalk. He gets out of his Audi and slams the door.

"Where the hell have you been? I rang you twenty times and you never answered!"

Super embarrassed, I turn to Romeo and then back to Gavin. "Sorry, I didn't look at my phone."

"I'd better go now," says Romeo. "I'll see you at the ASEL tomorrow."

"Oh, yes, sure. Thanks for walking me home."

He nods by way of a farewell, barely acknowledges Gavin and walks off.

"Who is that guy?" asks Gavin, as I watch him leave.

He didn't even recognize him.

"A student at the association I work at."

An unpleasant smile comes over Gavin's face. "I should have guessed, his outfit gives it away."

"No, it doesn't!"

"Come on, it's like you're wearing blinders. He looks so lame in those moth-eaten clothes!"

I am not in the mood to hear this kind of bullshit. "Whatever. You wanted to see me?"

"Well, yeah, it's been ages since we caught up properly."

I'm almost ashamed to admit that it's done me a world of good.

"Why don't we go up to your apartment?"

I sigh and am just about to open the door when I see Ines further up the sidewalk. She's walking at a furious pace. When she reaches me, I look at her in surprise. "Hey, are you all right?"

"Yes."

She opens the door and practically runs up the stairs.

I turn to Gavin. "I'm sorry, but something's up with Ines. Can we take a rain check on this until tomorrow?"

Gavin nods indifferently. "Whatever you want."

He doesn't ask me to let him know how things go, he just leans over and gives me a peck on the cheek. That's weird. He's never done that before. Then he gets in his car, starts it up and speeds out onto the road with a squeal of the tires.

I sigh and hurry up the stairs to catch up with Ines. She's in the bathroom and is splashing water onto her face. I can tell she's been crying.

"What happened?"

"I don't want to talk about it."

"OK. But at least tell me if it's serious."

She dries her hands and looks at me. "Annie, don't get annoyed with me, we can talk about it tomorrow. But right now, I just want to go to bed."

She leaves the bathroom and shuts herself in her room. It's not even 7 o'clock.

What's going on?

8
December

For obvious reasons, I don't sleep well, and when I get up, at around 9, Ines is still in her room. I make myself a coffee, grab a slice of brioche and go and sit on the couch with my ethno-anthropology textbook.

For someone who wants to give up university, I'm surprising myself. But I manage to do it because I know that there are guys like Romeo who work in a snack bar during the week, which can't be fun. And girls like Ines who would rather be doing anything other than working in a primary school at the end of the day.

No one gets to do exactly what they want, not even a girl like me. "No pain, no gain," as my mother would say, so yes, I'm going to take my exams and if I don't pass, at least I will have tried. No regrets, no shame.

At 9:30 Ines still hasn't got up, and that's not like her.

I go into the kitchen and prepare her favourite tea, cut a kiwi, put some plain yoghurt in a bowl and grab some crispbread. That's what she eats every morning. I put it all on a tray and go knock at her door.

"Hmmm?"

When I go in, I find my housemate all wrapped up in her duvet like a caterpillar.

"Breakfast is served!"

I put the tray on her desk and open her shutters. Ines closes her eyes against the light. "What are you doing?" she mumbles.

"I've come to help the caterpillar out of its chrysalis."

Her curly hair is all mussed up. She leans back against the headboard and takes the mug I hand her.

I sit down next to her. "Are you feeling better? Did sleeping help?"

She holds the mug and breathes in the perfume of the jasmine tea. "Yup."

"Do you want to tell me what happened?"

She gives a deep sigh.

"It's my boss. I don't know what he has against me, but it's really starting to get me down. I went to see him before work yesterday, just like he asked. And it was only to make sure I stick to next week's timetable, during my exams. I mean, come on! And then, he decided to accompany me to school. That's the third time he's joined us in two weeks, and who does he always focus on? Me! He analyses my every word, gesture and decision. Yesterday, apparently, I wasn't strict enough with a pupil who kept colouring outside the lines. And then after that, he harped on at me about encouraging them to work independently and let them wash their hands on their own, even if they have paint everywhere. He finds fault with everything I do and nitpicks over the stupidest detail."

Ines is still totally worked up.

I get the tray and put it on her knees. "Is he only like this with you?"

"I think so, yes."

"Have you spoken to anyone about it?"

She gives a bitter laugh. "Who would I to talk to? He's the one in charge of the after-school lessons for that neighbourhood."

She grabs the crispbread and bites into it angrily. "He's always on at me, and it's doing my head in. Does he honestly not have anything better to do?"

"Have you tried asking him why exactly he's monitoring you all of a sudden?"

"No, but the less I have to do with him, the better. He's got this creepy way of looking at me. He kind of studies me, then gets this sickly-sweet voice and hovers around me while he's talking."

"Does he make you feel unsafe?"

"Not really, but he's not the kind of person I'd go and have a drink with, if you know what I mean. My contract only goes until Easter vacation, but I don't think I'll renew it. I'll find something else."

I smile at her. "You know what? To take your mind off things, why don't we go Christmas shopping together on Saturday!"

"We don't really celebrate Christmas at home, Mom has always hated it, but we do give gifts at New Years, so why not. That's a good idea!"

"Cool! And don't worry too much, I'm sure this'll all work itself out."

"Yeah, you're right! Anyway, enough about me, how did your date with Romeo the Dazzling go?"

I burst out laughing at the endless list of nicknames. "Got any others?"

"Eventually I'll run out."

I smile at her.

"He took me to a bar with board games."

"No way?!"

"Yup! He told me about his family and his financial situation. I think it was important for him."

"Did you talk about yours?"

"No. And I'm not sure I can. I told him my parents paid for most things, but I don't think it's a good idea to tell him they can afford way more than that. I know what that would look like."

"Maybe the opportunity will come up for you to tell him, but here's a piece of advice: don't wait too long or it'll seem like you've been dishonest. 'Cause something tells me that Romeo-who-glitters and you aren't about to go your separate ways for a while yet."

"Oh, come on, Ines, give it up!"

"Let's just wait and see, eh? Oh, while I think of it, we have to send in our assignment on Pierre Bourdieu today."

"Argh… I'll get my notes in order and give them to you!"

"OK. Right, it's time you left, unless you want to see me in my full glory. I slept butt naked and now I'm about to get up."

I shake my head and giggle.

If Ines Abad didn't exist, someone would have to invent her.

Despite sending a message to Gavin this morning, I didn't hear from him all day. I think he's annoyed. So, just before I leave for the community store late afternoon, I send him another message and try to be as light and fun as possible.

Hi! I'm going to the food market now but should we get a burger after? I finish around 7:30.

Hi, I was just about to reply to your message from this morning. I couldn't answer earlier, I went to Belgium with some friends.

Tonight sounds good. I'll come and pick you up. Where's your community thing?

Great! Meet me at Place du Marché in Wazemmes at 7:40?

OK, sounds good.

His messages are kind of neutral, with no "Hi angelface," and my kiss emoji goes unanswered. I start to feel guilty. I haven't been very nice to Gavin lately. I've been irritable and keeping him at arms' length.

I think I might have put him off.

OK, so there are some things about him that annoy me, but even though we don't agree on everything, he's really nice to me. I'm in a phase where I'm questioning everything… though not necessarily Gavin, because before I freaked out about school, I was fine with him. I really need to get things back on an even keel between us.

I pull on my coat, gloves and a woollen hat, ready to brave the cold North wind. I've made a decision. Tonight Gavin and I are going to have a good time together.

There are fewer people at the market tonight, and they are practically all new faces. Elise tells me it's because most customers generally only come once a week. Romeo is among those absent, even though last night he'd said he'd be there.

I can't help feeling disappointed. I haven't been brave enough to send him a message since he left me with Gavin. It was so tense, just like the first time they met, and I would have liked to apologize for that.

"Annie," calls out Elise as I'm putting away the last of the empty crates. "Do you mind staying on a bit and explaining your Secret Santa idea to everyone? I asked the students who're going to be at the Christmas party to wait for us upstairs."

I look at my watch. It's 7:15.

"Yes, sure! I'll just finish what I'm doing and then head up."

When I go upstairs, four students are waiting for me in the room. A girl and three guys are sitting in some armchairs, but there's still no sign of Romeo.

All the decorations I brought on Tuesday have been put up. With the room's wooden walls and floor, it looks as cozy as a mountain chalet. Hopefully the students will be keen on my idea once I explain it to them!

"Ah, Annie, just the person we were waiting for!" says Elise, who's standing next to Anthony. "For those of you who haven't met Annie yet, this is our brand-new volunteer. She helps out in the food market, but she also has a great idea for our Christmas party!"

Everyone is watching me curiously in perfect silence.

"You all seem a bit nervous," interrupts Anthony. "Normally you're all cackling away like geese, and I can't hear myself think! Perhaps we could start off by introducing ourselves? Who wants to go first? Thea?"

He turns to a girl with purple streaks in her hair.

She's lounging back on the couch and straightens up with a sigh. "Thea, third-year art history."

Short but effective. I nod politely.

"Mathias, first-year master's in social sciences," continues another.

A third gets up and comes over to shake my hand vigorously.

"Ionut, I'm Romanian. Third-year medicine," he says, rolling his r's. "It's cool you're here. Thank you!"

Kowè, a second-year master's student in biology, is from Gabon and is just as friendly, and before I know it, everyone is standing around me and shaking my hand or saying hello.

"Thanks for your warm welcome, I was feeling a bit shy. So now it's my turn to introduce myself. I'm Annette, but you can call me Annie. I'm doing second-year sociology and..."

I break off as I hear the stairs creak behind me. I turn and see Romeo. It's crazy, but I automatically break out in a massive grin.

"Sorry I'm late."

"You're exactly on time," says Elise to reassure him. "Take a seat. Annie is just about to tell us about something quite fun."

He pulls out a chair and sits down with the others next to the couches.

"So," I begin nervously. "Elise has told me that quite a few of you will be here over Christmas, and she was wondering what cool activities we could do. So, if you're up for it, I'd like to suggest a Secret Santa."

"What's that?" asks Kowè.

"The idea is simple. We each pull a name out of a hat, and you have to give a gift to that person on Christmas Eve. Basically, you know who you're getting a present for, but you don't know who's giving you yours – it has to stay a secret. Which is why it's called Secret Santa."

Everyone looks at each other, and I can see a moment of panic on their faces. This is clearly about the financial problem caused by such a plan, so I hurry to reassure them.

"There's one special rule, though: you have to make the present, you can't buy it! You can use whatever materials you like. You can fix something up, make something yourself out of whatever you have at hand – wood or paper – anything that floats your boat. The only real restrictions are that you can't tell anyone who your gift is for, and you also have to learn about the person whose name you pulled out of the hat so you can work out what to give them!"

I watch the students exchange looks, I hold my breath a bit, and then, relieved, I see them start to look motivated.

"Will you be doing it too?" asks Romeo suddenly.

"Of course!" says Anthony on my behalf. "We're all doing it, or else it won't be as fun! And also, that means there'll be an even number. Eight of us!"

I tense up a bit.

"Oh, but… I probably won't be with you on the 24th."

"Don't worry! We'll make sure you get your gift beforehand, or if the worst comes to the worst, it'll be waiting for you under the Christmas tree when you get back."

I look at Romeo, as he was the one who'd asked the question, and agree. "OK, sounds good to me! But I'm warning you, I'm not very good at making things. I'm practically a walking catastrophe, and I mess up pretty much everything I try!"

Elise and Anthony look at each other knowingly. "We ate your cookies and we're still here to tell the story!"

I wonder how I should take that comment, but I already know: the cookies must have been disgusting!

"We'll provide you with various materials," Anthony tells the students. "Glue, scissors, string, cardboard, fabric, paper. Once you've had a think, just let us know what you need."

"Is everyone OK with this?" asks Elise.

Heads nod in agreement.

"OK, then, it's time for the lucky draw!"

I look at my watch again. It's 7:35, I'm going to be late. But I don't see how I can sneak out now seeing as how I'm the one organizing the event. I rush downstairs to grab my phone, which I had left behind, and send a message to Gavin.

I'll be ten minutes late, sorry.
Is that OK?

I add a kiss emoji and run back up to join the others. Elise and Anthony are already cutting up bits of paper for us to write our names on. Just as I'm about to write my name, I smile. I didn't think I'd even be participating, but now it's official. And imagine how funny it would be if I got Romeo!

The pieces of paper are all in a Santa hat; all we need to do now is pull out a name each. Thea is asked to pass the hat round. Everyone grabs a piece of paper and looks at it, trying not to let their expression give anything away. I surreptitiously sneak a look at Romeo. He reads the name without blinking or making the slightest movement of his face, and casually stuffs the piece of paper in his pocket. But I almost die when I unfold mine.

Romeo

If Thea hadn't been right in front of me and asked me to close my eyes before I put my hand in, I could have been accused of cheating. But nope, it's just the universe and its strange sense of humour.

It's so hard not to give anything away. What can I make him that's not going to totally embarrass me? Not to mention the fact that I'll have to practise what I preached barely fifteen minutes ago and get to know him so I don't give him something completely off the mark.

Hang on… fifteen minutes ago? Oh no, it's 8 o'clock!

"Oh no, is that the time? Elise, I'm really sorry, but I have to go. I'll come in on Monday, or give me a ring if you need me? Actually, that goes for everyone," I say, looking around. "Just ask Elise for my telephone number."

"No problem, you can go, we've been over the main points!"

"Thank you! Bye, everyone!"

I'm sorry I don't have time to talk to Romeo, so I just make a gesture to say I'll call him later. He gives me a killer wink.

Seriously, I'm repeating myself, but how can he have such incredible eyes?

I leave the building and run towards the square. Gavin is waiting for me, double-parked. I open the car door and slide into the Audi.

"I am so sorry. It lasted longer than I thought it would."

I lean over to give him a kiss, but he's as stiff as a board. I lean back, confused. "Are you upset with me?"

"No, but I just don't understand you anymore. We barely even see each other, we barely speak to each other, you organize for us to meet up and then you turn up late?"

"I'm sorry, I didn't have a choice."

"Yes, you did, and you chose to spend your time with those losers rather than me."

"Stop calling them that, Gavin, they're anything but losers. Some of them are studying medicine. They might end up saving our lives one day. I get it if you're upset with me, but stop taking it out on them."

"Annette Reynaud, the newest member of the French Red Cross! And what about us? Are you still my girlfriend or do you want us to take a break?"

Deathly silence.

Did he truly say that?

"What kind of a question is that? You're allowed to do whatever, head off to Belgium with your friends, and I never ask if I can tag along. Am I not allowed to lead my own life too?"

"You call that a 'life,' do you? Looking after deadbeats who can't even get by without other people's charity?"

"Seriously? That's an awful thing to say. You realize that most of them work?"

"Not enough, obviously."

"That's rich coming from someone who's never had to work a day in his life! Listen, either you accept that I have other interests, or you don't. And if you don't, then we have a problem, because I'm not going to put a stop to them just because of you."

"I can't believe it. Given the choice between them and me, you choose them?"

"I'm just asking you to accept that my life is changing."

"Your life is turning to shit, and I'm not going to pretend otherwise."

The point of no return. How did we get here?

There's such a massive gulf between us, I can't imagine what could bring us together again.

I grab my bag and open the door.

"What are you doing?"

"I'm going home."

He doesn't try and stop me.

Good. I don't want him to see me cry.

9
December

This morning, the roofs and sidewalks of Lille are covered in a layer of snow, and the grounds of the Vauban Citadel are so white, it's like being in garden in Quebec.

I had a terrible night thinking about Gavin and our fight the day before, but when I get up, the idea of a walk around in the fresh powder is impossible to resist. Snow always has such a calming effect on me. I put on my shoes, a big sweater, a scarf, gloves and a hat, and set off towards the park.

It's so beautiful, and even though it's overcast, the white light of the snow is dazzling. The trees are covered in hoar frost and the frozen puddles look like tiny skating rinks.

"Ha! Take that!"

I turn around in surprise and get a snowball right in the face.

"Ohhh, I'm sorry, Ma'am! I didn't mean to."

My eyes widen – I'm more shocked by the use of Ma'am than by the snow cascading from my face.

The culprit looks barely twelve years old and is cowering next to the friend who was obviously the intended victim. Their horrified faces make me want to laugh.

"Hey, don't worry, no harm done!"

"Yes, but we're sorry anyway!"

"Don't you have school this morning?"

"No, it's closed because of the black ice."

"You guys are lucky."

They really shouldn't trust my friendly tone of voice, but they do… So I bend over, grab some snow and throw it at the boy.

Bam! Bullseye.

"That'll teach you to call me Ma'am!"

He is so surprised he almost falls over backwards.

"Take cover!" I shout as I grab another handful of snow. They don't miss a beat. In no time at all, they're firing snowballs at me like the ruthless kids they are. I manage to keep up for a couple of minutes, then I surrender, throw my arms in the air, and retreat at full speed.

I go back to my peaceful walk.

It's just past 11 o'clock and despite the snow, there are still joggers running around as if nothing was out of the ordinary. I draw in a deep breath, lift my head, close my eyes and turn my face up to an imaginary sun.

"Soon there won't be anywhere in Lille we haven't bumped into each other!"

All the hairs on my arm stand up.

"Romeo?"

"Annette?" he replies teasingly.

My smile is so wide it threatens to split my face in two. His expression is exactly the same.

He's wearing leggings with grey shorts on top, a black windbreaker with a hood, and his earphones. Yup, going by the beads of sweat on his forehead, he's a jogger.

"It's much nicer running in the park than in Fives," he explains. "Especially on a day like today. Hey, were you doing roly-polys in the snow?" he asks, pointing to my hat and jacket covered in snow.

"I was ambushed by a couple of Christmas elves along the way."

"I see," he says sceptically, raising an eyebrow.

"Twelve-year-olds, they're the worst!"

"I was about to go home, but do you want to walk together for a bit?"

"Sure!"

I am really happy to see him.

"Your Secret Santa idea is really great," he goes on. "Who did you pull out of the hat?"

I give a snort.

"You don't believe in elves, but you do believe in Santa Claus? You really think I'm going to tell you?"

"I could give you some tips about the lucky person. To help."

If only he knew!

"My lips are sealed. You're not getting anything out of me."

This makes him laugh. "I didn't think I'd see you here."

"I just love the snow. I couldn't resist."

"Oh, me too! It might be the only cool thing about mainland France."

"The only one?"

"Nah, I'm exaggerating. Living on the continent has its advantages, but I miss the vegetation, the fruit, the mountains and the ocean. The smell of the tropical forest too, and the colours of the sky. Everything here is so different. It's duller somehow. But fair enough, today the mainland definitely wins points!"

Suddenly I realize that this must be the first time he's seen so much snow all at once. I bend down and pick up some snow.

"Here, now you can taste it."

"I'm going to be honest with you, that was the first thing I did when I got to the park. And it's not great!"

"OK. And have you already done this?"

Without thinking, I throw the snow at him, which lands right on the collar of his jacket. I freeze. Romeo seems just as surprised as me.

"Oh really? It's like that, is it?"

"Sorry! I couldn't help myself!"

"I get it," he says, in a pretend tone of forgiveness and bending down at the same time. "I'm not used to these winter traditions yet, but I learn quickly."

I see. Payback is imminent. But frankly, there's no point in trying to run away, I know he'd catch up in zero seconds flat with his giant ostrich legs. So I open my arms out wide, close my eyes tightly and slightly twist one of the few lines from Romeo and Juliet that I know.

"OK, you win. 'Be not so long to act; I long to die!'"

Totally pretentious, and I've even changed the word 'speak' to 'act' to fit our situation!

Then I open one eye. Romeo hasn't budged an inch. He's laughing, which is how I know I've won. I walk towards him with a smile.

"How about we make a snowman? That's another time-honoured tradition!"

"When I left home this morning, my aim was to go running, but… Come on, I want to show you something!"

He turns on his heels and walks so quickly I practically have to run to keep up. He takes me on a path between the trees into a little, out-of-the-way clearing, and we stop in front of the most ridiculous snowman I've ever seen. It has a deformed body and a head so tiny it looks like a scoop of ice cream. Its nose is a twig, it has two minuscule bits of gravel for eyes, and a dried leaf sticking out of its skull. I struggle to hold back my laughter.

"Go on, I can tell you're trying not to laugh!"

"Noooo, not at all! Your snowman is gorgeous! It's just that it looks like its head got stuck in a shrinking machine…"

"This is my first ever attempt. At least I tried!"

"Do you want to make a friend for him? One that's a bit more handsome?"

"Sure!"

To be fair to Romeo, it's not easy to make a snowman out of fresh snow, as it crumbles really easily, but together we manage to make something slightly better than his crooked garden gnome.

Standing among the conifers and birches, we admire our work.

"Makes a change from sandcastles," he says.

"Is that what you do for Christmas in Réunion?"

"No, we make bonfires on the beach… we drink infused rum… we eat chilli candies, samosas, cari, duck with lychee…"

"When did you last go home?"

"It'll be two years in May."

I can't hide my surprise. "But I guess you've seen your family in between?"

"Just Mom, in March last year. She stayed for two weeks."

Ohhh…

"It won't always be like this. Hey, look at that!" he says, coming to a stop in the middle of the path.

He points to the branch of a beech tree heavy with snow and moss. My eyes fly open. Two birds with bright green plumage and pink necks are preening each other.

"They look like parakeets. But they're out in the wild… in this weather?"

"They're ring-necked parakeets," he explains. "They're really cute, but they gradually invade the territory of other birds."

"I've never seen any before, they look so… exotic. It's unreal to see them here."

"They're like me: far from home but perfectly adapted to their new environment!"

I smile at him, and we start walking again. Finally, I say what's on my mind.

"I wanted to say… I'm sorry for the other evening."

He doesn't seem to understand.

"When you walked me back, Gavin was a bit stressed."

"Because of me?"

"No, not at all! Because I hadn't answered his calls and he'd been waiting for a while. You know, if he has something he wants to say, he doesn't worry about whether other people are around."

Romeo nods without saying what he thinks.

"Have you been together for long?"

"Almost a year. And you?" I venture to ask. "Are you with anyone?"

"I'm married to my studies! Hey, I'd better go or I'll be late. I start work at the snack bar at 12:30. But will I see you on Monday at the ASEL?"

I nod. I'm already looking forward to it.

Is this wrong?

Do I need to be thinking about this now?

I know the only correct response is no!

"See you on Monday!"

I head towards the city centre with a grin stuck to my face. This morning, I really needed to have some fun, and Romeo made sure I did just that. I almost managed to forget the fight with Gavin.

Automatically I look at my phone. Not a single message from him, which gets on my nerves. I have my faults; I know I've been neglecting him a bit lately, but I feel like he's been so judgmental, I can't bring myself to make the first move. If he's not going to call me, I'm not going to call him either.

These thoughts are running through my head when my phone rings. It's my parents. I answer the phone while continuing to walk.

"Hi, darling!" says Mom in a bubbly voice. "Are you busy?"

"Nope, just walking home, I went to the park. It's snowing here!"

"Lovely, but I bet it's not the same as Canada," she says teasingly.

"Yeah, that's hard to beat. Did you want to tell me something, Mom? 'Cause usually you call on Saturday."

"Dad and I just wanted to find out how your volunteering is going."

My parents have always been curious, so I explain things, and they seem happy.

"What's the association called again?" asks Mom.

I scowl. "Why?"

"We'd like to make a donation."

I come to a sudden halt. "A donation?"

"To support your work in our own way."

"Mom, you don't need to. This was my decision, not yours."

She seems surprised. "Maybe you don't need me to, but I'm sure the people you're helping do. We're not trying to interfere, Annie, but just help out where we can. I'm sure you know that we donate to several different causes, so why shouldn't we help the one you're working for? That's what solidarity is all about."

I sigh and give in. I won't be able to make her change her mind. And although it annoys me, she's right. It's the association that counts.

"Association Solidaire Estudiantine Lilloise. But, um… please don't tell them I'm your daughter? As you can imagine, I haven't told them about my financial situation."

"Of course, no problem, we'll be totally discreet," promises my mother. "Hey, with your Secret Santa business, are you still coming home for Christmas?"

"Yes, absolutely."

"Perfect! I'd better go. Dad and I send you a big hug. And look after yourself," she says, as if she thought I was spending my whole life studying.

I'm definitely not doing that, but that is what I'm going to do now!

And I sure did study. Ines and I didn't even catch sight of each other all afternoon. But at 6:30 pm, she opens the door to my room and rushes in like a hurricane.

"Hey, girl! Shall we go out tonight?"

"Wow… you're on form!"

"I've had enough of being cooped up inside. The girls from our tutorial group are all going to the pub tonight. It's happy hour from 7 to 9."

I frown. "How come you know about this, and I don't?"

"Cos you never read the messages in our WhatsApp group! So do you want to come?"

I leave my desk covered in notes, get ready quickly, and at 7 on the dot we get to the pub.

It's packed, and there are no free tables left. We get a drink at the bar and go join the others. There are quite a few students from our year.

What the… Don't tell me they're playing truth or dare! The last time I played this, I must have been fourteen.

"I love it!" I say to Ines excitedly. "Wanna play too?"

"Totally! But I'm warning you, you better not hold anything back!"

"In your dreams! There is no way I'd choose 'truth,' I'm not totally insane."

There are still a few rounds before our turn, and I don't think I've ever laughed so much in my life. The 'dares' are by far the best. The deal is that if you don't do the dare, you have to pay a round. Obviously everyone tries hard not to mess up. Then Joy, one of the girls in my tutorial group, looks at me.

"Truth or dare?"

"Dare!"

She barely needs to think before telling me what to do.

"You have to hop to the entrance, hop outside, count to thirty on the sidewalk, then hop back inside on the other leg!"

General laughter all around. I'm going to look like an idiot, that's for sure.

As I get up, Ines is in fits of laughter, me not so much as I see how many people are in the pub. Then one of the guys in our group starts yelling at everyone to move out of the way. There's literally an airplane runway all the way to the door. Now I just have to do it.

I hop like a total moron, with people I don't even know shouting encouragement. I almost fall over a couple of times but manage to keep it up. As I get to the door, it opens without me touching it. Perfect! Luck is on my side.

Once I get to the sidewalk, however, it's another story. It's so icy that bouncing around like a kangaroo isn't ideal, but I can't even cheat, Joy has followed me out to make sure I go through with it.

"Annie?"

And… disaster strikes.

I turn around: it's Gavin. He just catches me, but it's too late, both my feet have touched the ground.

"This round's on her!" yells Joy.

A huge cheer goes up inside the pub. But a deal is a deal. I'm going to have to shell out.

"What are you doing?" asks Gavin.

"Truth or dare. I lost."

He smiles.

"It's happy hour, I'm just off to meet my friends, but I'm glad I ran into you."

"Really?"

"Come over here," he says, taking me by the hand. He leads me to a stone entrance way, out of sight of passers-by.

"I… I didn't call you because…"

He's struggling to find his words. He runs a hand through his hair and looks a bit sheepish. This is not like him at all.

"You're really important to me, angelface, and I don't like it when we fight."

I open my mouth to say something, but he stops me.

"Wait, let me finish. I was out of line… but it's because I was jealous. I hate having to share you, and also I don't really get the choices you've made, but I shouldn't judge them. You can do what you like, I'm fine with it."

I didn't expect this. Gavin is not usually the type to apologize. But now that we're talking, I want things to be clear.

"You shouldn't be jealous, just like I shouldn't be when you're with your friends, right?"

"I know, but I can't help it."

I sigh. I have to say exactly what's on my mind.

"Look. I realize I might not have been very present lately, and I'm sorry about that, but just because it annoys you, that doesn't give you the right to say that I'm hanging out with losers at the slightest opportunity. It's unacceptable."

"OK, OK. It's just that you're so different from them. I don't get it."

"They're not different, they just don't have as much money, that's all."

"It was a euphemism…"

"Gavin, I'm being serious. Please stop it."

"OK, look, I don't want us to fight anymore. You and I are good together, right? We need to try and compromise. You stop putting me after the association, and I'll stop mocking them?"

I raise an eyebrow. I can't believe it.

"No, that's not how it works. I'll try and make more time between my study, my exams and everything else, and you will stop criticizing my choices, what I choose to do with my time, and the people I hang out with."

His brown eyes flash. He doesn't agree with what I'm saying, but I don't give him a choice.

"OK, if you say so." he finally says. "Come here."

He takes me in his arms and strokes my hair. "I love the colour of your hair. It's so blond, so perfectly blond."

His lips join mine in what he wants to be an intense and passionate kiss. I close my eyes and lean into his embrace. His fingers curl around my neck and he draws me in closer, before letting go with a sigh.

"It's Saturday tomorrow, do you want to go to Bruges?"

"Oh, sorry, I promised Ines we'd go Christmas shopping."

I wait to see how he'll react. To my surprise, he doesn't take it badly. "How about Sunday?"

"Sounds good."

Gavin leans over to kiss me again, then pulls away reluctantly. "Shall we go inside?"

"Yup, I have a round to pay."

He laughs, then takes me by the hand and heads back into the pub.

He joins his friends, and I join mine, still surprised by the fact that he even apologized. But I'm disturbed by something even more surprising: for the first time ever, his kisses left me totally indifferent.

For the first time ever, I didn't feel a thing.

10
December

It snowed again last night. The streets are totally white and there are hardly any cars around.

For a Saturday afternoon, it's amazing!

Ines and I decide to skip the shopping malls and instead go to the city centre. The blanket of snow is so thick that it turns our trip into an incredible experience. Our footsteps make a funny noise on the sidewalk. Our shoes sink ten centimetres into the snow in some places, and if we had wanted to sit down on a bench, it would have been like sinking into frozen cotton!

Ines is not the sort of person who gets excited about shopping, but I am. The air is crisp, the people around us are smiling, we studied like crazy all morning, and now I'm ready to shop!

So instead of just admiring the window displays, I go into each store and buy a little something here and a little something there. Then we walk past a place not far from our apartment that is part florist and part second-hand store. You wouldn't believe what they have in there, and everything is for sale! Their flower arrangements are stunning, and there are really great preloved clothes. Whenever I go there, I always want to buy everything, and today, in the window, there's a Christmas wreath with holly and a big red satin bow. I'm not thinking of my place but of the one on the door to the association. It's so bedraggled it's lost the connection it once had with Christmas. So I drag Ines into the store.

"Hello!" I call out merrily. "Do you deliver?"

"Of course," answers the woman with a friendly smile. "Lille and suburbs."

"I'd like the big wreath in the window, please." Her mouth turns downwards, and she shakes her head in apology.

"I'm really sorry, that one has been reserved. But if you'd like, I can make you another similar one, with holly leaves, red berries and sparkly LEDs. A bit like that one, but bigger," she adds, pointing to a gorgeous wreath hanging from the ceiling.

"Oh, that would be great, thank you!"

"I can deliver it on Tuesday, if that suits you."

I think quickly.

"Since you haven't made it yet, perhaps deliver it on December 20th so it stays fresh until Christmas?"

"I can do that for you!"

As the florist goes into a back room to get her delivery book, Ines turns to me with a frown. "Are you collecting them? We already have one at home, two if you count the one on your bedroom door."

"No, it's for the association. You should see the state of the one that's hanging on the door. I feel like I need to put it out of its misery!"

Ines raises an eyebrow. "For someone who didn't know what use you'd be, you're really getting into it."

"Dad has an old saying that I really love: 'I'm like a good wine, I get better with age!'"

Ines laughs and goes to rummage around the store while I pay and give the woman the delivery address.

Once we're out on the sidewalk, we look at our purchases: Ines has found a present for her mom – a pretty floral scarf – and so have I – a porcelain pocket mirror that opens like a tiny jewellery box.

We spend the next hour or so hunting for bargains in the old town, then around 3 pm, half frozen to death, we decide to go and get a hot drink at the Grand Place with all our bags. There are lots of people. The snow hasn't put anyone off coming into town. Even the Ferris wheel is turning non-stop.

"I'm going to get a Liège waffle big enough to stuff the belly of a 300-kilo giant!" says Ines. "With chocolate sauce and whipped cream on top. I'm staaaarving! And what about you?"

"Just a golden latte, but it's my shout!"

"What's the occasion?"

"Putting up with me going into every single store I could find!" I giggle as I lift up the bags I'm holding. Despite my gloves, my fingers are frozen. I put everything down once the food is in front of us, grab my mug with two hands and blow on the strange, yellow-coloured hot milk.

"I don't know how you can drink that," says Ines, sniffing at it. "What's in there again? Turmeric, ginger, cinnamon?

Why don't they put in a cube of veggie stock while they're at it? And it doesn't even have coffee in it, so other than stripping your esophagus as it goes down, what good is it?"

"My mother, who is a very wise woman, says that a cup of golden latte a day keeps the doctor away. You should take a leaf out of her book!"

"You have to be joking. Hey, look! Isn't that your Romeo Rhinestone?"

"Where?"

"There, just next to the churros stand."

As I turn around, our eyes meet. Neither of us moves.

And for good reason… He's not on his own.

There's a girl with him.

I frown as I inspect her. She has her back to me, and under her white woollen hat with a pompom, very long, straight, dark hair tumbles down her cream puffer jacket. She turns around holding a huge packet of churros, covered in sugar. She is gorgeous and looks like she has Indian ancestry.

So why did my heart lurch?

"Is that his girlfriend?" asks Ines, taking a bite of her waffle.

"I don't know. I thought he said he was single, but maybe I misheard."

Our eyes meet again, and he starts walking towards us, accompanied by the girl. I bet my smile is slightly over the top, but too bad.

"Hi," he says, stopping right in front of us.

"Hello! You don't know Ines, my housemate, but you saw each other at the library. Ines, this is Romeo. Hello!"

I say to the brunette, as I put my hand out to shake hers. "I'm Annette."

The girl looks at my hand in surprise but ends up shaking it.

"I'm Serena."

Even her name is gorgeous.

Ines intervenes, far more cheerfully than me.

"I'm Ines. Your hair is beautiful! Unlike mine."

"Are you kidding? I've always wanted curly hair! You're so lucky!"

And the two of them start up an in-depth conversation on haircare as if they've known each other forever. Romeo and I look at each, slightly overwhelmed.

"Are you taking a break from your studying?" I ask.

"Yup… Serena came and picked me up. She was worried I was going to suffocate in my studio. She wants to be a pulmonologist, go figure," he laughs.

"Oh, are you both studying medicine?"

"She's in fourth year."

"Here, sweetie, eat some of these. Otherwise I'll end up finishing them all."

I nearly choke. Sweetie? Oh, come on! Romeo – 6 feet 5 inches, shoulders like a furniture removal man and a three-day beard – does not look like he should be called Sweetie.

Serena takes a churros and stuffs it in his mouth.

"Hey, do you want to come grab a Christmas beer with us?" she goes on to say. "We thought we'd go to this cool bar just a bit further on."

"Count me in!" says Ines excitedly.

Looks like I don't have a choice.

I've never been to this bar before, but it's awesome. Outside, everything is covered in snow and Christmas decorations, but in here the decor makes you feel like you're at a beach with a tropical forest at your back. There are three floors with colourful furniture, indoor plants, woven straw on the walls, fake parrots, flip flops on the ground and striped sun loungers. I love it!

We order at the bar and then sit down at a table in a quiet corner. There are leather Chesterfield couches and armchairs in pink, blue and yellow: it's unreal!

Romeo sits down automatically next to Serena, with their shoulders and knees almost touching. It's kind of annoying. I can't work out if they're together or not. He told me he wasn't with anyone; why would he have lied to me?

Although now that I think about it, he just said he was married to his studies, and I interpreted the rest. But I guess that doesn't stop him from… wanting to… have fun!

OK, now, calm down. No need to start imagining things.

I look up at Serena, who lets out a shriek of laughter. Romeo just said something completely incomprehensible.

Then I realize. It was Creole. Things start to click into place.

"Are you from Réunion Island too?"

"That's the one! I'm so happy Romeo and I met each other," she says, laying her head on his shoulder and a hand on his thigh. "We're studying the same thing, we both like beer and rum, we're from the same place. And we both love eating samosas in bed and watching TV!"

OK, mystery solved. They're definitely together.

I feel irritated without even knowing why, but I have to admit they go together well. Exceptionally well even: they're both really tall, they both have Italian names, and they come from the same island. They'd be perfect for a *Vanity Fair* photo shoot.

"Are you guys both from around here?" asks Serena.

"I'm from the Paris region, and Annie's from the south of France."

"But you have mixed origins, right?"

Ines gets that little look of pride she does whenever someone asks her that question.

"Yeah, my dad's Algerian and my mom's half-French, half-Irish."

"No wonder you have those incredible eyes!" says Serena in rapture.

All I can do is look at Romeo, and *his* incredible eyes. He's smiling and not saying anything. As if being surrounded by three girls has put him in a kind of fourth dimension.

Ines and Serena continue to chat, and they barely stop speaking when the waiter brings us our order.

We get beer for everyone except me. I order a mocktail, which is served in a half coconut with a paper straw and a mini cocktail umbrella with little dots on it.

The first time I tried one of these, I was in Hawaii. My parents and I spent eight months there. And the coconuts were so fresh that all I wanted to do was throw out the drink and eat the flesh. I'm not sure that this one will have the same effect, but it's fun anyway. I bring the straw to my lips and take a small sip.

I look up. Romeo is looking right at me. "All you need is a tiaré flower in your hair."

"What?"

"You'd fit right in at home."

I have no idea why he said that. But I laugh gently.

"Like a tourist, you mean! Going by the colour of my skin, I'm presuming that was a joke."

"I'm sure you'd get used to the sun."

Unfortunately I can't tell him that in Hawaii, my skin stayed pasty white the whole time. I even got allergies from the sun.

"Have you ever been to the south of France?" I ask him.

"Nope. I haven't been anywhere except my island, Paris-Charles-de-Gaulle, and… Lille."

I feel uncomfortable and look down. I can't believe how brainless I can be sometimes. He has no money; how could he afford to travel? And what am I meant to talk about now? The tiny little Mediterranean coves he's not going to see anytime soon? The super-rich villages along the Côte d'Azur?

I'm even boring myself.

"Have you started your Secret Santa present?" I ask, in an attempt to change the subject.

"Ha ha! I don't know who he got," interrupts Serena, "but whoever it is had better not expect too much. Last night he was trying to glue matchsticks together and after ten minutes he gave up and they ended up flying everywhere!"

"Keep your mouth shut, please!" says Romeo. "You never know, I might have picked Annie, and now you've given it away."

"Oops!" Serena pretends to zip her mouth closed. I look at Romeo, wide-eyed. "I'm your Secret Santa?"

He smiles. "Nah, don't worry. You'll be getting a present from someone far more skilled than me."

"I'm a bit of a klutz too. These hands are no good at crafts."

Immediately he starts to study my fingers. "Do you play the piano?"

"How did you guess? I mean, I haven't played since I got to Lille, but yes."

"Your fingers are so long and slender."

It's stupid, but now I don't know what to do with my hands! I hide them under the table and give a silly laugh. "If you had seen the huge paddles my piano teacher had, you'd think differently."

They were incredible. His hands looked like they were strong enough to crack walnuts, but when he played the piano, they seemed unbelievably light, almost otherworldly.

"Maybe the two aren't mutually exclusive!" laughs Romeo. "Who knows…"

The four of us continue chatting for a while. I'm about to suggest another round, but Ines calls an end to it. She wants to study some more, and I should probably do the same.

It's 4:30. It's started snowing again, and the daylight is almost gone.

Around us, the Christmas decorations are starting to light up. With the falling snow, it's magical.

I pull on my woollen hat and wind my scarf around my neck, ready to brave the cold.

"That was really fun, we should catch up again soon!" raves Serena, clinging to Romeo's arm. "But let's hurry up and go home, Sweetie, I'm not made for the snow!"

I hate that nickname. Really hate it.

Then she releases him and decides to give us a hug. Romeo leans towards me to follow suit, and even though I'm tall, I have to stand on my tiptoes.

Our cheeks touch.

Damn, he smells good.

I have to fight not to close my eyes.

Oh, come on, this is ridiculous. Calm down!

I back off, smile at everyone and then grab Ines by the arm to lead her away. All the people coming and going have barely made a dent in the snow, it's still so soft.

"Home sweet home!" I sing out as we reach our place.

"That girl is so cool," says Ines enthusiastically.

"You think?"

"Yes! Don't get jealous, she really is great."

I shrug. "Whatever."

"You're jealous!"

"No, I'm not."

"Yes, you are! But I get it. He's cute."

"Ines!"

She bursts out laughing and pulls me across the street.

"But she's even better looking than him! I'm not used to meeting girls who are prettier than me," she says jokingly.

"Now you know what it's like for me."

She stops dead in her tracks. "Are you nuts? You're beautiful, Annie! Have you seen your hair? Your beautiful pale skin and pink cheeks! You look like a Russian doll!"

"Yeah, without the curves," I add, looking down at my non-existent chest.

"Pfff. If I was a guy, I'd think you're hot!"

And she starts walking again.

"Hey, wait a second," I stop her. "Look at this pop-up store!"

In front of us there is a window display unlike any I've seen before, full of Christmas objects. There are little teddy bears, stars, wooden reindeers, Nutcrackers, cuddly toys, Father Christmases made of all sorts of materials, all sparkly and shiny. Everything is so pretty.

"Um, no!" says Ines firmly. "We already have everything we need at home, and I'm sure your precious association doesn't need anything else."

"Don't be a party pooper, we're going in!"

I drag her in with me and then come to complete halt as the scent of gingerbread and then cinnamon fills my nostrils.

Wow, I love this place!

I start looking around everywhere, on all the shelves, in all the half-open drawers. Even Ines gets caught up in the wonderful atmosphere. This is like heaven for kids *and* adults!

I'm wondering how I'm going to get out of here without buying something when I stumble on a magnificent painting. A landscape in the style of Henri Rousseau. A jungle, with incredible, deep-red flowers, perfectly ripe fruit, wild animals and, on every branch, a thick layer of snow making the leaves bend under its weight. And right at the bottom, painted in gold letters: 'Christmas on My Island.'

My heart starts to beat more quickly.

I know what my Secret Santa for Romeo is going to be.

A forest, exotic birds on branches, vibrant foliage and the deep blue of the ocean.

I'm going to give him his island in a snow globe.

11
December

Gavin comes to pick me up at around lunchtime to drive us to Bruges. I had just gotten back from a craft store, where I bought everything I need to make my snow globe. I was lucky enough to get the very last base, as the shop won't be restocking them. I have no idea what I've gotten myself in for, but it's not going to be easy. The person who sold it to me warned me that I would have to be really meticulous. And everyone knows that 'meticulous' is my middle name!

I came back from the store with a bag of leaves and synthetic moss, paint, Fimo* clay that I don't even know how to use, special tools, and lots of bits and pieces that I'll have to fiddle around with using tweezers. There are even some gorgeous tiny bird figurines that look as if they were stolen from a Playmobil factory.

"We'll be there in ten minutes," says Gavin, all smiles as he drives. "We're lucky, it's great weather today."

It sure is. It snowed again last night, but the skies have cleared to an azure blue. My parents are utterly convinced that there's no light in the North, so I send them a couple of photos to prove I'm not a pathological liar.

---

* TN: Fimo is a brand of polymer clay sold worldwide.

I smile at Gavin. I am determined that today is going to be super fun, to make up for the past ten days we spent being annoyed at each other. He seems to be in a really good mood. Ever since we left he's been laughing, telling jokes, and he hasn't once mentioned my studies or the association. It's so easy when he's like this!

"I'm going to park in the t'Zand underground garage," he says. "I don't want anything to happen to my car. Did I tell you that the last time I was in Belgium some jerk scratched the passenger door?"

"No, but is everything OK, did your car survive?" I say jokingly.

"I dropped it off at the workshop of a guy my dad knows, he's an auto body mechanic. He fixed it the same day."

Gavin and his car. He didn't even realize I was teasing him.

"You still don't want to get your driver's license?" he asks.

"No, I don't really need one in Lille."

"Yeah, especially 'cause you have me to drive you around!"

I raise an eyebrow, but don't bother mentioning that there's this incredible invention called the train that's been around since 1804. It's not always on time but it's really practical, and it goes pretty much everywhere. I know my way around an airplane too, apparently.

Gavin pulls into the garage, and as I look around, I see that the whole of the Nord département must have arranged to meet up in Belgium today. There is an incredible number of cars with its 59 number plate. Bruges really isn't far from the border, and it's maybe one of the prettiest towns in Belgian

Flanders. When you come here, you can expect to hear as much French as Flemish.

We park, and ten minutes later we find ourselves in a big square full of construction work going on. It's 2 pm and my stomach is making the most outrageous noises.

"Are you hungry?"

"Starving!" I answer. "And dying to eat some fries."

I love fries in all their many forms: big, small, crispy, soft, cooked in oil or beef fat, French, American or Belgian! If you want to put me in a good mood, feed me fries. And Gavin knows this better than anyone.

"Why do you think I wanted to take you to Belgium?" he says with a wink, putting an arm around my neck. "Let's go! Your wish is my command!"

The last thing we want to do is go to a restaurant; they're all full and people are lining up outside, so we buy a big bag full of fries to take away, and Gavin orders a *mitraillette** as well, before we go and sit down on a bench next to the Reie Canal.

The sun is shining brightly and there's not a cloud in the sky, and even though I'd love to lie down on the grass, there's still snow everywhere. I'm living each moment to the fullest and not feeling guilty about missing an entire day's worth of studying, which is what Ines is busy doing. Exams start tomorrow afternoon, so spending a whole day away from my studies is the best thing I could do.

---

* TN: A mitraillette is a type of sandwich common in Belgium and the North of France. It usually consists of a portion of baguette filled with fries, sauce and sometimes meat. It's also called an *américain*.

Or at least, that's what I tell myself. I need a break.

We stay there a while, watching the boatloads of tourists visiting the town by canal, surrounded by ducks paddling in the cold water. It's such a romantic spot, with the trees covered in snow, the little stone wall on the bank of the river and houses with gables on the other side, but Gavin doesn't seem to notice. All he does is talk non-stop about his car races, the Porsche his dad is going to buy, the one he wants. He has always been like that, totally focused on what interests him and nothing else. Why did that not bother me before? I don't know… So I convince myself that simply being here is a good start and listen to him without saying anything, but at some point, absorbed in my own thoughts, I lose track of what he's saying.

"So what do you think?"

"What?"

"Do you want to go for a beer at the 2be Beer Wall or not?"

In *Vampire Diaries* any opportunity to drink whisky is a good one. In Belgium and the North of France, the drink of choice is beer. I'm used to it.

"OK!"

We plunge into the town centre, and like every time I come here, I'm struck by how beautiful it is. Bruges is incredible and unique. You feel like you could reach out and touch its medieval past. With all the red-brick buildings, the cobbled streets, the little stone bridges, the city walls and gates, it's like travelling back to another time.

We walk a few hundred metres and reach the heart of the old town, the Burg, with the city hall and its mighty belfry, surrounded by historical buildings. Tourists line up to ride in a carriage drawn by big, black horses. They line up to visit the basilica and the many museums. They line up to buy sandwiches. It's overflowing with people, and I totally get it.

This is the first time I've seen Bruges in the snow in the period leading up to Christmas, and it's mind-blowing! It's extraordinarily beautiful.

"Wow…"

"What?" asks Gavin.

"It's so gorgeous."

He shrugs. "It's Bruges."

"You look so blasé. We could be in Trifouillis-les-Oies for all you care!"

"It's just I've been here so often, that's all."

Well, I still think it's amazing. This town is the greatest! And when it's Christmas, with all this snow, it's just unbelievable. It makes me want to sing 'We Wish You a Merry Christmas' at the top of my lungs!

"OK, so what shall we do then?" I ask, super excited. "We don't have to go and get a beer right away, what do you think? I'd love to climb to the top of the belfry. Imagine looking out over all the snowy rooftops! And then there's the Fries Museum, that could be fun!"

Gavin gets an awkward look on his face.

"Um… Actually, some of my friends are at the 2be Beer, and I said we'd meet them there."

I have to make a real effort not to lose my smile.

"Your friends? We're not spending the day together, just the two of us?"

"Yes, totally, but they're there, and I thought we could go for an hour, just for a beer or two."

Make sure the day goes well. Make sure the day goes well. I keep my cool and push my disappointment down as far as it will go.

"OK, if you want."

"Cool! Come on, it's over here!"

He takes me by the shoulder, and we head down a narrow street lined with bars, chocolate shops, restaurants and… the Torture Museum, which is unbelievable. I went there once with my parents while they were on a visit. It's in a basement and once you get inside, even the smell is a kind of torture, an unbearably musty combination of sewers and mould.

The 2be Beer is practically next door, in an exquisite Flemish building with tall windows of cross-hatched stained glass, sculpted stone lacework and a huge turret. We go through a carriage entrance and continue along a passage that had left my father in awe.

The bar is at the end on the right, and on the walls, on each side, hundreds of different beers are displayed behind little windows, showcasing all the beers produced in Belgium. It's so spectacular that it's a real tourist attraction. There are so many people you can barely see a metre ahead. We force our way through the crowd and end up on a wrought-iron balcony overlooking the canal.

Below us, the water slips quietly by, with waterlilies and the odd swan, not disconcerted in the least by the amount of people. It is so charming and romantic that I can't resist.

"Shall we take a quick photo first?" I suggest to Gavin.

He pulls a face. "They're waiting for us…"

"Just one or two!"

I pull him by the arm, get out my phone, and with our backs to the railing I take a barrage of selfies. Gavin smiles briefly, while keeping an eye out towards the bar. I give up.

"Right, let's go!"

Some tables have been set up outside and at one of them, a group of three guys are watching us arrive, cracking up.

"Didn't know you liked having your photo taken!" says one of them mockingly. "You looked like a total dick!"

"It's his wannabe playboy side coming out," says another.

Gavin's infamous friends. Just as I thought, I don't know any of them. They keep roasting him for a bit more, then shuffle round and pull in two more chairs.

"Sit down! What do you want to drink? A Cassadura for you and a Brugs Tarwebier for your girlfriend?"

Gavin says yes without asking my opinion, which annoys me. I don't say anything though; I don't want to make him feel uncomfortable. But I know exactly what the vibe is. These guys are here to drink, and they don't give a damn about what's around them and how beautiful it is. They haven't even asked me my name, and honestly, I don't care. I already know I'm not going to like them. We'll have our drink and then leave.

But things don't go exactly as I'd planned. Gavin is on his third beer, and I haven't even finished my first. All they talk about is cars, their last cannabis- and alcohol-fuelled trip to the Netherlands, girls – as if I wasn't there – and Gavin doesn't look like he's going to budge. I'm over this. I'm not the sort to make a scene, so I lean over to him and whisper in his ear that I'm going for a walk. He barely listens.

I get up and leave without anyone noticing.

I pace through the streets of Bruges in a rage. This is not at all how I had imagined today would go. I had made a real effort to make up for my absence over the past few days. And if it was just for Gavin to go drinking with those three losers, I would have been better off not coming instead of wasting my time here. Not only am I angry, I'm also really sad. Gavin and I have absolutely nothing in common anymore. Nothing at all.

I go into the first store I see and decide to finish my Christmas shopping. I may as well make the most of being here.

I keep myself busy until 5 pm, then go back to find Gavin. They haven't moved an inch, but they're in a sorry state.

"Ah, there you are!" says Gavin as he sees me, in a voice I barely recognize. "I thought you got lost somewhere!"

"That's what you hoped, you mean," sniggers one of the three guys.

"Come here, babycakes, I want you to try this amazing beer. And I'll get another one too."

"I think you've had enough to drink. Come on, let's go."

"Look at her!" cries the drunkest of the three. "She thinks she's your mom!"

"Gavin…" I say again in a steady voice.

Luckily, he still has just enough sense to listen to me.

"Nah, guys, I'd better go. She has her exams tomorrow."

He gets up, staggers and nearly knocks the table over in an effort to keep his balance.

He is in no condition to drive, and I don't have my driver's license. This is not looking great. There's no train or bus, so I only have two options: call a taxi or spend the night here.

"Let's just get a hotel for the two of us, eh?" slurs Gavin.

"I'm going to call a taxi."

"Oh, go on, a five-star hotel with rose petals and champagne."

His eyes are bright, and I know exactly what he's thinking. But given the state he's in, that's the last thing I want.

I try the first option and ask the waiter for the telephone number of a local taxi. I end up calling about fifteen different taxis, but not one is willing to take us all the way to Lille.

So, even though it totally sucks, I'm left with no choice, I have to fork out for a hotel. It costs a fortune, when all Gavin deserves is a straw pallet on the floor. That would set him straight.

Once we get to the hotel room – far too beautiful and romantic for the pitiful couple we are – Gavin flops onto the bed in his clothes and falls asleep instantly, only to start snoring. I watch him for a few long seconds without moving, before grabbing my phone and letting Ines know where I am. Her reply hits me like a bucket of cold water.

Why in the hell don't you dump this loser?

I have to go. I'll let you know how things are tomorrow.

Hey, don't miss your exams because of him, OK? If you need someone to pick you up, just let me know.

Don't worry, I'll sort it out. See you tomorrow 😘

😘

I lie down next to Gavin, totally over today, totally over his behaviour and totally over my life, which feels like it's spinning out of control. Negative thoughts are racing through my mind. I'm this close to crying but manage to hold back the tears. He's not worth it. I finally fall asleep. It's not even eight pm.

What a fantastic day…

When I open my eyes, awakened by a hand roving over my stomach, the room is pitch black. I've no idea what time it is, but Gavin is glued to me with his alcohol-laden breath. Seeing how he's touching me, he's obviously back to normal and knows what he wants. I push him away gently, but he doesn't give up. His fingers try and burrow under my t-shirt. I grab him by the wrist.

"Stop it."

"Oh, don't sulk. I feel much better now and really want to give you a cuddle."

A cuddle? He must be kidding.

"I said no."

He ignores me and leans onto me even more. He grabs my hips and rubs against me.

"Babe… you can't leave me like this, I need you."

I leap off the bed, turn on the light and push him over to the other side of the bed.

"What part of the word 'No' do you not understand? I do not want to sleep with you, I do not want you to cuddle me. I don't even want you to touch me. I am REALLY not in the mood."

"You sound like an old woman who's been married for thirty years," he grumbles.

"No. I sound like someone who's going to walk out right now if you keep this up. It's your fault we're here, so leave me alone and let me go to sleep."

I lie down again and turn my back to him.

"You are such a drag! I didn't bring you to Bruges for this to happen."

"I could not agree more."

"Oh, come on… I overdid it a little this afternoon, but it's not like anyone died. It was just a few beers."

There's no point replying. He wouldn't understand.

"We'll talk about it later. My exams start tomorrow, I need to rest."

"Bullshit! They're a total waste of time, I already told you. But do what you want. And when you finally realize how stupid you've been, you'll come running back to tell me I was right, and all I'll do is laugh at you."

In a rage, he gets up and shuts himself in the bathroom, slamming the door behind him.

I turn out the light and lie back down, with tears in my eyes and my heart aching.

This cannot go on.

12
December

We leave Bruges at 10 o'clock in stony silence.

When we get to my apartment, I barely have time to get out of the car before Gavin revs the motor and speeds off, tires screeching.

My head is spinning with bad thoughts, the same ones that plagued me all night and on the drive home. I wonder if Gavin even realizes that it's over between us. I haven't spoken a single word to him since last night. At the hotel, he went and had breakfast, as if nothing had happened, whereas I couldn't even get a single coffee down. But today is an important day. I have to put all that aside.

As I'm about to put the key in the lock, the door opens with Ines behind it.

"Oh, there you are! I was so worried you wouldn't make it back in time! How are you? How do you feel?"

I put my bag on the ground and sigh. "Like someone who needs a litre of coffee, a hot bath and a Tylenol. Some peace and quiet too."

"What happened? Talk me through it."

Which I do. Ines is appalled.

"I can't believe what a loser he is. Does he ever think of anything apart from himself?"

I reply without an ounce of irony. "Yes, his car. Don't take this the wrong way, but I'm going to lock myself into the bathroom to try and clear my mind. Then I'll see if I can study for an hour or two before I head off."

"Do you want me to stay with you?"

I raise an eyebrow and give her a weak smile. "Why, do you want to scrub my back?"

"In your dreams!"

I know what she means though, so I answer seriously.

"That's nice of you, but I think I need to be on my own for a while. But let's hang out tonight if you want?"

"Sounds good."

I shut myself into the bathroom, choose a playlist on my phone and turn on the Bluetooth speaker before running a bath.

My head feels like a giant watermelon.

Nothing is going right at the moment, that's for sure. And what is also sure is that all it would take to completely finish things off is failing my exams and letting my parents down. OK, so I've left things a bit late, and I haven't studied as much as I should have, but I make myself a promise: if I pass my exams, I won't make any hasty decisions. I'll think seriously about what I want to do with my life.

When the bathtub is full, I get in, shut my eyes and sink under the water.

Empty my mind, for just a few minutes: that's all I want.

When Ines and I come out of our first two-hour exam, I have the weird feeling that it didn't go too badly. Everything seemed so clear and logical that I start to doubt myself. But after talking things over with Ines and other students in the metro, it looks as if I didn't write complete nonsense after all.

"Maybe the subject suits you more than you thought," she says with a wink.

"Let's not get ahead of ourselves. I want to wait and see what the results say first. And not before the start of the next school year anyway!"

"What'll you do if you pass everything?"

My thoughts from this morning come racing back. "I dunno. I'm sure it'll be obvious when the time comes."

"Obvious? 'Plain and evident to the mind; perfectly clear or manifest,'" she recites. "Yup, 'obvious' is the right word. Just like it seems pretty 'obvious' to me that you need to break up with Gavin."

I sigh. "I really don't want to talk about this right now. And anyway, you're about to get off the train and I'm staying on until Wazemmes. I'm going to the ASEL."

She smirks at me, which doesn't bode well. "Hey, didn't you say you wouldn't go in during your exams? You're not going to meet up with something else that's 'obvious,' by any chance?"

I roll my eyes. "Ines, I'm warning you. If you say that word one more time, it's going to give me indigestion!"

"OK, OK! But when you see him, say hi from me and tell him you love his eyes! See you tonight!"

Ines skips off the train, and the doors close behind her. She's definitely not going to let me off the hook that easily!

That said, she's not wrong. When I first met Elise, I had said I wouldn't be available during my exams. But I feel useful when I'm there. And I want to show them I'm taking this Secret Santa idea seriously.

I reach the food market with a smile on my face but come to a halt as I see the crowd waiting on the sidewalk. I'm fifteen minutes early, and there's already a huge number of students queuing up. Twice as many as the other times. I cast my eyes over them in the hope of seeing Romeo, but he must like taking me by surprise.

When I go in, Mathilde and Hassan, the two volunteer students, are already there, filling the crates with fruit and vegetables on the display stand behind the counter. Same rigmarole as the last time – it's December, so a Santa hat is required. But this time I'm organized and pull one out of my bag before putting it on my head.

"Hi!" I say. "There are so many people outside."

"Don't remind Elise," replies Hassan. "She only received half of the food she ordered. She was expecting the rest to arrive today, but it wasn't delivered."

"Really?"

"There was an issue with the supplier, she's going to have to tell some customers that even though they signed up, they won't be getting a food bag. She's so frustrated."

I look around for Elise. She's on the telephone at the back of the store.

"There are bags for how many people?"

"About twenty," replies Mathilde, wiping her forehead with a hand.

"But... there are at least fifty waiting outside."

Mathilde screws up her face and shrugs.

"Yup. It's awful."

"Annie!" cries out Elise behind me. "Were you just passing by or did you make time to come especially?"

She looks frazzled. Her hair is all over the place.

I take off my coat and put it on the counter.

"I've come to help! And it looks like I chose the right day."

Elise huffs out a sigh. "Yup. Right, we're opening in five minutes, everyone gather round!"

Mathilde, Hassan, Anthony the treasurer, and Veronique and Pierre, two retired volunteers, congregate around Elise.

"As you know, this has been a challenging day: we only have twenty food bags for the forty-eight people who signed up, plus all those who didn't sign up. I had hoped we'd receive another delivery by 5 pm, but it's 4:55 now, so I think we can assume it won't get here until tomorrow morning. I will explain the situation and make sure the customers can come and collect them later. But considering the number of students waiting outside, I'm pretty sure we're going to run out of shower gel, toothpaste, sanitary pads and shaving cream. Seeing as you're here, Annie, can you go to the mini-mart and buy some extras? We have an account with them, I'll let them know you're coming."

"Of course. How much of each do we need?"

Elise rummages in her pocket and pulls out a piece of paper.

"Here's the list. Thank you, that's one less thing for me to worry about. OK! Places everyone, it's time to open."

While she opens the roller door and the customers start to enter one by one, I dash to the mini-mart to buy the missing items. But when I get to the checkout and see how much it all costs – 135 euros for twelve bottles of shower gel, eighteen tubes of toothpaste, ten spray cans of shaving gel and twenty packets of sanitary pads – and I think about how much I spend on a single visit to the hairdresser, I find myself unable to tell the checkout assistant that I'm here on behalf of the association. I get out my credit card and pay.

I leave the store as if nothing were up and hurry back to the food market.

There are still people on the sidewalk, and when I come in through the main door, I run into Romeo, who is coming down the stairs.

"Oh, you were upstairs?" I ask with a smile.

I always smile when I see him. He does too, but he's more discreet about it.

"Yeah, I needed a couple of things for my Secret Santa."

"Matchsticks that'll do as they're told, I suppose?"

'Sweetie' pokes his tongue out, which just makes him look even cuter.

"Let me give you a hand!"

He comes over, grabs two of the three bags I'm holding and takes them into the store. Just as we go in, we hear shouting in the aisles.

It looks like two students are arguing over toothpaste. We go closer to see what's happening.

"Hey!"

"Piss off! I saw it first! And anyway, your teeth are so shit, it wouldn't even do you any good!"

I can't believe what I'm seeing.

"You're such a jerk, you know that?" says the guy who had wanted the tube of Colgate.

"First come, first served, dude!"

"Yeah, except that *I* was here first!"

"Then too bad, it's every man for himself. See ya!" And he heads over to the checkout, without a care in the world.

"What's going on here?" asks Anthony.

He's not particularly tall nor solid, but he's still imposing. Except that the student who took the toothpaste doesn't give a damn, and once again voices are raised. Anthony speaks a little louder and everyone falls quiet.

"You have already been warned," he says to the troublemaker. "This is the last time you pull a stunt like that. This is a place for supporting one another, not walking all over each other."

The student laughs scornfully. "We're not living in some fairy-tale world. If you don't fight, you don't get anything!"

"You're welcome to fight if you want, but fight against those who deserve it."

"Screw you!"

He drops his shopping bag and leaves. I can't get over what I just saw.

"Let it go, Annie," says Romeo, with a neutral expression. "Even poor people can be jerks. And he's a regular.

It's like he has a sixth sense and only comes when there's not enough stock."

"The worst thing is that there's plenty. I just got more."

"He's a jerk. And being a jerk has nothing to do with where you are on the social ladder."

I feel a little disturbed. I hand over the bags to Anthony and then hang back, giving a sympathetic look to the student ridiculed by the other.

"Actually," says Romeo, catching my attention again. "I'd like to ask you something."

"Yes?"

"Come over here."

He leads me over to the foot of the stairs in the entrance hall. "Do you have Ines's phone number?"

His eyes are shining, and I feel totally gutted. "What?"

"I was wondering if you could give me Ines's telephone… Oh," he cuts himself short, noticing my expression. "It's not for me, it's for Serena."

I know I must look like a fool, but I start blinking madly.

"Serena?"

"Yup… She's got the hots for Ines."

I gape at him, speechless. But not for long.

One plus one equals two, so…

"She's not your girlfriend?"

"My girlfriend?" He bursts out laughing. "I'm not that crazy! And anyway, she's not into guys."

"Oh…"

I feel relieved. But why do I feel *so* relieved?

Romeo drops his head and looks me straight in the eye. "Did you think we were together?" To my extreme embarrassment, I get a moronic expression on my face. Like I'm the world's greatest ditz.

"Yes! You just looked so cute together."

"Well, nope."

He shakes his head with a smile and looks at his watch. "There are too many people here today, and anyway, they don't have enough food bags. I'll come back tomorrow. Tonight I've got a date with my textbooks. You'll message me her number?"

"Will do!"

"Thank you!"

He turns around and heads towards the main door, but at the last minute, looks back at me with a little smile on his face.

"Actually, I prefer blondes."

And out he goes.

Why is it so hot in here all of a sudden?

It's exactly 7:30 when I get home.

I'm surprised to find a bouquet of flowers in front of my door. Surprised but not amazed.

I know who it's from.

I pick it up and read the accompanying card.

There's nothing that flowers can't fix.
G.

I go inside and nearly let out a cry as I discover Gavin sitting on the couch. I put the flowers on the little table in the entrance way and turn to look at him.

"How did you get in?"

"Your housemate let me in. She was just off to run an errand. The flowers on your doorstep were the first surprise. And I'm the second!"

He gets up to kiss me, but I back away.

"Oh, come on, angelface. I know I was a bit of an idiot, but you and I love each other."

I am calm, too calm. Gavin should be able to guess that something's up, but he's totally relaxed and sure of himself. Totally unfazed.

I face up to him.

"You invited me to spend the day with you in Bruges, and then you got drunk with some guys I don't even know. You almost made me miss my exams, and then that night, you thought you could touch me, as if nothing had happened, and then got shitty because I didn't want you to. And, to top it off, you didn't apologize once."

He runs his hand through his hair and gives a little smile. "Come on, Annie. Let's not blow things out of proportion. I'll make up for it. OK, so I messed up in Bruges, but what about this; how about we go to London for the weekend, just the two of us? We'll stay in a luxury hotel, just the way we like it, and go on a restaurant cruise along the Thames. It'll be a dream trip."

I look at him without a word, my jaw clenched tighter than ever.

"What do you say?" he insists.

"You are completely deluded."

Gavin furrows his brow.

"You'd rather go to Amsterdam? Stockholm? Rome? Just tell me where you want to go."

He really has no idea.

"We're not going anywhere together, Gavin. You and I are finished."

"What? What are you on about? Just because of Bruges?"

I sigh. It's discouraging to see how little he understands.

"We just don't have anything in common anymore, Gavin. Maybe you don't realize it, but it's true. The things I do don't interest you, and the things you do don't interest me either. We don't agree on anything, we're always arguing, we're not on the same page."

Suddenly his eyes blaze. "Not on the same page? Are you kidding me? You and I come from the same background. I know this, but you seem to have forgotten that you're not like those losers who need help to get through life!"

"Oh, give it up, Gavin. It gets tiring hearing you repeat the same thing all the time."

"Shit, Annie, are you blind?!"

I am so sick of how bigoted and offensive he is. "I think you should go. I don't want us to start fighting again."

"And what if I don't want to leave?"

I turn around and open wide the door to my apartment. "You don't have a choice."

"So, that's it? The two of us are over? After all the cool things we've done?"

I am not a nasty person, and I hope I never become one, so I don't answer that question. The things we did together were superficial and nothing special. We had fun but all we did was think about ourselves. We were even superficial towards each other.

"Gavin… we're no good together. It's better to end it now before we start hurting each other."

"You're the one hurting me!" he hisses bitterly. "But what else should I expect from you? You're just like every other super rich person. You take whatever you want then throw it away once you find something better!"

His words are like a slap in the face. "How can you say that? That is so not true!"

"You probably only got together with me because you felt more powerful, and you wanted to help me. And now that you've found your stupid association, I'm not enough for you. You want to prove you're better than everyone else!"

My heart starts racing. The things he is saying are horrible. "Please go, Gavin. It's for the best."

"Yeah sure! See you round, *angelface*."

He leaves the apartment like a shot, leaving me trembling in front of the open door. I close it and pull myself together.

I just did what was best for the both of us.

For me.

I don't regret anything.

13
December

"Oh man, I am so useless! I mean, honestly. Have you ever seen anyone so useless? Even a chimpanzee could do this a hundred times better. I think I'm going to give up and make him a macaroni necklace instead, that's more my level."

From the living room couch where she is studying, Ines lifts her head to look at me and raises an eyebrow. "Perseverance not one of your strong points?"

Unlike her...

We left the campus at 4 pm and as soon as we got home, Ines immersed herself in her textbooks for tomorrow's exams. That girl is a machine. She never gives up. And me? Well, initially I just wanted a bit of a break and thought I'd start Romeo's snow globe, but that was before I remembered I had two left hands. And now I'm on the verge of despair. I've spent an entire good hour trying to make mini tree trunks with Fimo for the tropical forest. It's a disaster.

In theory it's easy enough: you open the globe in two, you stick all the decor on the base,

you add the artificial snow and screw the globe back together. You turn it over and hey presto!

So where am I at? I bought synthetic moss, which I've already stuck on half of the wooden base. The other half will have beige glitter for the beach and blue glitter for the sea. Once I've finished, I plan to put a layer of glue on top to properly seal everything. But before that, I have to make the tropical forest and insert the birds and flowers… Given my technical prowess, I'll still be here in ten years' time.

"This is a total mess," I grumble. "It doesn't look like anything. Hmm, actually, yes it does. It looks like hedgehog poop."

"You know what hedgehog poop looks like?" asks Ines in surprise.

"I sure do! At my grandparents' place, in the south of France, they have lots in their garden. You have to keep an eye out if you want to go running outside in bare feet."

Ines pulls a face. "Sounds charming."

"The thing is, if I had an incredible housemate to give me advice, I know it'd be a thousand times better," I say innocently, as I roll out a piece of Fimo on the table.

Unlike me, Ines is good with her hands. When she saw me buy all this paraphernalia, she told me she used to make jewellery out of Fimo when she was in high school, so I know she can do it.

She smiles and closes her folder with a bang. The table she's working on is littered with sheets of paper, I wonder how she manages to study them all at the same time. Ines Abad is a mystery to me in so many ways!

"OK, fine, you win! I'll show you what to do, then you'll be the queen of the baobab!"

"There aren't any baobabs in Réunion."

"Oh, yes there are! And that's probably the only thing I know about the island! There aren't many, but there are some."

Now it's my turn to look surprised. "How do you know that?"

"Serena called last night, and she talked about them."

I cast my features into a neutral expression.

Even though I told Ines that Serena wanted her number and that Romeo was going to give it to her, I didn't mention that it was because she liked her. I'd rather Serena did that herself. Having said that, I'm dying to know what they talked about.

"Hmm, I can't quite see the connection between the two. Did she call you to speak about baobabs?"

"No, just because. And to ask if I wanted to go out for a drink."

"Oh? Not to play Scrabble? Now that's a surprise," I tease her like she did for me and Romeo.

Ines pretends not to have heard.

"You should use this for the tree bark," she says, giving me a kind of cuticle pusher that's lying on the table. "Make little holes and lines. And work directly on the baking tray, then you won't break any while moving them around."

I do as she says and copy each of her movements. It's not extraordinary, but it's not hideous either. I'm making progress.

"Have you ever been attracted to a girl?" Ines suddenly asks me.

Ah ha! Now we're making progress!

"No, and you?"

Not at all a loaded question…

"I dunno. There are some girls I find sexy, but I've never imagined myself with them. I mean, I've never imagined kissing them!"

"And what about Serena?"

Ines's deep green eyes grow wide. Her mouth falls open.

"What? We were talking about her, and then all of a sudden you ask if I've ever been attracted to a girl. I'm just trying to work out the connection here…"

Then, with an air of total detachment, I insert a branch into my misshapen tree.

Ines runs a hand through her hair, through her curly, wild mane that everyone falls for, and lets out a deep sigh.

"We spent more than two hours on the phone, can you believe it? My phone got so sick of us, it hung up by itself."

Can I believe it? Not really. I've never spent more than fifteen minutes on the phone, and even then, it was under extreme duress.

"Two hours on the phone just to ask you out for a drink? That seems excessive!"

"Ha ha, no, we talked about lots of stuff. About her island, why she wants to be a doctor, her family. We talked about so many things: we have so much in common! She also did her childcare certificate when she was a teenager. She loves the sun, the sea, walking in the forest and baking. I think she's awesome. She *is* awesome! Oh, and, can you believe it, way back she also has North African ancestry."

"All that in one perfect package?" I say teasingly.

Ines gives a sigh of contentment. "Yes!"

"So do you think you're attracted to her?"

Purely a rhetorical question – the answer seems obvious to me.

"Do you think it would be weird? Seeing as how I've always preferred boys?"

"No. You can be attracted to whomever you want."

"This has never happened to me before. You know, I truly thought I was in love with Mehdi. We share the same background, we've known each other forever, and I was sure we were made for each other. At the time, I couldn't imagine being with anyone else."

"Life can be full of surprises!" I say, thinking about what she has just said and relating it to Romeo.

And feeling disturbed.

But just a bit.

No, quite a lot.

Actually, it disturbs me far too much.

"Did Serena say she was interested in you?"

"No, but she did say she liked girls and… you know, I don't think it's any different from how it is with boys. The signals are the same. Oh my god," she says in a dramatic voice. "I just don't know where I'm at!"

"Me neither," I grumble, as I notice I just broke my tree's one and only branch. I'm so bad at this.

Ines smiles, takes a piece of clay and rolls it between her fingers as if she's been doing it her whole life. "I don't think you're kneading it enough. That's why it doesn't hold."

And in the blink of an eye, she creates the shape, lays it down flat, makes lines with a toothpick and attaches it to the tree. It looks better than the real thing. I pout.

"I know you can do it," she says soothingly.

"I really hope so, otherwise I bought all this for nothing."

Ines smiles at me then narrows her eyes.

"What?" I ask.

"All we've done is talk about me, but you haven't spoken about word about Gavin since you told him it was over between you."

"That's because there's nothing to say."

"Hmm. Are you sure?"

I sigh. "It was just a matter of time, you know. I don't think anyone's going to be surprised."

"Do you still love him, despite everything that's happened?"

Huh. Now there's a question I haven't asked myself. It's as if the answer was patently obvious. I reply while kneading my Fimo clay. "No… and I wonder if I was ever in love with him at all."

Ines nods but stays quiet, giving me the space to keep speaking.

"I had a crush on him, I was really attracted to him. It's like with you and Mehdi, we come from the same milieu. Our lives were easy, we basically did whatever we wanted, we didn't need to worry too much about the future. But I came to realize that even though we were having fun – in the beginning, anyway – it wasn't enough me to truly fulfil me. Gavin didn't make me a better person. You probably think I'm being selfish saying that."

"No, not at all. You know what I've always thought of him, but putting that to the side, I think there's more to being with someone than just having fun. It's important to be challenged and go beyond ourselves somehow…"

"…and learn from the other," I add. "And I just didn't want to learn from Gavin anymore. That's what it boils down to. I think I eventually realized that if we had stayed together, we would have made each other unhappy. We are so different. It took me a while, but I got there in the end."

Ines smiles at me. "No, actually, I think it went quite fast. And you know what? I'd even say it started when you met Romeo Bling-Bling!"

You can always count on Ines to get straight to the point.

"You're imagining things."

"No, I'm not. You fell for him the first time you saw him in the library."

"I didn't fall for him! I just thought he had incredible eyes. Look, you can forget about your little fantasy. The break-up was triggered by the fact that I wanted to quit university and do something else. Plus the issues around the association and real-world problems. With hindsight, the experiences I had with Gavin seem so superficial."

"Whereas with Sparkling Romeo, it could be so much better!"

"Are you ever going to give that up…"

"No. Because I can see what you don't want to: you like him. And you have right from the start."

I sigh.

"You still don't believe me? Wait here, I'll prove it to you!" Ines leaps up, rushes into her bedroom and comes back with a magazine that she opens on a double page: **Quiz: Who is your ideal partner?**

"You're joking," I say.

"No. And while we're at it, I'll answer as if I like girls. Let's go!"

1. Imagine your ideal date. Would it take place...

- ■ at the movies?
- ♥ in a café?
- ★ at the library?

"For me it would be in a tropical café and for you it's obviously the library," she states. "Seeing as how the answer is right there."

I look at her in disbelief. This doesn't seem right...

2. In terms of your ideal partner, do you prefer men or women who have...

- ♥ a sense of humour?
- ★ a sense of maturity?
- ■ a sense of responsibility?

"I like women with a sense of maturity, and you?"
"Um… responsibility."
"OK."

3. Would you rather have a partner who is...

★ over-confident?
■ a bit quirky?
♥ from Réunion Island?

"Huh? What kind of a question is that? You're making these up, give me that."

She yanks the magazine away so I can't read it. "Go on, which one do you choose?"

"But…"

"OK, from Réunion Island! Me too!"

This girl is crazy…

4. When in love, would you say you are someone who...

♥ is super stressed?
★ is totally chilled out?
■ can't see what's right in front of her eyes?

"Right, number three for you, and 'super stressed' for me."

"Hey! You keep answering for me! And this Réunion Island business is garbage!"

"It's because I know you so well. And no, it's not. It's all written here in black and white!"

She gives me a wink.

5. You are most happy when...

- ■ you're with your friends?
- ♥ You know exactly what's coming up?
- ★ You have to make a snow globe for your future date?

I shake my head and smile.

"I know, it's number three. And number two for me!"

"You're unbelievable."

"OK, what about this one."

6. You could never be with someone who...

- ★ has the sense of humour of a tax agent
- ■ has the IQ of a barnacle
- ♥ has the soul of a hippie

"I'd say the IQ of a barnacle."

"OK. I pick number two as well! Last question."

7. You could imagine going out with...

♥ an accountant?

■ an artist?

★ A doctor?

"No, don't even bother answering," she says as I open my mouth. "I already know! A doctor! Like me."

This time I can't help but burst out laughing. A quiz, yeah right!

"OK, now for the results."

She pretends – because her test is 100% invented, of course – to tally up the scores, then clears her throat.

"Here's what it says for me."

★ Your ideal partner is older than you and possesses the element of maturity you are looking for. He or she will bring serenity and confidence.

You are drawn to the exotic, so he or she will come from a far-off island that you would love to visit. Because you have a need for security, he or she works in the health sector.

Your ideal partner is tall, with dark skin and long hair!

See!"

"Oh, whatever… Go on, ya clown, read out my quiz results."

Another clearing of the throat.

♥ Your ideal partner is the same age as you and will prove him or herself trustworthy in all circumstances. Because you persist in refusing to see the truth, he or she will be revealed to you by an amazing friend, who saw the truth right away.

You are drawn to the exotic, so he or she will come from a far-off island that you would love to visit.

Hey, that's just like me!

Because you have a need for security, he or she works in the health sector.

Well, what do you know!

Your ideal partner is tall, with dark skin, curly hair and blue eyes!

"There you go," she says as she closes the magazine. "It's irrefutable, undeniable, inevitable: Romeo Supernova and you are made for each other."

I'm about to die from laughing so hard!

"You're something else."

"Mmm, I know. I should start writing these kinds of quizzes. Imagine the plaque on my office door: Ines Abad, sociologist and designer of love quizzes."

"You'd be a hit!"

I look at the snow globe on the table, the two ridiculous lumps of Fimo lying next to it and wonder if I might need to try and motivate myself a bit more. Maybe Ines is right. I have to admit that… actually no, I have no idea. Or maybe I do.

"How about some music?"

"And then we study after that?"

"OK!"

With a tiny smile at the corner of her mouth, Ines gets up and turns on the television. She logs in to YouTube and plays the first song that comes up as a suggestion. And what a surprise, it's All I Want for Christmas is You.'

The first notes ring out, ready for us to butcher the song and burst our neighbours' eardrums. But Ines and I don't care, we love a duet!

I get up, Ines plops a Santa hat on her head and some fairy lights around my neck, we stand in front of the TV screen and…

I don't want a lot for Christmas,
There is just one thing I need.
I don't care about the presents,
Underneath the Christmas tree.
I just want you for my own,
More than you could ever know.
Make my wish come true,
All I want for Christmas is you.

14
December

All exam days are the same, or almost.

Get up early, have breakfast early, start stressing out early…

But this morning, it was get up late, leave late and run to the metro so I don't miss the train and have to wait another five minutes.

I didn't hear my alarm go off, and as Ines had left at 7:30 to go to the library, no one was there to give me a kick up the butt. And today is my biggest exam day.

I got up, got dressed and left the apartment as fast as I could, without even showering or doing my hair.

Arrival at the lecture hall: 8:58 am.

"Hello," says the supervisor standing at the door. "Two minutes later and you wouldn't have been allowed in."

As if I hadn't realized.

I hand her my ID card in silence.

"Hurry up, everyone is already in place."

I nod, look at my seat number on the list on the door and go into the room.

It's far from full, and there are empty chairs all over the place. Second year is when the numbers start to taper off, and if my parents hadn't insisted, I would also have been one of the absentees.

It's obvious what time of the year it is: more than half the students are wearing a Christmas beanie or jumper. Merry Christmas and happy exams!

Ines motions to me; as fate would have it, I'm sitting just two spaces away from her and there's no one in between.

"I was freaking out! I didn't think you'd make it. I left you three messages."

"My alarm didn't work, and I haven't had time to look at my phone. It was a close call; if I'd been one minute late, the harpy at the door wouldn't have let me in."

Our statistics professor is on the stage right in front of us, prim and straitlaced, dressed in a suit, tie, white shirt and perfectly shined shoes.

It's just his hairstyle that doesn't quite match the rest: the strands of hair he usually folds over to hide his bald patch are a bit higgledy-piggledy.

He taps the microphone, causing it to feed back. I've never understood what's this thing all professors have with the microphone.

Here we go again for the hundredth explanation of the rules since the beginning of the week. It's the same for each exam.

"We're going to hand out the exam papers now, and may I remind you that these are anonymous, so no need to sign yourselves off as Einstein, Omar Sy or Houdini the Master Illusionist. All we need is your student number written on each page, including the separating pages. Don't bother putting little hearts either."

Everyone starts to laugh.

He turns around and writes a time on the whiteboard in big letters.

"You are not allowed to leave the room until at least halfway though the allotted time. If you finish before then, you may count the hairs on the back of your hand, but please do so quietly."

Another round of laughter in the room.

"And, as a reminder, please be informed that any act of cheating is punishable by a five-year ban on sitting exams," the professor says. "Let's hope your Christmas hats have been keeping your brilliant ideas on the boil. Good luck everyone."

A supervisor places a blank copy of the exam in front of us, and inside is the subject we are going to be examined on. I quickly glance over it; these are basically analysis exercises based on opinion polls or data from x or y sample.

I hate this subject, but needs must…

Ines and I leave the last exam at 4 pm. I think I'm even more spaced out than when I arrived. Two hours of exams, two hours for a quick lunchbreak and another round of revisions, and then another two hours of exams. I'm shattered. It feels like I just ran a marathon.

In the metro with Ines, we go over our answers together. She tries to be reassuring, but I feel like I totally bombed out.

I didn't hand in any blank sheets, in fact, I wrote quite a lot, but it seemed devoid of content somehow. But what surprises me the most is that this thought annoys me. I hope I didn't screw up. Why? So I can continue my studies or so

I don't have to attend extra classes to get the credits anyway? It's too early to tell, but I have to be honest with myself: doubt is creeping in.

The train arrives in Lille-Flandres; Ines is ready and waiting at the doors.

"I hope I won't be late. I have a feeling my boss is going to come down hard on me."

"Things aren't any better?"

"I try and ignore him, but now he's coming to the school every second day. And he's always watching me. I wonder if he's getting ready to write a report on me. I am so sick of it."

As soon as the doors slide open, she rushes out.

"See you tonight!"

I take my time going home, and just as I get to the Grand-Place, I finally give in to my desire to see what Romeo is up to, casual-like.

Hi! Just to let you know that Ines and Serena seem to have clicked.

Hey there! I heard.

How're your exams going?

*Alea jacta est!** And you?

---

* TN: A Latin phrase meaning "The die is cast," used to indicate that there is no turning back.

I'm just leaving one now. *Alea jacta est!*

We're such polyglots!

That must be the only thing I know in Latin! My train's about to arrive at Lille-Flandres, are you nearby?

Yes!

Actually, I'm almost home. But he doesn't need to know, does he? I stop in the middle of the sidewalk, ready to do a U-turn.

Wanna go for a beer?

Again? This guy must have some Northern French blood in him! But it still makes me smile like an idiot.

Cool! I'll meet you at the square in front of the station.

I don't run, I fly, and I don't stop to think why. I don't care; the main thing is that life is great.

I'm totally out of breath when I get to Lille-Flandres. Romeo is already there, waiting for me next to Romy, Lille's wonderful statue, the bright yellow bust of a young woman that stands in front of the station. It's the town's darling. A contemporary Mona Lisa weighing 500 kilos, no less.

"You're chatting her up while waiting for me?" I joke.

"Yup, but she's not very talkative, plus she's kind of looking down on me, so I gave up. I think she prefers men in suits."

Unlike me. I prefer his look.

Gavin once said that Romeo wore clothes like a hobo, by which he meant 'second-hand.' But Romeo is so good-looking that he could wear whatever he wants. Today, it's a simple pair of blue jeans and an open jacket over a black sweater.

It's enough to throw me into disarray.

The fault of Ines and her stupid quiz. Obviously.

"Shall we go?" he asks, motioning with his arm.

Yesterday the sky was blue, and the air was dry, but today it's overcast and damp. I forgot my scarf as I left this morning, so I raise the collar of my coat and hold it against my neck.

"Here," says Romeo.

I look at the grey plaid scarf he's holding out.

"Thank you."

I wrap it around my neck and can't help breathing in the smell of him. The same smell that had such an effect on me when we hugged. The way I keep overreacting is starting to get embarrassing, so I try to stay calm.

We walk past a Nord beer stand, where Romeo stops and asks me what I want.

"I know this isn't what we came for, but… a hot chocolate? And once I've warmed up, I'll go and get us a beer!"

The guy has hot chocolate in a glass vat spinning behind him. It's thick and dark brown. A hundred calories per hundred millilitres, I bet! Romeo nods and orders one for each of us.

"Come on, let's sit over here," he suggests.

The preferred spot of all Lille residents: on the edge of the fountain.

We sit down while the town buzzes around us. It's Wednesday and there are people everywhere – families, couples, groups of students at each stand and in front of all the activities. The Ferris wheel is jam-packed and turns practically non-stop. There's an impressive line of people waiting.

"Have you ever been on the Ferris wheel?" asks Romeo.

"No, never."

"Do you want to try? I won two seats on Wéo."

"The local TV channel?"

"Yeah! It was totally random. I clicked out of curiosity, and it worked! So, what do you think?"

I look up at the big wheel, I look at Romeo, and I give a huge smile.

"Yes! But I'll buy some roasted chestnuts first, because with the size of that line, we'll be waiting for a while! Are you sure the seats are free?"

"Yes, don't worry, you won't have to take out a mortgage!"

Do not, I repeat, do not start with your nervous laugh.

"Are you OK with roasted chestnuts?" I manage to avoid giving a direct answer.

"Done!"

He accompanies me to a stand that looks like a train locomotive, decked out in Christmas colours: red, green and white. There's even smoke coming out of the chimney!

And, as opposed to most of the other stands, there's practically no queue. The waffles and *croustillants** are far more popular.

"One large bag, please," I ask the man standing there, whose hands are black with soot.

"Coming up!"

He lifts a section of the locomotive body to reveal a blackened metal plate with holes in it, on which dozens of split chestnuts are roasting. Underneath it, red-hot charcoal is burning.

"That smells incredible," says Romeo.

"It's the best smell in the world! You'll see, these are so delicious!"

"OK, I can't wait."

Then, at the worst possible moment, just as I'm grinning at the salesman, one of them detonates, explodes and bursts open all over me.

I step back and widen my eyes in surprise.

"Oh my god!"

Roasted chestnut flesh everywhere. On my cheeks, in my hair, on my coat, on Romeo's scarf. I spit out some bits and raise my eyes to him, a little disoriented. With his lips clamped shut and his forehead wrinkled, I can tell he's trying not to laugh.

"Sorry!" says the man while continuing to stir. "That was one happy chestnut! It just got a bit overexcited to see you, you'll have to excuse it."

---

* TN: Croustillons are a type of doughnut common in Belgian Flanders and Netherlands, but they are also enjoyed in northern France. They are usually sprinkled with powdered sugar.

Huh? What did he just say?

Now it's Romeo's turn to explode. With laughter.

"You should see your face!"

"It's not funny."

"Oh, yes, it is!"

I pretend to sulk and dab at my clothes and cheeks.

"Wait, let me help you."

Romeo, still grinning, reaches out a hand to remove pieces of chestnut from my hair.

"Don't move, you have a piece on your eyelashes."

I freeze and let his fingers delicately brush across them.

I can feel my heart beating fast.

"There," he says in a gentle voice. "As good as new!"

"And I'll give you a bit extra to make up for it!" interrupts the salesman. "Be careful, they're hot."

I pay and take the bag. "Thank you!"

Just as the final rays of sun disappear, we move off and join the wait for the Ferris wheel. Romeo seems to enjoy the chestnuts and puts all the skins in his pocket, making sure not to drop any on the ground.

"Did you always want to be a doctor?" I ask, without preamble.

He pulls a face. "I wanted to be a botanist or a zoologist. I'm fascinated by the tropical forest."

"What made you change your mind?"

He turns to me with a coy smile. "You mean, when is it that little boys and girls start playing doctors and nurses?"

I laugh.

"Ha! I always wanted to be the nurse!"

"Ah, that's your practical side coming out."

"But even the sight of a needle makes me shudder, so it wouldn't have been a good idea! And what about you?"

He sighs. "I'm not too sure. I guess studying natural sciences heightened my attraction for medicine. And the situation around me too, I think. One day I realized the extent of the poverty in my part of the world and that we need people to help deal with it."

"Do you want to work for an NGO?"

"Ideally, yes. Maybe in Madagascar. A large percentage of the rural population there lives below the poverty line, and some barely earn €1.90 a day. Access to healthcare is limited."

I'm not surprised to hear his reasoning. I knew straight away that he has a good soul.

"If you want to work in Madagascar, why didn't you stay and study on Réunion Island?"

"Because there's more choice here, and I wanted to travel a little. And also, we wouldn't have met if I hadn't come here!"

I blink.

"And what about you and sociology?" he asks.

I just manage to contain my nervous laugh. My answer won't be as principled as his.

Because I didn't know what else to do? Because I didn't have any particular aim? Because I picked the first idea that cropped up? Of course, I won't put it exactly like that.

"Unlike you, I've never known exactly what my path is. And to be honest, I still don't really know what I want to do with my life or even if I'm on the right track."

"Helping others suits you," he says, as if it were a given.

"Oh, you think?"

"Elise thinks so too."

"Really?"

"Of course. You are committed, compassionate, generous…"

"... and single," I say quietly, speaking aloud without realizing it.

Too late… As the queue moves forward, Romeo pauses.

"You're not with Gavin anymore?"

"No."

"Oh, I'm sorry."

"Don't be, we weren't right for each other. It's for the best."

Romeo's eyes start to shine. But why? What should I read into it? Compassion? Joy? Opportunity? I have no idea. I have absolutely no idea and that makes me frustrated.

"You know what they say," he says. "Being single is better than being in a bad relationship!"

"Or that there are plenty of other fish in the sea!"

"That too!"

Finally, we get to the ticket stand.

"Two tickets, please," asks Romeo, handing over his voucher.

"You're not allowed to eat during the ride," the stallholder tells us.

Romeo folds the newspaper above the final few chestnuts and puts the whole thing in his pocket.

"Let's go!"

We move up the metal walkway and then climb into a cabin, next to one another. I counted; it goes around three times.

As we near the top it is so cold I start to shiver.

"I don't have another scarf," Romeo says with a smile.

No, but you do have warm arms.

Cut it out! This is getting out of hand.

But I can't help thinking it. Thinking about it a lot. I tense up a bit, straightening my collar in an effort to compose myself and put my hands in my pockets. A few seconds later, we get to the top. Romeo instantly puts his hand in his pocket and pulls out the bag of chestnuts, which aren't so hot anymore.

"What are you doing?"

"I'm going to eat some."

"But… we're not allowed to."

"What the guy doesn't know, won't hurt him!"

I stare at him open-mouthed.

"Oh, this one's no good."

And he throws it over the side.

"Oh! But… there are people down there, you can't do that!"

"Yes, I can, watch!"

And he does it again.

"Romeo! Why are you doing that?"

"To see if you'll loosen up, you seem tense. Another bad one!"

And it follows the same path as the previous one.

"No, no, stop, I'm not tense at all!"

"Oh yes, you are. And anyway, it's biodegradable."

He keeps up his little performance until we're nearly back at the bottom. I'm dying of embarrassment at the idea that he might get caught, but then as I watch him fooling around and throwing the skin out in one direction, and looking in the other, as if nothing were up, I start to laugh. And he continues for two whole revolutions until he's finished all the chestnuts.

On the third round, the wheel stops to let more passengers on. We happen to be right at the top; all the people down on the Grand-Place seem tiny.

The city stretches out before us, with the belfry and buildings all lit up and wisps of smoke drifting from the chimneys.

"It's beautiful," says Romeo, without needing to add anything else.

"And there's still so much snow on the roofs."

A few long seconds pass before Romeo speaks again. His voice is faint, as if he were talking to himself.

"I've had two incredible encounters this year."

I look at him, my lips parted in silent interrogation. He doesn't take his eyes off the horizon.

"The snow and you."

The snow and me.

I can't speak, but something is happening, right now.

Something that I didn't think would happen so soon.

Oh no… I'm starting to fall in love.

15
December

"When? How? Why has this happened? Because of his blue eyes? His thick black hair? His unbelievably long legs and sexy stubble? You don't fall in love just like that!"

I'm in a total dither, but Ines just looks at me in amusement before drinking her glass of orange juice in one go and clapping it down on the table.

"Because it's your destiny and the planets are perfectly aligned? There doesn't need to be a specific reason. There was a spark between the two of you and it just went ziiiing!"

Ziiiing?

I've always been someone who's reasonable, rational and realistic. I don't believe in things that go ziiiing! But Mom laughs and calls those things 'the three R's.' She claims that the first never lasts and that one day, we all leave it behind. That it's impossible to always remain reasonable, and that there are days when we all lose our reason.

Well, there you go! For me, it looks like the time has come. I'm severely lacking in reason, or at least I'm about to be.

Get it under control, Annie, come on!

"You know what? I'm just going to pretend this isn't happening. I've only just broken up with someone, I'm not going to launch myself into another relationship three days later!"

"Why not? Have you got some deontological code you're meant to be following that outlines good conduct? Can you give an example?" says Ines. "Life is meant to be lived. We're not meant to create our own obstacles."

I look at her with one raised eyebrow. "I guess you're talking about yourself now, too, huh? With Serena are you living life or going round in circles?"

Ines gets an offended look on her face. "Me? Go round in circles? Clearly you don't know me at all. Firstly, if I want something, I go get it. Secondly, I'm totally falling for this girl. But at least I accept it! Even though I'm at a compete loss as to how it happened."

I scowl and get up to put my bowl in the sink. "It's not that I don't want to accept it, it's just that this situation is completely bananas. How is it possible to fall in love so fast?"

"It's called chemistry, darling! And the best thing is, it's probably mutual. Come on, we have to be at school in an hour, and I still haven't showered. Here's my advice," she adds as she disappears into the corridor. "Stop thinking about it so much. *Carpe diem**!"

I sit back down and rest my elbows on the table with a sigh.

Yeah, sure.

---

* TN: A Latin phrase that means "Seize the day!" and is used to urge someone to live life to the fullest.

We finish our exam at 4 o'clock. Just like the day before, Ines goes straight to her after-school job, and I wonder whether I should go home and rest for an hour or go straight to the ASEL. While I was in my exam, Elise sent a group message. Tonight, she's planning some Christmas drinks for those who want to stay, as well as a little surprise.

I've got butterflies in my stomach, and it's not because I'm going to be distributing food bags or having a few drinks.

Association = Romeo = explosion of hormones = wildly racing heart.

This is going to be the death of me.

I spent all day thinking about what I feel for him. While I got my exam paper, while I wrote my essays, while I read them over. I wouldn't be surprised if I had dropped his name in somewhere between Mancur Olson's free-rider theory and an analysis of flu vaccination for senior citizens.

Woe is me. I hate being like this.

No, actually, I love it.

I find him so… and…

I freeze. What if he doesn't feel the same way?!

"Aaaaaaahhhh! Think about something else!" I cry out loud, making the girl walking past me jump.

"Sorry, I'm talking to myself."

I give an embarrassed smile then look up at the sky. It won't be long before it starts to pour down.

Right, I've made my decision. I'm going to keep myself busy at the association. That's more sensible.

I walk through the campus to the metro. It's a direct line to Wazemmes and I arrive just fifteen minutes later.

It's pouring rain when I get there and I'm completely soaked, my hair plastered to my cheeks and my hat dripping like a floor mop. I hate to think about what my mascara looks like.

Only in the North do we get downpours like that!

A girl I've never seen is waiting at the door. She looks to be about my age, petite, with short brown hair and big blue eyes, and despite the fading light, I can just make out her pale skin.

She doesn't have an umbrella either. She's practically an hour early and is in much the same state as me.

"Hi! Have you already pressed the doorbell?"

"No, it's not time yet," she says, revealing a slight Slavic accent.

"Oh, that's no problem. There's a common room upstairs, and you can't stay outside in this weather. We'll go in together. Is this the first time you've been here?"

She nods and starts to cough. I can even see her shivering. Who knows how long she's been waiting for.

I ring the interphone.

"Yes?" Anthony's voice emerges from the speaker.

"It's Annie!"

We hear the door beep, and I dash inside. The girl hesitates.

"Come on! You're allowed to come in, I promise. You can even have a hot chocolate if you want."

Her eyes seem to light up, and she decides to follow me.

"My name's Annie, and I'm a volunteer here at the ASEL."

"My name's Radana."

Upstairs, Anthony is putting big supermarket bags onto the table and… oh! A giant Christmas tree still in its netting has been set up in front of the bay window.

So that's the surprise.

"Hello!" I say as I take off my hat. "I'm a bit early."

"Hi, Annie! You brought the rain with you."

"Yup. This is Radana. She was waiting at the door."

"Oh! You should have rung the bell," Anthony says to her.

He walks over and comes to a stop as she puts out her arm to shake his hand.

"Radana Nováková, I have just signed up."

Surprised, Anthony shakes her outstretched hand.

"OK, welcome! You're both completely soaked. I'll go and get something for you to dry yourselves with. And don't just stand there, take off your coats! You can hang them just here," he adds, pointing to a row of hooks along the wall.

While we do as he says, he disappears into the kitchen and comes back with some towels.

"You chose the best day to come," he says to Radana. "After we've handed out the food bags, we're going to have a drink together and decorate the Christmas tree!"

Radana looks at me, a little lost.

"This is the common room, and the food market is on the ground floor. Some students like to come here and play cards or board games, or simply chat and have a coffee."

"OK. But I don't want to bother anyone."

"You're not bothering anyone," Anthony interjects. "Quite the contrary. Right, I'll leave the two of you, I have to make a phone call. Elise won't be far away. And help yourselves to a hot drink, you'll find everything you need in the kitchen!"

I do as he says and put on some milk to heat for the hot chocolates. There are some cookies in a bowl, so I grab them too.

When I come back out, Radana is sitting near the radiator, under the bay window. She's all hunched over and seems numbed by the cold.

"Are you all right?"

"I've just got a bad cold," she answers as I hand her a mug. "Thank you."

The rain would definitely not have helped.

"You have a cool accent. Where are you from?"

She sniffs and looks up at me with weary eyes.

"The Czech Republic."

"You speak really good French. Have you been here for long?"

"Just a year, but I learned French at university in Prague."

She takes a sip and closes her eyes with a shiver.

"You look sick. Have you been to see a doctor?"

"Yes, yes, it's just a cold," she says again. "Are you a student too?"

"Yup, second-year sociology. And you?"

"Second-year master's in chemistry. I study the transportation of pesticides in soil and groundwater contamination."

A million light-years away from any of my aspirations.

"I never imagined a place like this could exist," she goes on in perfect French. "The university information services told me about it. But I was scared to come."

I'm not in the best position to tell her I understand and that it must be hard dealing with all the challenges, but I want her to know that no one will judge her here.

"There are lots of students in your position, international students too. But everyone is welcome here. No one will bombard you with questions."

"You know, my parents are paying for my studies and housing, but… the rest is hard. I can't ask them for anything more."

"Hey, you don't need to justify yourself. If you're here, it's because you have a good reason."

She smiles at me and then starts coughing again. More violently this time, to such a degree that I need to take the mug from her hands.

"Are you sure you're all right?"

"Yes, yes. I had–what do you call it here? Bronchitis? I still cough, but it's much better."

I don't insist, as I can see she feels uncomfortable.

"Have you been told how the food market works?"

"No, not yet."

Elise would be able to explain it better than me, but I try and give her all the basic information about the market, the common room and the various forms of help she can receive. Radana seems more reassured once I've finished.

No need to be a genius to realize that the ASEL is heaven-sent for her. If a student turns up here, it means that they're really on the edge.

I glance out the window. It's still raining heavily, and there are far fewer people waiting for the market to open than on the other evenings. There are barely twenty, including those who are doing the Secret Santa.

Romeo is so tall that he stands out, even hidden under his hood.

And what do you know, a smile comes to my face of its own accord.

There aren't many people who signed up for a food bag tonight, so we finish at the market earlier than expected. Elise explains that many of the students have already gone home for Christmas.

Last time's dream team ends up in the common room to decorate the tree and have a drink together.

Radana has decided to stay as well, which reassures me. She seems truly exhausted. I don't know where she lives, but I'm not going to let her go home on her own.

Romeo comes over and hands me a glass of sparkling wine. Because of the rain, his hair is even curlier than usual.

He is so hot.

If my smile were any bigger, it'd leave the sides of my face!

"Hey, thanks!"

"You look worried, or am I imagining it?"

"It's Radana, the new girl. I've been watching her for a while. She can barely stay upright."

He turns around to look at her. She is sitting on the couch talking to another student. Listening to him, more than anything, given how little she's actually saying. She's struggling to keep her eyes open and is coughing more and more.

"Has she been to a doctor?"

"She told me she had."

Then I look at the bags full of decorations lying on the table. They're almost empty; everyone has taken a turn at decorating the tree.

"We're the only ones who haven't put anything on it! Shall we do that now?"

Romeo follows me, more amused by my enthusiasm than anything else. I've already gathered that Christmas, with its profusion of baubles and garlands, isn't his thing.

As we both put our hands in the bag, our fingers touch. For me, there's an instant electric shock, almost like a spark.

Ziiiing!

"Oh, sorry!" I apologize as I take a step back.

"No worries. I got a really ugly gnome. Your turn!"

I rummage inside and pull out a red heart with a pretty gold ribbon to hang it with.

"A heart for Christmas?" he jokes. "That's adorable!"

We walk up to the tree, and each hang our little bauble. Then Romeo turns to me with a satisfied look, just as a lock of my hair falls across my face.

Spontaneously, he gently moves it aside and slides it behind my ear.

I'm no longer breathing.

"Your cheeks are all pink," he whispers with a very slight smile.

It's because of you.

"It's the wine!"

I don't think he believes a word of it.

He looks me straight in the eye for a few seconds without saying anything, then his gaze drops to my mouth.

My lips open of their own accord; I feel like I'm on fire from head to toe.

His smile vanishes.

I think this is something that everyone experiences at least once in their lives, when time seems to stand still, when you find yourself alone with the only person who counts.

For me, that moment is now.

I don't even hear the hubbub of clinking glasses, the peals of laughter or the lively conversation. Everything around me has gone blurry, and all I can see is Romeo's deep blue gaze, shining with desire.

My heart starts to beat faster. My breathing becomes shallow.

I want to kiss him.

In front of everyone.

Romeo slowly lowers his head to mine.

It's going to happen. It's going to happen…

"Who's going to put the star up?" cries Elise suddenly. "Romeo! You're the tallest! You can have the honour!"

I wasn't even born when records were around; I've never used one in my life, but I bet the sound of the needle scraping across a record produces exactly the same effect as Elise's interruption right then.

Everything comes to a screeching halt.

Romeo lifts his head and smiles, taking the star that Elise is handing him, as if nothing was out of the ordinary.

This guy must be a master of self-control, otherwise I can't see how…

The Christmas tree is almost two metres tall, but Romeo, with his long arms, reaches the top without needing to stand on his tiptoes. A wave of cheers breaks out.

"Yayyyy!"

While everyone is focused on the pretty golden star, while the magic of Christmas is at its pinnacle even though it's only December 15th, Radana suddenly captures my attention.

She has just stood up and is swaying unsteadily. I go over to her just as she leans against the wall, her cheeks red and her eyes half-closed in fatigue.

"Hey… you really don't look well."

"My head is spinning a bit, but I'll be fine. It's because of the wine. Can you tell me where the bathroom is?"

"It's upstairs. The ones next to the kitchen are out of order. I'll go with you."

I watch carefully she walks up each step in front of me. There aren't many, but they're uneven and can be tricky. Radana holds on tightly to the banister. She seems increasingly feverish.

"Are you all right?"

"Yes… I… no…"

Then, just like a slow-motion sequence in a bad film, I see her let go of the banister, lose balance and fall backwards, her arms flung out wide.

I try to hold her up, but she takes me down with her.

Boom.

16
December

It's past midnight when the intern at the emergency services tells me I can leave.

I was lucky; I got away without any serious injury. Radana and I had tumbled head-over-heels down the stairs and ended up in a heap at the bottom. Result: I have a big bump on my forehead, a little cut and an enormous bruise covering almost my entire right thigh. No visible damage in the x-rays. However, my appearance later today will be another story.

And of course, today is my biggest exam day.

But Radana wasn't so lucky. When the emergency services came to get us, she had blurred vision and couldn't stand unassisted.

I'm allowed to leave, but she is still under observation. The little information they deigned to give me doesn't tell me much: "She's still being examined."

Since 9 pm…

When I get to the waiting room with my precious release form, Romeo and Elise are still there. They both jump up as they see me.

"How are you?" asks Elise.

"Fine, thank you. Just this big bandage on my forehead and a bruised leg, but nothing broken. It looks worse than it is."

"That's a relief. Do you have any information about Radana? No one has been able to tell me much."

"Not really," I reply. "I just know that she went in for a head x-ray before me, and that she's, and I quote, 'in good hands'."

"OK. I'm going to see if I can find out anything more. I've already said that the ASEL will act as a guarantor for her if needed. I don't know if she's insured. Wait here, I'll be back soon. I'll be driving you home in any case."

I look at Romeo, who hasn't said a word. He looks tense. His jaw is clenched.

"Are you OK?"

He nods, his eyes glinting. Then he lifts his hand to delicately brush my hair away and look at the ugly bandage I have on my forehead. I can't help giving a little nervous laugh.

"You want some practice examining me?"

But he doesn't even crack a smile.

"I saw you head upstairs with Radana, and the next minute we all heard a big crash. You got up almost straight away, but I was really worried about you. Falling down the stairs like that can often lead to serious damage."

"I'm fine, I promise."

He takes my hand and holds it tightly.

"I'm glad you're not hurt."

Woah! Here we go again; another interplanetary storm is taking place in my veins. It's giving me goosebumps.

Suddenly the attending physician who has been looking after Radana comes into the waiting room.

"Are the people who came with Ms. Nováková still here?"

Elise, who was speaking to the woman at the reception desk, comes over to us.

"Hello, I'm Elise Presle, president of the ASEL. Radana is one of our customers. She was at our premises when she fell."

"I'm Dr. Duchatel. I examined Ms. Nováková. She asked me to inform you of her condition. There are no serious consequences from her fall apart from a few bruises, but the examinations have shown a serious vitamin deficiency that cannot be explained by the fact she has the flu. I don't think this young lady is eating sufficiently, so we are going to put her on a drip until tomorrow, just to be sure. Does she live in a damp apartment?"

We look at each other. Obviously, none of us have any idea.

"OK," he says. "I'll leave that for you to discuss with her, but any information you can provide us with will help us treat her cough, which seems to be due to an allergy rather than a virus. We are going to transfer her to a room on the second floor, and you can see her during visiting hours."

"Will she be in the hospital for long?" asks Elise.

"I imagine she will be out by the end of the day, if all goes well."

"OK, thank you, Doctor. Could you give her my telephone number? If she needs anything at all, she shouldn't hesitate to call me."

He nods, takes her business card and disappears behind a door.

Elise turns to us with dark shadows beneath her eyes, but also with a smile.

"Good! We're finished for the evening. It's time for me to take you home."

"We did it! Hooray! Lead the way!

Do do Dora, do do do, Dora!"

Ines sings and dances her way out of the lecture hall. I knew it. The exams were too much for her. She studied far too much and now her brain has exploded. Why am I not surprised?

"Who is *not* going to be studying tonight? Meeeee! It's party time!"

And on she dances.

As for me, I'm still half-fried after last night.

"So do you think it went OK?" she asks, more seriously.

"We'll see."

To be honest, I can't say either way. I feel just as strongly that I passed as I do that I failed.

"I'm sure you'll be fine!" she insists.

I check my phone and see a message from Mom, who is impatiently waiting for my news, and three others from Elise that I hurry to read.

Hi Annie, Radana was discharged from the hospital at 3 pm, all good. She has medication and now just needs rest! Is everything OK with you?

Mathias has cancelled for the 24th and so Radana will take his place.

Also are you free on Sunday? The ASEL has a stand at the Halles des Wazemmes Christmas market and we're selling *papillotes*. Anthony is dressing up as Santa Claus for children's Christmas photos. We need volunteers... dressed as elves!

I reply, with a smile on my face. Ha! I can just imagine what I'll look like disguised as an elf!

Hello, I'm relieved to hear about Radana. Thanks for letting me know! Sounds great for the 24th, you'll have fun! For Sunday, I don't have my train tickets yet, I'll see if I can make it. But in theory, yes!

Hmm, looks like I'm not in such a hurry to go home after all.

"Actually," says Ines innocently, as we arrive at the station, "you got home late last night, so I forgot to tell you. Because Serena isn't on call tonight and isn't working at the hospital tomorrow, I invited her over to the apartment to celebrate the end of exams."

"OK, no problem."

"Why don't you invite Romeo?"

Just like each time I hear his name, my heart skips a beat. I can't control anything anymore. This is getting freaky…

"You think I should?"

"I'm sure you should! He'll come with his best friend, and I'll come with mine!"

"Um, technically I won't be coming, I'll already be there."

Ines giggles, as happy as I've ever seen her, and pulls me along.

She's as excited as a little kid!

We go shopping on our way home, and Ines gets it into her head that she wants to do a Savoyarde fondue.* Yeah, great! We'll have to leave the windows wide open for three days afterwards! But it's worth it, I love cheese.

Once we get home, Ines decides to scrub the apartment from top to bottom, and I video call my parents a day early. Dad answers.

"Hi, darling. So how did your exams go this week?"

"Well, I tried my best."

"I'm sure you did just fine!" calls out Mom in the background.

Dad turns the camera towards her; she's in the kitchen with her back to us.

---

* TN: The Savoyarde fondue is a dish from the mountainous Savoie region in France. A mixture of different cheeses is melted and then eaten with bread picked up at the end of a fork.

"Your mom is trying her hand at churros. But for the moment, apart from the smell of burning oil, there's not much to show for it."

"Oh, ye of little faith! I haven't even started cooking them yet!"

"I'm not sure I'm in any hurry for her to start," whispers Dad.

I snigger. I inherited my lower-than-average cooking abilities from my mom. She often tries new things, and 90% of the time they fail.

"So anyway, how do you feel about your exams?" asks Dad again.

"I don't know… I think some of them went OK, but I'm not sure about others."

"Have you thought about what you'll do next semester if you pass this one?"

I clear my throat. I want to say that I'm making progress, even though I don't know exactly where I'm heading, but I'd rather not say too much, because then I'd have to mention Gavin and… Romeo.

"Not yet, Dad."

"OK. And how is the ASEL going?"

"It's really interesting and quite an education. The people I work with are great. This Sunday I've been asked to help out selling *papillotes*. Would you and Mum mind if I didn't go straight home?"

"As long as you're back by the 24th!" calls out Mom.

We chat for another five minutes about this and that. Then I hang up. It's 7 pm. I've got thirty minutes to get ready.

The major question is: What I am going to wear?

Serena and Romeo arrive at 7:45.

The fondue set is ready on the table, the bread has been cut into little pieces, the beer has been chilled and the sliced meat is waiting in the fridge.

For the occasion – and I've definitely gone overboard – I pulled my hair back into a plaited bun, but if I shake my head around too much, it probably won't last fifteen minutes. I put on a little make-up but wasn't able to hide the mammoth lump on my forehead, and, because I want to feel comfortable, I put on a pair of black leggings and an oversized pale pink wool sweater.

Romeo looks gorgeous, as usual. He's wearing a simple white t-shirt – because everyone knows that in December the temperatures are tropical – and a pair of worn jeans that might seem basic, except that they reveal his sensational legs! I'm going to have to be careful where I look.

This guy really does things to me, and now that I've admitted to myself how I feel about him, it's like riding a bike without your hands. And when he leans towards me for a hug, something in my lower abdomen is set alight.

Someone help me…

"Your place is so cool," says Serena once we're settled in the living room. "It must cost you a fortune!"

I catch Ines's eye. She knows I'm on thin ice here.

I open my mouth to answer, but she beats me to it.

"Split between the two of us, it's not too bad, and we got a grant for living costs, which helps."

A grant, as if! We don't have anything of the kind.

"And what about you, do you work?" Serena asks me.

"Um… no, I'm lucky."

"Oh, that's cool! What do you parents do for a living?"

I look over at Romeo and those blue eyes of his, waiting for me to answer. He has told me about his parents, but I haven't. I've done everything I can to avoid it.

I swallow.

"Um… my dad works as a legal advisor and my mom has an e-commerce business."

An 'e-commerce business' that is so well-known millions of people use her app to sell their clothes, books and anything they don't want anymore. I bet they both have it on their phones.

"It's always useful having a legal expert in the family!" laughs Serena.

"Hey, I have news about Radana," I say to Romeo, in an effort to urgently extricate myself from the conversation. "She got out of the hospital today."

He nods. "Yeah, I know. I was at the ASEL before, and one of the students told me that her housemate had moved out and that Radana was going to take her room. She's moving in tonight."

Immediately I think back to the doctor asking about her living conditions, which could have contributed to her poor state of health.

"Was her apartment that bad?"

"It must have been. Apparently when Elise took Radana home, she couldn't believe it. There was mould on the walls, no ventilation, the windows were rickety and there was no heating at all."

"Are people even allowed to rent out places like that?"

"Have you been living under a rock?" says Serena. "Everyone knows what it's like. When I first got to Lille, you should have seen the hovels I was shown… and the rent was astronomical!"

Ines and Romeo chime in; they all had the same experience. Whereas I just visited my apartment, liked it, and my parents bought it. I've never had to struggle for anything in my life.

I try and keep my expression as neutral as possible, but my silence gives me away. I notice Romeo's curious gaze. He's looking at me intently.

"I'm hungry!" I say to create a diversion.

"Just to let you guys know, the first one to drop their piece of bread into the cheese has to do a dare," Ines warns us.

I bet that will be me.

We move to the table, and no surprises here but I'm just as bad at stabbing my fork into the bread as I am at baking! The pressure I'm under for the duration of the meal is very high, but in the end Romeo is the one who loses his piece of bread, just as we're about to finish eating.

"Naked in the stairwell, naked in the stairwell!" Ines starts chanting, banging her cutlery on the table.

I nearly choke on my last bite of cheese. Is she trying to finish me off for good?

Romeo looks at me with a coy smile that I can't for the life of me interpret, and Serena fakes a grimace.

"Oh, please, no! Not that!"

"Well, we have to think of a dare! Those are the rules," decrees Ines mutinously.

And then, who should drop their piece of bread into the cheese? Yours truly!

"Excellent," she says. "Seeing as no one is prepared to strip off, the two of you will have to play a round of Twister together."

Romeo and I look at each other in horror.

I hate Twister. What on earth is she up to? I am most definitely not ready to start entwining my limbs with Romeo. Well, not like that anyway…

But I can't get out of it. In no time at all, the coffee table has been shoved against the wall, the couch pushed back a metre, and the Twister mat laid out. I clearly don't have a choice.

And, of course, Ines is the referee. Romeo starts. Right hand on a red circle, left hand on a yellow circle.

"Annie, your turn!" says Ines.

I spin the wheel. Right foot on yellow, left foot on red.

So far so good, but two rounds later, Romeo is looking up at the ceiling with his arms and legs beneath him, holding himself up in a kind of reverse hands and knees to keep his butt off the ground. I tense up. So far I've managed to avoid touching him, but now he's taking up practically the whole mat.

"Annie," says Serena. "Right hand on red."

And then a left hand on a green circle.

I hate them.

They're doing this on purpose.

I'm going to have to straddle him.

I find myself in the exact same position as Romeo, but reversed, with my face looking down at the mat. Except that Romeo's face is just ten centimetres below me! If I had known this would happen, I would have skipped the cheese.

Romeo seems to find this funny, the girls are snorting with laughter and me? I'm struggling to breathe. I can't tear my eyes away from his lips.

"How long do you think they'll last in that position?" asks Serena.

"Not even five minutes," answers Ines.

"Shall we bet on it?"

"OK! But while we wait, there's something I just have to show you."

"Oh?"

"The djellaba I inherited from my grandmother. Come and have a look."

"Hey!" I protest, as I see them leave the living room.

But Romeo doesn't take his eyes off me.

"How long do you think you'll last?"

With your mouth that close to me? Another ten seconds. Probably less.

He looks at my lips and keeps staring at them. Does he have any idea of the effect he's having on me?

Yes, he does. I'm absolutely sure of it.

"I dunno if you're aware of this, but we look like total fools," I say, unsure of what to do next.

I can feel his warm breath on my skin. I swallow hard.

"Not sure I agree. I think we're almost perfect like this..." he says in a rough voice, stretching slightly upwards.

Closer to my mouth, closer to my tongue and my overwhelming desire to eat him alive.

"That fondue was a set up," I murmur, my breathing jagged.

"A cunning ruse."

He is so close to me he's blurry. I'm burning up. I'm about to explode. So why am I even waiting?

I don't give a damn.

"Romeo…"

"Yes?"

"You're a pain in the ass."

There is nothing but the urge, the desire, my limbs that are starting to shake and a heart that's going to explode, it's beating so fast. I give in and place my lips on his.

If he was expecting a gentle touch, he's hot out of luck. There's no way I can control myself; I've waited too long.

But Romeo doesn't hold back either. He sits down, puts one arm around my neck and pulls me in tightly, devouring me in turn. He's burning up. So am I. When Ines and Serena come back, we couldn't care less. It's like we're the only people left in the whole world.

I give myself up to the kiss. I give him everything.

And it's the best kiss of my entire life.

17
December

When my parents and I left Canada to return to France, I knew what I would miss the most: the snowstorms that confined us to the house for days, leaving in their wake an expanse of white so vast that it was as if the roads, prairies and gardens had never existed. Last night it started snowing again, and now all the streets in Lille are practically deserted once more.

Why does this weather put me in such a good mood? I don't really know, it goes way back, but last night when I went to bed, and this morning when I opened my eyes, it was with a smile on my face. And the reason for that smile has a name: Romeo.

I stretch and give a deep, satisfied sigh. Romeo and Annette…

It's crazy!

When Romeo left last night, I was on cloud nine, and I still haven't come off it. I left Ines and Serena to themselves and shut myself in my bedroom, where I relived that extraordinary kiss at least five hundred times. It was the most intense kiss of my life, but also the most longed-for.

And now obviously, Twister is the best game in the world.

Ines and Serena left us on our own in the living room, and we shifted to the couch, where we could not stop kissing. It felt so good being in his arms. As if nothing was as important as what we were experiencing together. When the time came for him to leave with Serena, I knew he wanted to stay just as much I wanted him to stay.

I don't even know why we held out.

I look at my phone. It's still early, not even 7:30 yet. Ines must be sleeping in, so I get up and tiptoe into the living room. The smell of cheese is still so strong that I can't help making a face. It's quite full-on, first thing in the morning! I open the window a little, tidy up the last of the things on the dining table and go and sit in the living room to have my breakfast. Then I get Romeo's snow globe, more motivated than ever to finish it just the way I want it.

Last time I completed a tree, the only one I've managed to make. It's been baked and varnished, and although it looks like a cutting that has taken a turn for the worse, I reassure myself with the thought that if I add a few more, as well as plenty of greenery, I'll be able to camouflage my lack of skills.

Is it because my heart is full to bursting that I'm suddenly able to work the clay like a pro? Definitely! The second tree, which I complete in record time, is much better than the first. I add lots of little branches and foliage, which I mark with fine lines. I also make tiny red fruit and even take the time to create a tree stump, on which I'll stick one of the bird models I bought. Time just flies by, and after almost two hours, it's finally starting to look like something real. All I have to do now is bake it and then stick the elements together.

Thirty minutes at 110 degrees and… ta-dah!

I'm so proud of myself and so lost in my own thoughts that I don't hear the door to Ines's bedroom open.

"Awww, she's so cute with her modelling clay!"

I look up at Serena with a start and drop my beautiful tree on the table. The trunk breaks in two.

"Oh, no, my tree…"

Serena comes closer with an apologetic look on her face.

"Oh, I'm sorry! I didn't mean to startle you."

"No, don't worry. I thought you went home with Romeo last night."

"I did. Then I came back…"

I look a little closer at her. She's wearing a pair of Ines's pyjamas. No questions needed. Clearly my evening was not the only one that ended well.

"Is it completely broken?"

"Yup… but I'll try and glue it back together. That might work. Otherwise, I'll just make another one."

I'm a little disappointed… This one was really good.

"What's it for?"

"A snow globe."

She studies the little bits and pieces spread out in front of me.

"It looks like a cartoon tropical forest."

I give her a sideways look. I'm not sure whether that was a compliment.

"I pulled Romeo's name out of the hat for the Secret Santa," I tell her.

"Really?"

"Yup. And as he misses your island but loves the snow too, I thought I'd make him a snow globe with a bit of both. But unfortunately, I'm not the most talented at doing things like this."

Serena sits down. She seems impressed.

"No, no, it's really good. I mean, it's not totally realistic, but it works!"

"I spent quite a bit of time on the internet looking at botanical websites trying to get the leaves to look right. This is supposed to be a tamarind tree, but I haven't quite got it, have I?"

"It's really cute," she says, as she gently picks up the first crooked tree I made. "Are you sure you're going to be able to stick the other one back together?"

"We'll see! I have to do more things anyway. I have to add birds, moss, and sand. So I'll just do another one."

"He's going to be really touched."

"You think?"

"Absolutely! I've known him for just over a year, and the first time we met, when I said I was from Réunion, he was so happy to have found a bit of his island here that I thought he was going to cry. It was really hard on him leaving his family, friends and lifestyle behind. It hasn't been easy getting used to life and the people here. It's so different to back home."

My chest tightens in sympathy for him.

"He's really going to love it," Serena says again.

"Already hard at work with your crafting?" says Ines as she comes into the living room.

Wow! I've never seen her hair so dishevelled. It's like a firecracker went off inside her pillow. I'm not going to ask her how her night was, but it looks like it was fun!

"Is there any coffee?" she asks with a yawn.

"In the kitchen."

Just before she leaves the living room, Serena grabs her by the hand.

They smile at each other.

They look so cute together that I can't help smiling too.

"So, what shall we do today?" ask Ines as she comes back with a mug. "I see it snowed a lot again."

"Do you feel like going skiing?" Serena asks.

I look at her in astonishment, as does Ines.

"Skiing? Where?"

"Nœux-les-Mines, my dear!"

I've never heard of the place, or the fact that you could ski in the north of France.

"It's in the Pas-de-Calais, not far from here. It's about three quarters of an hour's drive. It's an artificial slope, but with all the snow that fell last night, I bet it's totally white. The conditions should be perfect. We can rent skis there, and I know a store that rents out sports clothing too. We'll definitely find something to wear for the snow. What do you both think? We could bring Romeo along with us too? But we'd have to get going. I bet it'll be packed today!"

"Let's do it!" I say, filled with enthusiasm.

"Oh, and don't forget to change your bandage before you leave!" she adds as I head to my bedroom.

"Whatever you say, doc!"

In the back of Serena's Ford Fiesta, Romeo and I brush our fingers against one another and smile. I rest my head on his shoulder. He smells so good… The two of us are official, and my cheeks are pink with happiness.

On the way there, I can't help looking out the window. The landscape is unusual for the north of France. There is snow everywhere. The slag heaps look like miniature mountains that have been generously sprinkled with powdered sugar, and the trees without leaves are covered in frost.

"Look," Romeo says, handing me his phone. I look at the photos of the dry ski slope in Loisinord.

I have to admit that I find it a bit weird, all this snow and then an artificial ski run.

He cracks up.

"You should see your face! But for my first time skiing, this is perfect. I don't want to fall flat on my face."

I laugh out loud. "I'd pay to see that! And I can't promise I won't laugh!"

He tickles me in retaliation, and then I cuddle up to him again.

It's almost 2 pm when we get to bottom of the hill at Nœux-les-Mines. Romeo and I get out of the car hand in hand. There aren't as many people as Serena had feared, but more importantly, the artificial run has been transformed into a snow-covered slope. It's like a real ski resort, with a button lift and a bar where you can order crepes and have a hot chocolate. Despite the sun, it's so cold that the tip of my nose has turned red.

"I'm not sure if you realize," whispers Romeo into my ear, "but I've never seen so much snow in my whole life. It makes me want to roll you around in it."

"What? Why me?" I pretend to be offended.

"Because I already know that out of the two of us, you're the only one who's not going to fall over!"

Yup, I'm guessing that's a safe bet!

"Who's already been skiing?" asks Serena as she comes over to us.

Unsurprisingly, Ines and I are the only ones to raise our hands.

"Cool!" she says. "You're going to be able to teach us! Come on, the sports store is just over there."

We all giggle when it comes time for Romeo to try on his ski boots. Size 14! I've never met anyone with such huge feet.

He slides them into the boots, struggles to close them and then stands up hesitantly.

"Are there really people who are willing to pay all this money just to look stupid? Every year?" he asks in all seriousness.

I laugh and gesture for him to follow me outside while the girls get ready.

We sit down on a bench to wait for them. I put my feet next to Romeo's: the difference in size is enormous! I wear a size 8.5 for my 5'9 height.

"You don't have any trouble keeping your balance with such small feet?" he teases me. "You never fall over?"

"And do you not ever trip up with those giant clodhoppers?"

He laughs, grabs the edges of my woollen hat and pulls it down over my face.

"Hey!"

I bend over, grab some snow and throw it at him before running away.

War breaks out. In fewer than ten seconds, snowballs are flying in every direction. Anyone foolish enough to walk between us is in danger of being hit by a projectile. Almost all of my shots miss him, but on the last throw, bam, I get him right on the nose! Immediately he lowers his head and covers his face with his hands.

"Hey… are you OK? Did I hurt you?"

But I should know by now that my naivety is my greatest enemy. In one agile movement, Romeo grabs hold of me by the shoulders, sticks a foot out and trips me up, and I find myself flat on my back in the snow, arms akimbo.

He laughs out loud.

"Beaten at your own game," he says with a grin, holding out his hand.

Which I take hold of and pull hard on, and because the hard shell of his shoes has already made him unsteady, he loses his balance and falls right next to me. Face down. With his mouth full of snow.

I smile. "You were saying?"

Romeo lifts his head, spits and turns towards me, resting on one elbow while looking at me with a crooked grin. "I guess that means it's a tie."

I laugh, lean over him and give him a leisurely kiss on the lips in encouragement. "That won't be the last time you fall over! Shall we go?"

"OK, kids, who doesn't know how to walk anymore?" teases Ines as she comes out of the store, dressed as if she was going to ski down a mountain cliff: helmet, ski goggles, backpack.

"Romeo slipped over because of his giant clown feet! I was just saying to him that he probably doesn't even need skis."

Romeo gives me a knowing smile as he gets up, reaches out his hand and brushes the snow off my shoulders before leaning and whispering in my ear.

"Careful, I might bring you down with me and bury you alive under the weight of my body. And that would be such a shame, as I had planned a less dangerous meeting between the two of us."

I look up at him with burning eyes. "Is that an invitation?"

"Why just one?"

Pow! An explosion of butterflies in my stomach.

I stretch up and murmur something into his ear too. "I accept all your invitations…"

If he manages to stay upright after that, I don't know what else to do!

He bursts out laughing, kisses me and looks over towards the button lift.

"Come on, it's time to run rings around me on the slopes. But in other domains, you might be surprised!"

I can't wait to find out…

The four of us head towards the beginner's slope. The button lift experience is going to be interesting, I can tell.

I explain what to do – hold the ski poles in one hand, don't sit on the disc but slip it between your legs so it rests under your butt, and hold the lift pole with the other hand. Let yourself be pulled along, while keeping your balance as you go, and don't lean over, whatever you do.

I lead by example and go first, no problem.

I look behind me. Romeo is next in line. He's nervously clinging onto the lift pole but doesn't fall. Unlike Serena, who falls over but then isn't able to get off the track in time, making Ines fall over right after her. But after a while, once Romeo and I are at the top, we see the girls arrive. Serena is managing, until she has to let go of the pole and… bam! She topples over, followed by Ines, in a hilarious twin roly-poly.

Ines gets up, completely unnerved. I don't think she thought she'd fall over so often!

"Sorry," apologizes Serena, who despite her crooked hat still manages to retain her elegance. "I really don't think this is my thing!"

"Come on, going down is much easier."

"Quicker too, if I fall and roll the whole way down," Serena says jokingly.

Ines and I each have our learner skier: Ines with her darling and me with mine!

Romeo turns out to be a good student. He falls over a few times – quite a few, actually – but he gets up immediately, obviously proud when he manages to ski ten metres without falling. After an hour, he is an expert at the snowplough stance, a common skiing technique all beginners learn, and makes his way down the slope with his skis in a V in front of him. With his long legs and arms out to the side he looks like a moving X. But it's important to keep your balance, so I refrain from teasing him.

"You should have warned me that my knees would be wrecked," he says as we both arrive at the bottom of the slope for the fifth time. "I can't even feel them."

"Yup, that's the snowplough for you! The sun's already going down. Shall we wait for the girls at the bar?"

"Yeah!"

We sit down in the outside seating area and… woohoo! Beer is out and hot chocolate is in, with sugar-dusted crepes all round. And this time, I insist on paying.

From our new vantage point, we don't miss any of Serena's antics. She insists on leaning back with her knees bent and her arms outstretched, and inevitably falls over each time. This is where I see just how patient Ines is, the after-school teacher. She never quits and keeps on explaining, again and again. Between the odd tumble, Serena steals a kiss from her. Even from where we are, we can see that they complement each other just as much as Romeo and me.

"Are you going to the market for the *papillote* sale tomorrow?" asks Romeo.

"Yes, and you?"

He nods and adds, "I'm pretty sure I'm going look like the most deranged elf in the world."

"Then I'll have to come just for that!"

Romeo smiles, reaches out a hand and, with his thumb, wipes the corner of my mouth.

"You have a milk moustache."

I run my tongue over my lips. Romeo follows the movement and our eyes meet.

"You're beautiful."

A huge smile on both our faces.

"Thanks. You're not bad yourself."

"I'd really like to kiss you…"

"And what's stopping you?"

"I want to make sure you want to too."

I smile even wider. Smart alec!

"I want to."

With his hands, he gently takes me by the cheeks, leans over and opens my lips with his, mixing his breath with mine, and leaving no doubt as to his desire. It's the softest yet most passionate kiss I've ever had.

And in front of everyone too. Never has my heart beat so fast.

"I've liked you since the very first day," he murmurs.

"Me too."

He wraps an arm around my shoulder and draws me closer to him with a smile.

I don't know where this relationship is going, but I do know one thing: I'm going to make the most of it.

18
December

“Ohhh, so cute!” says Ines teasingly, as she notices me sulking in front of my reflection.

A green dress with striped red-and-white tights, a black belt with a large buckle, a pointy collar, an elf hat, pompoms stuck to my brown ankle boots… and a pink with yellow polka-dots band-aid on my forehead – I didn't have anything else. My oval, full-length mirror has spoken: with just a little more effort I could participate in the ‘Looking Stupid Never Killed Anyone’ world championship.

“You are going to be a hit!” she assures me with a laugh. “The kids are going to finish your *papillotes* in no time, that's for sure!”

Last night on our way back from the ski slope, Romeo and I stopped by the ASEL to pick up the costumes that Elise had hired for the *papillote* sale today. And boy oh boy, she does not do things by halves.

“All you need now is a few more freckles,” Ines adds, pinching her cheeks with the tips of her fingers. “I can do some for you if you want.”

“No one touches my freckles!”

“Well, at least braid your hair!”

"You must be joking."

"Go on, it's the perfect vibe! Hang on, I'll give you some pigtails."

She dashes over despite my protests, separates my hair, and the hairstyle is done in no time.

"Are you serious?" I say, looking at the result. "I look like Pippi Longstocking."

"They're ideal! You'll have plenty of strength for the day ahead! Um, I don't mean to be a pain in the ass, but you should go or you'll be late."

I look at my phone: it's 10 am.

Things kick off at 10:30.

Well, you gotta do what you gotta do.

I ignore the amused looks in the metro, not to mention the surprised and confused faces, and hide myself as much as I can in my long coat, before arriving at Wazemmes in the freezing cold.

Yesterday's snow hasn't melted; even the benches and car roofs are still covered in it. On the square, the snow has been cleared along the sidewalk to allow space for the farmer's market stands. There is music, children are playing and building snowmen, and some city workers are decorating a huge tree in front of the glass frontage of the Halles. I just love the atmosphere of this place during the festive period!

I walk to the Halles and stop in front of the huge art-deco, red-brick building, with its stunning glass and ironwork.

I don't know much about architecture, but there's no doubt about it, it's super impressive. And even more so at this time of year. Through the windows you can see all the flashing Christmas decorations, twinkling lights, and branches of holly and fir tree hung all around.

Inside, the atmosphere is electric. The festivities have just begun, and the aisles are packed with families and children everywhere. The usual food stalls have all been taken by storm – the café in the middle of the Halles and the smoothie bar – but so have the stands with wooden toys, candies and tea. The place is swarming with people, and I struggle to find where the ASEL has their stand. Finally, I spot them in a corner, right next to the fair-trade grocery store. There's an impressive number of children lining up in front.

I hurry to join them and discover an adorable little wooden structure with a counter and the cash machine from the association, and behind it, an armchair, shelves filled with bags of *papillotes* and cushions dotted over the floor. It looks a bit like Santa Claus's living room; it's really cool! And on the red and gold couch, flanked by two children, is Father Christmas himself. Normally Anthony doesn't have the same potbelly as Santa, but he has padded out his stomach to complete the illusion. He has reddened his cheeks and is wearing a great bushy beard along with a hat topped by a big pompom, small half-moon glasses perched at the tip of his nose. Not bad at all!

A sign written in big letters says: 'Buy one packet of papillotes and get a photo with Santa Claus FREE.' No wonder the line is so long.

The photo printer that the association hired is going to start smoking soon if things don't calm down.

Elise comes over to me dressed as Mrs. Claus, her blond curls escaping from under a green hat. But the main attraction are her red platform shoes that give her an extra ten centimetres at least. It's extremely effective, but I do wonder how she manages to stay upright.

"Hey, Annie! Anthony has just started the photo session. You look delightful! And I love the hairstyle!"

I feel like giggling. As delightful as an elf, that's a new one!

"Mathilde, Hassan and Radana are already here. And Ionut too, the Romanian student. Do you remember him? He's taking the photos. And Romeo shouldn't be far away. I didn't think there would be so many people, it's incredible! One of our partners donated one hundred kilos of loose *papillotes*. I thought we'd struggle to sell them all, but with this crowd it'll be much easier than I expected! Although it might be a little calmer in the afternoon."

For the time being, things are certainly going well. Mathilde and Hassan are behind the counter, taking people's payment, one after the other. They are also dressed as elves and also look completely ridiculous. Mathilde has the same costume as me, with piercings and tattoos into the bargain, and Hassan has the male version with green pants, a red tunic, a big black belt and a hat.

"Where's Radana?"

"Just behind the stand. We've set up a quiet spot for her to fill the bags with *papillotes*."

"I'll just go and put down my stuff, and I'll be back!"

What's my job going to be? I'll have to wait and find out!

I find Radana in a kind of storage room without a roof. She's sitting in front of a tiny round table and is carefully filling up the bags. I smile as I see two or three empty wrappers on the floor. As I've always said: chocolate is life!

"Hi! Have you been here long?" I ask, hanging up my coat.

"Oh, hello there! I got here around thirty minutes ago."

Her accent and her rolled Rs bring a smile to my face.

"Do you feel better?"

"Yes, thank you. And I just wanted to say that I'm sorry. I could have hurt you when I fell."

"Oh, no, Radana, don't apologize. It wasn't your fault," I say as I pull up a chair and sit next to her. "And I'm totally fine."

She looks at the band-aid on my forehead.

"Not totally…"

"Oh, that's nothing. It'll be gone in a week. Romeo told me you'd moved into another apartment. How is it?"

"I've only been there since Saturday, but I really like Thea. She's very nice."

"Thea with purple hair from the Secret Santa?"

Radana nods.

"Cool!"

Then there's a pause in the conversation, so I open an empty bag to fill with *papillotes*.

"Um, I feel a bit awkward asking… but is there anything you need for the new apartment that might make you feel a bit more at home?"

Radana has extremely blue eyes, and as she looks over at me, they are glimmering a little with unshed tears. "This situation is so embarrassing," she says.

I'm mortified.

"Oh, Radana, I didn't mean to make you feel bad, I'm sorry."

"No, it's not you. It's just that I need so much. All my clothes, shoes and even my hairbrush were damaged by the mould in my old apartment, so I threw them away. And now I have hardly anything."

I try to stay chill, but it makes me so mad to hear this.

"I'm sorry," I repeat, for want of anything better to say.

"When I came here, I didn't think it would be so hard. My parents already help me a lot, but the cost of living is so expensive in France compared to the Czech Republic. I can't ask them for anything more."

She had already mentioned this, and it breaks my heart to hear her justifying herself again.

"What size shoe are you?"

"I think here it's an 8.5."

"The same as me! How would you feel about me lending you some clothes and shoes?"

She looks at me, caught off guard.

I would rather have said that she could have them or even that I'd buy her some new ones if she'd rather, but in addition to the fact that I'd have to explain my situation, I also don't want to make her feel worse. Elise had told me that those who come to the ASEL hate being pitied, and I would just loathe it if Radana got the feeling that's what I was doing.

Because despite what Gavin might have said about them, it's not pity that we should be feeling for people like Radana, but admiration. They are so courageous and are worth one hundred times more than people like Gavin and I.

"You want to lend me some clothes?" she repeats, as if she hasn't understood.

"We're about the same size, and we have the same shoe size, and I'd really like to. Truly."

"But what do you want in exchange?"

"Nothing."

Seeing her surprise, I understand that until she discovered the association, Radana must never have been able to count on anyone here. And there are hundreds of students in her position. My guts are twisting, and I really want to help her get back on her feet, that's all.

"I don't know what to say," she murmurs.

"How about yes! And if one day I come to your country and am totally lost, you can come to my rescue!"

She runs a hand through her hair and smiles.

"OK."

"I can bring a couple of things to the association tomorrow. Will you be there?"

"Of course."

"Cool! We can just meet a bit earlier. Anyway, I'd better go, I'm meant to be doing something on the other side," I say as I get up. "I'll take the bags you've prepared."

"Annette?" she says, just before I disappear around the wooden wall.

I turn back and look at her. I think she's about to cry.

"Thank you so much."

I play things down with a wink and go to put the bags of *papillotes* on the counter, which get sold as soon as they arrive.

"We need more!" says Elise. "Who can come and help Radana and me?"

"I will!" says Mathilde hurriedly, who is clearly sick of handing out *papillotes* right, left and centre. "Annie, can you take my place?"

"Sure!"

It's intense, to say the least. Everyone seems to want a packet, no matter how long they have to wait.

"What in the heck does this chocolate have that's so special?" I whisper to Hassan.

He gives a weary little sigh.

"The chocolate, nothing, but the photos with Anthony are hysterical. I think that's the only reason the parents are buying them."

I turn around. On Anthony's right, a little girl is sitting quietly, with her finger up her nose, carrying out a thorough search for an intruder she's clearly finding hard to locate. On his left, a kid of about three is intently yanking on his beard. And Ionut is snapping away, come what may!

"Every single child behaves as if they were possessed," says Hassan. "And it's only 11 am. It's going to be a long day."

"They're all excited by the magic of Christmas, it's not their fault!" I watch for a couple of shots and sympathize with poor old Anthony. Then my attention is caught by something, or rather someone, who has just come into the Halles, leaving behind him a trail of startled expressions.

Romeo…

With an elf hat perched atop his curly hair, he is moving through the crowds with as much dignity as his costume – which looks as if it were made for his much younger brother – allows him. His green pants are so short they only reach half-way down his calf muscles. But he had the brilliant idea of covering them up with stripey socks. As for his minuscule red tunic, it basically looks like a crop top. Everyone can see just how flat his stomach is! And, of course, he wasn't able to do up the belt, so it's just hanging off his hips. The truth is that I actually find him super sexy, but at the same time, I have to stop myself from bursting out laughing.

"Don't say anything," he warns me.

I clear my throat.

"Did you go through a hot wash and only your clothes shrunk? Jeez! Those pants really make you look like you're up to some kind of funny business!"

"Go on, laugh as much as you like. It's no worse than what I've already been through on the metro. Anyway, Pippi, you do know that funny business has more than one meaning?" he teases in return.

"Umm…"

"You know, when two people get involved in some hanky-panky of a more personal nature…?" he explains with a meaningful look.

"Oh…"

"So no, I haven't been up to any funny business, but I'm definitely up for it if you are."

And there's that phrase again that keeps cropping up whenever I'm around Romeo: is it getting hot in here, or is it just me?

Before I can say anything, he leans over to kiss me.

"Hi…" he breathes against my lips, and at exactly the same time, we hear a clicking sound. We turn around to see the official photographer for the event with her camera pointed towards us.

"Perfect!" she says. "You guys look so cute! You'll be able to see the photo in the local paper."

Romeo and I look at each other and laugh.

"Ready to enter the arena?" I ask.

He makes a face. "What do we have to do?"

"Get rid of one hundred kilos of *papillotes*. That's four hundred 250-gram packets!"

"Easy-peasy! Come on, let's go."

Initially we take turns doing all the different jobs, and it's practically non-stop.

Then around 3 pm, as the crowds start to thin and the market stalls on the square are being dismantled, Romeo and I turn into streetsellers, going through the aisles, outside, and even into bars. We don't stop for a moment. People buy *papillotes* from us either because our matching outfits look great or because they feel sorry for us. By the time 5 pm comes around, as the doors of the Halles are being closed for the day, after two snowball fights, multiple stolen kisses in the street and several hot chocolates knocked back in a hurry, only ten kilos of *papillotes* are left!

Ninety per cent of the stock has been sold.

Once we tidy everything up, take down the stand and remove everything from the site, it's 7 o'clock. Romeo and I collapse onto the couch in the ASEL common room, completely exhausted.

Elise and Anthony have planned a *raclette*,* and I think to myself that after the fondue on Friday, I'm going to turn into a piece of cheese if this keeps up.

We leave the ASEL just before midnight. In the metro next to Romeo, I lean against his chest, with his arms around my shoulders.

With our costumes we attract a few weird looks, but we don't even care.

"That was a cool day," he says quietly.

I give a huge yawn. "Extremely tiring too."

"Do you want me to walk you home?"

"Oh no, you'd miss the last metro."

"I have long legs, I can walk."

"No way. I'll be fine."

I snuggle into him a little more and realize how long it has been since I felt so good with someone.

Felt so good, period.

Because I like everything about Romeo – his mind, his gentle spirit, his simplicity and what he does to me: he makes me want to do something with my life.

---

* TN: A raclette is a traditional meal from the Alps, where special cheese is melted and served with boiled potatoes.

He does something that Gavin was never able to: he makes me a better person. When I first started at the ASEL, I wasn't sure of what I was doing, and without realizing it, Romeo has made me feel sure about what I really want.

What I want is to feel useful.

What I want is to help people.

And what I want is to be with him.

I sigh.

"What's up?" he asks.

What's up is that I don't want to leave him tonight.

I close my eyes, unsure how to respond.

He strokes my hair, and I don't move until the metro stops at the Lille-Flandres station. Romeo will continue on until Fives.

"Hey… we're at your stop."

I sit up straight, look him in the eye without moving and wait for the beep to sound and the doors of the train to close again.

"What are you doing?" he asks with his eyebrows furrowed.

"I'm walking you home."

"But there won't be another train for you to go back?"

I smile. "I know."

Romeo narrows his eyes at me and finally understands.

I won't be going home tonight.

19
December

I had pictured Romeo's apartment in an apartment block, but it's on the top floor of an old building right in the middle of Fives.

We push open a big gate leading into a courtyard where a few cars are parked and then climb a metal staircase. He lives in an attic studio and by the time we get there, my heart is absolutely racing…

"It's small, but functional," says Romeo, as he invites me to come inside.

There is one room with a tiny kitchen, a table and two chairs, a two-seater couch and an old cask cut in half for a coffee table. Right at the back, pushed up against the wall, is an unmade bed and a nightstand. Opposite, there's a desk covered in books and Romeo's study notes.

It's cute.

"The bathroom is in here," he says, leading me through a door. "It's not fancy, but it's clean and there's hot water!"

He's talking quickly and justifying himself, as if he's scared I'll judge him.

I touch him on the arm. "I'm really happy to be here, you know…"

"I'm really happy you're here…"

But he still seems tense.

"If you want to take a shower, go ahead, the towels are just here in the clos –"

I stop him by stretching up on the tips of my toes and placing my lips on his.

"Sorry," I say, as I end the kiss.

He smiles. "I've had more unpleasant interruptions. That kiss wouldn't have a sibling, would it?"

This is the first time we've truly been on our own. We don't need to hold back or worry about being disturbed, so I let myself go.

Romeo can tell how I'm feeling and pulls me tighter to him, holding me with greater urgency.

"So, what about that shower?" he asks against my lips.

"I really need one, but I love kissing you too much…"

So he starts again, then moves his lips to my ear. "I love it too."

He pulls away slightly, takes a moment to look at me, then opens the wall closet where he keeps all his clothes. He gets out a towel and a gigantic t-shirt.

"For bed."

A shiver runs over my entire body.

Sleeping in his t-shirt and in his bed…

He smiles at me. He gets it.

"There's a hairdryer under the sink if you need one. I'll be just in the other room."

"OK."

"Oh, wait!"

He goes back to the closet and grabs a hoodie and a warm pair of socks.

"Just in case you get cold."

"Thank you!"

He leaves, and I take a deep breath. There's hand-washing laundry detergent on the edge of the sink, so I run the water and pour in some detergent, then get undressed quickly and dunk in my underwear. Once I wring them out, they're almost dry. The magic of microfibre.

The shower does me a world of good. I pull on the t-shirt, hoodie and socks that are all way too big for me, then untangle my hair as best I can with Romeo's comb. I make do with a bit of toothpaste on my finger to brush my teeth and the job's done.

By the time I leave the bathroom, Romeo has straightened the duvet and arranged the pillows on the bed. He has dimmed the lights and put on *Hunky Dory*, an album by David Bowie that I love. He's waiting for me on the couch and scrolling on his phone, still dressed in his hideous elf costume.

"It's all yours!"

He gets up, still with bare feet, comes over to me and caresses my hair. My heart is going to explode if he keeps this up.

"I won't be long. I don't have much to drink, but there should be some tea around somewhere if you want. Just help yourself."

I nod and watch him disappear behind the door.

I look around and notice the little details I had missed when we arrived. The half-finished packet of chips on the counter, his class schedule stuck on a whiteboard, an empty mug and a spoon on the kitchen table. A pair of running shoes sticking out from under the bed, a novel by Stephen King on the bedside table and, right next to it, a frame with some photos in it.

I sit on the bed and take a closer look.

It's his family. I immediately recognize his brothers, who are posing on the beach. They look like him. There's a shot of his parents. Romeo gets his curly hair from his mom and his blue eyes from his dad. They're in front of a cafe with a smile on their faces. Then a photo of Romeo hiking. He's pointing at the Piton de la Fournaise, a volcano on Réunion Island.

"So you've met my family?" he asks from behind me.

I turn around to see him in shorts and a t-shirt, with damp hair.

"You seem very close-knit."

"We are. Do you have any brothers or sisters?"

I sigh. I'm not going to be able to get out of talking about myself.

"I'm an only child."

Then I look back at his photos.

"Are your parents standing in front of their bar?" I ask him.

"Yes, in Saint-Denis. People go there to play cards and dice, talk about football and put the world to rights."

Romeo sits next to me and takes my hand. "You must be tired."

I hold my breath. "No…"

"Nervous?"

"A little."

"Me too…"

I look down.

It feels good to know we feel the same. Gavin was always so sure of himself, and he never gave me space to say whether I wanted to slow things down. Romeo is different.

"You're making me lose my head a little, Annette Reynaud."

I smile. "You're making me lose my head a lot, Romeo Payet."

He gently slides his hand behind my neck. I lift my head to look at him properly and am reassured, because I know I'm not the only one whose heart is hammering. Romeo leans over and stops a few centimetres from my mouth.

My breathing accelerates.

I close my eyes and slightly open my lips, as if in a signal, as if giving him the permission he's waiting for.

He kisses me with the utmost tenderness. His breath smells like toothpaste. My tongue meets his and we fall back onto the bed. My head sinks into a pillow, and I wrap my arms and legs around him.

I don't want to let him go; I don't want to let him leave.

Romeo sits up, strokes my face, looks at me, takes his time and makes me feel what no other boy has every made me feel: that there is nothing more important than the two of us, that we are connected, and that nothing is more meaningful that what we are about to do. It's amazing, and I know he respects me.

I trust him.

The fire within me spreads everywhere, exploding like a nuclear fission reaction, making an intense heat radiate outwards from my stomach and all through my flesh.

I want him so much.

"Wait," I murmur against his mouth.

He freezes, and I can see the desire blazing in his eyes. I reach out for my bag at the end of the bed and take out a little silver packet, which I hand to him.

He smiles at me, he eyes shining more brightly than ever before.

I am burning up.

Our clothes fly off into the room and all that remains is the two of us, our jagged breath and the desire to share our innermost being with the other, without artifice and without fear. He gives himself up to me and I to him, without limits, until our bodies consume each other.

With my cheek resting on Romeo's chest, I look at our folded legs and the goosebumps dotting my thigh.

I'm cold, but I wouldn't move for anything in the world.

Romeo notices my little shiver and reaches out to gather up the duvet that had fallen onto the ground. He covers us with it and holds me tightly.

"Sorry. I don't often turn on the heating in here. I've gotten used to it, and I don't realize how cold it is anymore."

"Don't worry, I'm fine."

I cling to him with a sigh and breathe in the smell of his shower gel combined with the scent of his skin. I'm so happy to have met him. So happy to be here with him tonight. There's nowhere else I'd rather be.

"Tell me about yourself," he says as he caresses my hair. "I hardly know anything about your life."

The question was bound to come up sooner or later. I could – I *should* take the opportunity to tell him everything, but not now. I don't want to spoil the moment. I choose to go with humour.

"Hmm, let's see… I was born in the south of France. I used to swim a lot, but I gave it up the day my horse nearly drowned."

"Huh? You had a horse that nearly drowned?"

"Yes, we were doing aquapony, but he was too small for it, so he went under."

I feel his head twitch, and he starts laughing.

"You're nuts, you know that? I actually believed you!"

He waits a few seconds before starting up again.

"What kind of childhood did you have?"

'Privileged' is what I should say.

"Comfortable," I say instead. "Loving parents who were attentive and present. I was a good girl, but a bit of a loner."

"That only half surprises me. I was a real tearaway, all over the place!"

"I would never have thought so, you seem so calm."

"Appearances can be deceiving!"

His arm tightens around my shoulders, and I nestle into him even more.

"When did you go to the ASEL for the first time?" I ask, without knowing why the question popped up now.

At the worst possible time.

Under the duvet, Romeo lightly caresses my shoulder with his fingers.

"I only signed up in September. It took me ages to decide."

"Do your parents know you go there?"

"No, and there's no way I'm telling them."

"Why not? What are you worried about?"

He doesn't sigh or hesitate. His reply could not be any firmer.

"I'm worried they'll make even more sacrifices for me, that it'll be at the expense of my brothers, who shouldn't have to bear the consequences of my choices. I'd rather manage on my own. Speaking of which, I start a new job tomorrow," he says to change the subject. "In a bar in the centre of town."

"Oh, why?"

"The snack bar near the campus didn't need me anymore. Anyway, I'll be working every day at lunchtime and some evenings too."

I remove my arm from under the duvet and start picking at the fabric with my index finger. For those who know me, it's obvious: something's on my mind.

Clearly, Romeo has worked it out too.

"What is it?"

"What if I stayed for Christmas?"

"But what about your parents?"

"They've had nineteen Christmases with me, I'm sure they'll be fine. I organized the Secret Santa, it makes sense for me to be there, and… I want to be with you."

Romeo turns around so that we're lying face to face.

"I don't want to deprive you of your family, Annie."

"You're not depriving me of anything, I just really want to be with you."

He smiles at me.

"Well, in that case, I would be delighted. That means I'll get to see who you're giving your Secret Santa gift to."

He has no idea how right he is!

I sigh and rub the tip of my nose against his.

"It's 3 o'clock in the morning. It's your first day at the bar and you'll be dead tired. Shall we go to sleep?"

He lifts his arm and turns off the switch above him, before pulling the covers over our shoulders.

"You better not snore!" he says.

"And you better not fart!"

He laughs out loud.

"Good night, Annette."

"Good night, Romeo, o Romeo."

Without moving, I listen to his breathing become more and more regular, until he falls deeply asleep.

I close my eyes, overcome with fatigue.

Romeo is the person I've been waiting for, the person I want to grow and develop alongside and share things with, even the things I'm hiding because I'm scared he'll judge me.

Tomorrow I'll tell him about my parents, about our true situation and how I grew up, and he'll understand.

And if he doesn't, I'll tell him that I'm in love with him and that nothing else matters.

Nothing at all.

I turn around and fall asleep with a smile on my face.

"Shit! We forgot to put an alarm on!" cries Romeo as he jumps out of bed. "It's 11:15 and I said I'd be there at midday."

I sit up a bit groggily. We didn't sleep much last night.

Romeo flies to the bathroom and comes out dressed in five minutes.

I just have enough time to pull on my tights and my elf costume from the day before. I make a face, but we don't always get what we want in life.

"Take your time and stay here if you want," he says. "I'll leave you the keys and you can put them under the doormat. Apart from me and the owners, no one comes into the courtyard anyway."

"Where's the bar you're working in?"

"In the old part of town."

"I'll come with you then," I say, as I pull my hair back into a ponytail. "Then I can go home and get changed right after."

"OK, let's go! I have to leave now, sorry. I can't even offer you coffee!"

He gives me a kiss, and we leave his apartment. The cold stings our faces. But at least it's not raining, that's something! In the metro I catch people looking at me, but unlike yesterday, I'm not sure what's making them cringe – my outfit or the bags under my eyes that are so big I could use them as suitcases.

We get off at Lille-Flandres and practically run to the bar. We get there five minutes early.

We stand back a little from the storefront, and he leans over to kiss me.

"Thank you for yesterday. I think it was the best night of my whole life."

His hair is all tousled, so I lift my hand and try to straighten it a little. But to no avail; clearly his curls just do whatever they want.

"I'd better go. I finish at 3, are you going to the ASEL tonight?"

"Sure am!"

He kisses me again, as if sorry to leave me, then pulls back for good this time.

"See you later!" he says, before looking back and adding, "Just to let you know, I've never seen a girl first thing in the morning who looks as pretty as you."

And he disappears as I laugh to myself on the sidewalk.

Suddenly my attention is caught by a double-parked car. A car that is all too familiar.

It's Gavin's.

He starts it up, slowly drives past, looks out at me without saying a word or waving and then revs up the engine as he speeds away.

One thing's for sure: he saw Romeo and me together.

At 5 o'clock, after barely getting any rest and acting a little distracted all day, I arrive at the food market. I had called my parents to tell them that I wouldn't be home for Christmas after all. Mom was upset, claiming she'd already organized everything. But I know that's not true. She hasn't bought the plane tickets because my parents always do things right at the last minute.

I explained why I was staying… well, I told them half of it – the association and the Secret Santa thing. Dad didn't get too worked up – I could tell he was looking forward to a trip just with Mom – but Mom's tone of voice when we hung up was a little stiff. I know she'll come around and that it's not really serious, but I hate situations that make me seem ungrateful.

This time, though, I want to focus on me.

Because most customers have already gone home, there are even fewer than last week, and we finish much earlier. As usual, Romeo and I, as well as the students who will be here on the 24th, meet up in the common room.

I discreetly give a bag of clothes and shoes to Radana, then tell Elise and Anthony that I'll be here for Christmas Eve after all. They are almost as happy as Romeo and decide a celebratory drink is in order.

In the North, it seems like any excuse for a toast is a good excuse, and I'm totally on board with that!

"How did the new job go?" I ask Romeo while we are in the kitchen putting glasses onto a tray.

"Intense but fun. And oh man, the meals are way better than at the snack bar! I'll have to take you there one day."

"I would love that. Do you want to come around to mine afterwards?"

I really want to talk to him about me and my parents. I want to be as honest as possible, just like he's been with me.

Because we're together now.

"Yes, of course."

"And I told my parents I was staying here for Christmas…"

I don't finish my sentence as I am interrupted by Elise, who has come to join us.

"Annie, there's someone here for you!"

I frown.

"Someone's here for me?"

"Yes, he's waiting in the common room."

He? A guy?

I don't have a good feeling about this.

And I'm right. When I go back into the room, Gavin is standing in the middle of everyone with a huge grin on his face.

20
December

"What are you doing here?"

No one is really paying any attention to Gavin: all the students are chatting amongst themselves and Elise has gone to the kitchen with Anthony, but I'm suspicious.

The fact that Gavin is here now, when only this morning he saw Romeo and me kiss, is not a coincidence.

And his smile is totally fake, I know it by heart.

"What's the problem? I can't come and say hi to an old girlfriend?"

I raise an eyebrow. "Of course, but you could have gone to my house. I'm a volunteer, I'm not supposed to meet friends here."

"Oh, of course, silly me. But I guess that doesn't go for him?" he says, turning to Romeo and looking straight at him.

Romeo is standing behind me, just to the side, without saying a word.

He's clearly tense, but unlike Gavin, he's not one to make a scene, for which I'm grateful. This is not the time or the place.

"Oh, my bad," Gavin goes on with a forced laugh. "You're a customer, I'd forgotten that. I got mixed up because you guys are sleeping together. You'll have to excuse me."

Red alert. I narrow my eyes at him.

"Have you come to create a scene?"

Gavin runs a hand through his hair unconcernedly.

"No, not at all, you always think the worst. I told you, I just came to say hi. But I am kind of curious to see what it is about this place that attracts you so much. Apart from the male students, that is…" he adds mockingly.

"You should leave, Gavin."

"No, not yet. You haven't even offered me a drink when I can see you're about to serve up some supermarket fruit juice. I wouldn't miss that for the world!"

Then he looks around, eyebrows raised.

"It must be reassuring for these poor students to feel so at home, except for the fact that their families aren't here."

His condescension is unbearable. I'm about to lose it.

"Come over here," I order him, while taking him by the arm and walking him over to the stairs that go up to the third floor.

"Why did you come here? What do you want?"

His eyes become black with fury.

"Did you dump me for him?"

"Absolutely not. Our relationship had come to its natural conclusion, and you know that just as well as I do."

"And when did you start telling yourself that? When you realized I was of no use to you anymore, because you'd already taken everything you needed?"

"How can you say that, Gavin? That's untrue, I never used you!"

"Of course you did, you wanted more fun in your life! Because before you met me, you were bored to tears. I was just a distraction for you, the spoilt brat who takes what she wants then throws it away."

"Oh, that's rich coming from you! Why do you have to ruin everything?"

"Because you've taken me for a fool, that's why," he says, his voice rising as he loses his temper. "You're trying to make me think that things ended the way they did because they were destined to, but that's not true, is it? You were already eyeing someone else!"

This is the exact moment when I realize that Gavin's heart isn't broken, he's just annoyed by the situation.

"You're wrong. I didn't leave you for someone else. I left because our relationship wasn't working anymore."

"And that just occurred to you all of a sudden? When was it exactly? When you started playing at being the good Samaritan? Your superhero syndrome miraculously opened your eyes?"

"I'm not saving anyone, I'm just helping however I can, like we all do at one point or another."

He gives a scornful laugh.

"You're joking, right? That's just what little rich girls like you say to make themselves feel better! And is that working out for you, is everyone OK with your pity?"

Automatically I look behind me to make sure no one heard.

Gavin gives me a speculative look.

"I don't believe it… You still haven't told them?"

"Gavin…"

"You've been coming here for two weeks, you're even hooking up with one of these hobos and you still haven't said anything? What are you really up to? An undercover sociology study? You've probably made them think you don't have any money either, so that you can better study them and pass yourself off as one of them! Oh, no, I forgot, it's not even as noble as that, you're only here because you were bored and didn't know what to do with your life!"

Gavin's pretending to be offended, but he has no morals, he just wants to hurt me and obviously he's prepared to do that by the worst means possible.

"Stop talking garbage!"

"I'm talking garbage?" he says in an even louder voice so the others will hear him. "I bet that everyone here has your mother's app on their phone, because none of them have enough money to buy new clothes. Did you tell them that each transaction on her site brings in more dough? Your parents are multimillionaires, damn it, and you're goofing around with the people your 'rents are making money off? While they're starving? You disgust me!"

My face drains of colour.

"Annie?"

I turn around to see Elise, her brows drawn. And behind her, Anthony and the other students are looking at us, completely dumbfounded.

But I have eyes only for Romeo.

And all I can see is his expression, cold and hard.

"Now they're all here, Annie, tell them the truth, go on!" says Gavin, getting nastier than ever. "Tell them just how rich you are, and that the only reason you're here is because you were bored shitless in your life as a poor little rich kid spoiled by her parents! Why don't you tell them just how much you took advantage of me, and now of them?"

"That's enough, young man!" says Elise, interrupting him. "I think it's time you left."

"Oh, sure, she's useful for you, she has to be protected. You're perfect for each other!"

"Out. Now."

Anthony intervenes. He is not very tall, nor heavyset, but the fact that he is a man is enough to make Gavin give way.

"Fine, whatever, I'm out of here. And happy Christmas, ya bunch of fleabags!"

He shoves me out of the way with his shoulder, walks the short distance between the two staircases and runs down the steps before slamming the door behind him.

I can't seem to catch my breath.

"Are you OK?" asks Elise.

I don't answer. I'm unable to tear my eyes away from Romeo. His eyes are so full of confusion, and disappointment too. I have to talk to him.

I take a step towards him but stop as I see him turn on his heels. He grabs his coat, slips it on and leaves via the stairs.

"Romeo, wait!"

I rush down the stairs and catch up with him on the sidewalk. It's pouring buckets again, and I've come out without a coat, but I couldn't care less even though I'm shivering with cold.

I clutch his arm.

"Please, wait..."

"Why? You must have found it funny seeing us struggle to make ends meet, while all you have to do is call your parents for them to deliver a load of caviar."

"I'm not that kind of person, Romeo. It's not how Gavin described it. Of course I'm not using the customers for my studies. I wanted to quit school, I had lost my way. You have to believe me!"

He looks at me under the flickering streetlight, his face wreathed in disappointment.

"Romeo…"

"You lied to me, damn it. I feel like such a fool."

I'm finding it hard to breath.

Romeo shakes his head.

"I'm going home."

I want to hold him back, tell him he's wrong, but it's no use trying to defend myself now, tonight. He's too angry.

Dripping with rain, I go back upstairs and collect my belongings without saying a word to anyone and without meeting anyone's questioning looks. Then I leave the building.

I feel like I'm standing on the edge of a cliff.

I'm suffocating.

I need to be alone.

By noon the next day, I still haven't gotten out of bed. I was awake for most of the night. forcing myself not to write a message to Romeo. Because the reality is, I just don't have the courage to hear him say again what a bad person I am.

I want to scream.

And I hate Gavin for what he did.

I never loved him like I love Romeo.

Shit. I don't want everything to be turned upside-down again, I don't want…

Three little knocks warn me that the door is about to open. Ines comes in, but I turn around and hide under my duvet.

I don't want to talk.

"Wow, in all the time we've been living together, I've never seen you stay in bed for so long. Are you sick?"

I don't answer, so I hear her walk across the wooden floor to my bed. She puts a hand on my shoulder and sits down on the mattress.

"Annie, are you OK?"

"No," I mutter. "I want to die."

"Does it hurt somewhere?"

I heave a despairing sigh. "In my heart."

It takes her a few seconds to understand.

"Oh. Have you had a problem with Romeo?"

"Yes…"

Because I can no longer breathe, I come out from under the duvet. My eyes are all swollen.

"Hey, darling, you're worrying me."

"I don't think he wants to see me ever again…"

"Is that what he said? What happened?"

I pull myself up to a seated position, while tugging the covers up to my chin. I crack and start crying.

"Oh, Ines, it hurts, it hurts so much."

"Oh no!" cries Ines. "Come here and tell me all about it."

I snuggle into her arms like a child. Ines is patient and listens to me explain the situation between sobs.

When I finish, my duvet cover is in the same state as my tissues.

"It was awful. Gavin totally ripped me apart. He was so unfair. I never saw things like that, never. I didn't decide to go to the ASEL for some sociology study, I never used anyone. All I wanted was to try and work out what I should do with my life, and I wanted to help people… I just wanted to help and to feel useful, I promise."

"I know, Annie, darling. I was there when you decided to go. Gavin is just jealous and sour."

"If you could have seen the look on Romeo's face. He was so disappointed, so bitter. I wanted to talk to him. I should have done it sooner. And I told my parents I wasn't going home for Christmas, but how can I go back to the ASEL after all this? I feel so embarrassed!"

"Hey, stop beating yourself up. OK, so you intentionally hid the fact that your parents are loaded, but you weren't obliged to reveal everything about yourself. I don't think for a moment that the president of the association would reproach you for that. You've done nothing wrong. On the contrary, you've been really helpful and super present the last couple of weeks. Has she tried to call you?"

I look at my phone. A message from Elise came in ten minutes ago saying I shouldn't hesitate to call her. I nod.

"Are you going to call her back?"

"Yes, of course. I owe her an explanation too."

"It's all going to be fine."

"With her, yes, but Romeo…"

Ines sighs.

"He feels betrayed, but you never actually lied to him, you just kept avoiding the subject. Annie, you haven't killed anyone, as far as I know, anyway. The situation isn't as bad as all that. Let's not go overboard. Everyone's allowed to make mistakes. I'm sure Romeo will come around."

I give a sniff. "You think?"

"Why don't you try and talk to him today? You could go and see him after he finishes work at the bar?"

My heart feels like it's going to explode just at the mere thought of it.

"Come on, girlfriend, it's not over yet," says Ines, trying to reassure me.

I cross my fingers and hope she's right.

A 3 o'clock I'm waiting opposite the bar where Romeo works. On the way here I repeated what I want to tell him a hundred times in my head, but I've forgotten everything. I can't even remember my own name.

At 3:10 he finally emerges, pausing as he catches sight of me.

"Hi. Can we talk?"

His face is completely expressionless. He's not giving an inch. My stomach is in knots.

"I'm listening."

I swallow down my saliva. He's not making this easy for me.

"I am so sorry for yesterday…"

"Yeah, I can imagine."

He is so cold.

"Look, I… I never intended to hurt anyone, especially not you."

"Well, you failed."

"I know, and I'm so sorry… I wanted to talk to you. I was going to…"

"But you didn't."

His words crack like a whip.

"You lied to me. *To me*. We spent the night together, slept in the same bed. I confided in you, but you lied to me."

"Romeo, I really wanted to tell you, but I just couldn't find the right moment. You have to believe me."

"And yet I gave you the perfect opening last night."

"What, confess everything at a time like that? Like pillow talk?"

"That would have been better than the way it turned out."

I feel like crying again. "I can understand why you're angry. I didn't want people to see me as the daughter of rich parents first off, I wanted people to get to know me and appreciate me for what I could offer."

"You've totally missed the point! You think I'm upset because of the association? That's not it at all. I thought I was more to you than just a *customer* that you had to hide the truth from. But I was wrong."

"But you are more than that!"

"That's enough. It was obvious to me that your parents are better off than mine, even though I hadn't realized quite by how much, and I still wanted to get to know you more. I confided in you, and I hoped that you trusted me too. But that wasn't the case," he adds, in a voice full of regret.

"You're wrong…"

He gives a bitter laugh. "You think? Well, it doesn't look like it from here, because what you did was put me on the same level as the others. You didn't want to hurt the poor dude who doesn't have a penny to his name!"

"What? No, that's not it at all, I just wanted to be careful."

"Careful? We're straying awfully close to pity now, aren't we?"

"Stop it! I haven't turned anyone into an object of pity. It's just that I didn't know how to bring this up, that's all. Damn it, I'm not defined by the money in my bank account. The girl you liked, that's who I am."

He looks at me for a long moment.

As he doesn't say anything, I try my luck.

"I like you, Romeo. Why does it have to be so complicated?"

"Oh, so what, we stay together and live out a remake of *Lady and the Tramp*? Sorry, Lady, count me out."

"I'm not going to apologize because I don't have the same life as you."

Romeo looks at me intently, lets several seconds go by and then delivers the final blow.

"Don't call me again. Ever."

I follow him with my eyes, unable to move. All I want is to go back in time. That's all. But I've played my hand, and I lost.

21
December

The sky is grey, just like my heart. Cloudy and dull.

I didn't want to, but I finally decided to meet up with Elise at the ASEL. She really insisted that I go in.

She obviously wants to talk about what happened on Monday night. And I need to speak to her too.

I'm trying my hardest not to get too depressed and instead tell myself that maybe Romeo just needs time to accept things.

But there's also a part of me that is angry, because even though I wasn't entirely transparent, I wasn't dishonest either. I wanted to take the necessary precautions and look out for the customers, but I also wanted to protect myself from judgement or misinterpretation. That's not a crime.

I sigh and leave the metro.

When I get to the front door of the association, the Christmas wreath I ordered at the florist has been delivered. Someone has hung it on the door, and it brightens up the street with its flashing little LEDs and scarlet holly.

Feeling a heavy weight settle in the pit of my stomach, I press on the intercom.

It's exactly 2 pm, and I expected to find a couple of students in the common room, but apart from Elise, it's empty.

She is sitting at the end of the table, near the window, with her phone at her ear. In front of her there are two mugs, a Thermos of coffee and a plate with Christmas cookies on it.

She's been waiting for me.

She beckons me over while finishing her conversation.

"OK, great. Yes, that would be perfect today between 6:30 and 8:30 pm. Thank you again for the suggestion and I'll see you later."

She hangs up while I'm still unbuttoning my coat and stands to give me a hug.

"I'm glad you came. Take a seat. Would you like a coffee?"

I nod. I feel so awkward.

She fills a mug and smiles at me. "Are you feeling better?"

"I am so sorry for what happened. Gavin is my ex-boyfriend, and I don't know what he was thinking coming here and causing such a fuss. He said a whole lot of garbage. It's true I was feeling completely lost, but not that I was using you."

"You don't need to justify yourself. The reasons for your presence here are not important. You've only been here two weeks, and your help has already been so precious."

"Thank you. But I do want to say that I'm sorry. Maybe I should have told you about my parents' financial situation from the very beginning."

"And why should you have done that? If I needed that kind of information before employing a volunteer, I would have asked the question at the first interview. The money in your bank account or the bank account of your parents is none of the ASEL's business. And anyway, I had understood how things were before your ex-boyfriend came here spouting all his bitter nonsense."

My eyes widen in surprise. "How?"

"A few days after you started here, someone made a very generous donation. It wasn't difficult to work out that it was your father, even though he made absolutely no mention of it. The same surname and a bank in the south of France. It might have been pure chance, but I didn't believe it for a moment. There was also the groceries and the Christmas decorations you brought that you said came from the residents in your building. You left the receipt in the shopping cart. No average student would have been able to spend 300 euros."

"Oh…"

"And on the day we didn't receive the delivery and you went to the supermarket, we never received the invoice for the personal care products you were meant to charge to the association's account. You were the one who paid."

"I wanted to…"

"I can imagine. You do not need to feel embarrassed about your parents' financial situation."

I look down. "I made a mistake. If I had been more open, then all this drama would never have happened."

She sighs, and the sigh conveys all her kindness.

"Our customers couldn't care less whether you are rich or poor. What is important for them is not feeling alone, and that's exactly what you do each time you come here. The rest doesn't matter."

I spent all day yesterday and last night thinking about it. But I just can't imagine coming back to the association after all this.

I feel embarrassed, and things between Romeo and me are still so bad that he might decide not to come back if I stick around. He needs the ASEL, and I don't want my presence to deter him from coming.

"I've decided to stop, Elise. After the scandal Gavin caused, I don't want to make people any more uncomfortable. I don't want people to think I'm being a volunteer for the wrong reasons. And I don't want to run the risk that some people might not come… because of me. I won't be there on the 24th."

"You're wrong, Annie. We need you, and the students need you. And not just because you also gave us a magnificent Christmas wreath," she adds with a wink.

"Oh, you guessed? Was the receipt with it too?" I manage to joke weakly.

She gives me a big grin. "No, but it's exactly the sort of thing you'd do. Because you like making people happy, and if you weren't so respectful of the customers here, you'd give one hundred times more. I saw you with Radana. If you'd listened to your heart, you would have paid for her to move to a new apartment yourself and given her money. But you hate the idea that anyone might think it's a question of charity."

"That's why I didn't want to talk about my parents."

"I know."

Elise reaches out and takes my hand in hers. "I would like you to be here for Christmas Eve. It's important, for you and for all those who have followed your Secret Santa idea with excitement."

"Not everyone will be happy."

"Do you mean Romeo? He's angry, but that will pass. Just give him the time to reflect on it. And as my mom would say: 'That's his karma.' And yours is to do what your heart tells you."

I can't help it; a tear rolls down my cheek.

"What would *you* like to do?" Elise asks gently.

"I'd like to come..."

"Well, that's settled then!"

She pours herself another cup of coffee and dunks a chocolate cookie in, which she downs in one mouthful.

"Actually, are you doing anything between 6:30 and 8:30 tonight?"

"No, why?"

Elise smiles.

This was not at all what I had planned, but I go with the flow and turn up at the agreed time at Place Rihour.

Night is about to fall so everything is lit up – the arch across the entrance to Lille's Christmas village, the little chalets, the decorations along the building facades and the trees, with the Christmas lights forming a star-studded sky above our heads.

The first time you take in the sight, it's totally enchanting. And the smells! The odour of mulled wine and *croustillons* is everywhere! It feels good, and for just an instant I forget my heavy heart.

I walk down one of the little paths, looking for the little stand where Elise has said she'd meet me. It's hard to miss. There are adorable snow-white cuddly toys for sale, as well as mischievous elves with pointy ears.

Elise is already there. She decided to come and try to sell the final *papillotes*, convinced they'll sell even more quickly here than at the Halles in Wazemmes. She's managed to find a stallholder willing to share a stand, and, of course, I said I'd come and help.

It'll do me good and give me something to think about other than Romeo.

I almost wrote to him a hundred times today. I chewed my nails down to the quick, but I didn't give in. I want him to understand on his own that what the two of us experienced together goes beyond the boundaries of money and differences in background.

I'll give *him* Lady and the Tramp.

"Ah, there you go!" Elise calls out excitedly from the platform in front. "This is Tabita. She's in charge of this stand, and she's the one who makes these gorgeous soft toys."

I shake her hand warmly.

"Come around the back, I'll open up for you."

Inside it's tiny; there's barely enough room for the three of us.

The bags of *papillotes* have been arranged on the counter, next to the toys and elves. There's a big sign to attract passers-by:

AT NIGHT, WHEN YOU'RE TUCKED UP IN BED, THE TOYS AND ELVES LOVE TO EAT CHOCOLATE.
PLEASE BUY A PACKET SO THEY DON'T GET INDIGESTION!

OK, here goes!

Ten kilos of *papillotes* equals fifty 200-gram bags, and by the looks of things, everyone wants one. After only an hour we've already sold half. Elise is delighted, the customers are satisfied, and so am I! I'm even having fun. The Christmas spirit that makes people happy and carefree is working its magic on me.

I've almost stopped thinking about things, and I'm surprised to notice how enthusiastically I'm working to sell the final bags.

I'm just handing over a bag to a little cutie-pie who is barely six years old when my internal radar orders me to look up.

And there he is, not even two metres away, with three of his friends and a beer in hand. Romeo.

He sees me but acts as if I wasn't there. He even turns his back on me.

All the joy I had felt until then disappears in a puff.

Right. That's it.

He doesn't have the right to behave like that. Not after all we've shared.

Even if he is mad at me.

I picture myself leaving my spot to give him a piece of my mind.

"Are you OK?" asks Elise, who obviously hasn't spotted Romeo.

"I'm buying this bag! And I'll be back in a sec!"

I take a random bag, open it and leave the stand to join Romeo and his friends.

"Hey!" I say in a merry voice. "I'm handing out *papillotes*! If you like it, you can go and buy more at the stand just there. Here, try one."

"Cool," says one of the friends, helping himself.

I pass round the bag and finally reach Romeo, making sure to plaster a big grin on my face.

"A *papillote*?"

"No, thanks."

"You should! They're good enough to fall in love with!"

Everyone bursts out laughing, even though they have no idea who I am.

Romeo looks at me without blinking, without a smile.

He is so pigheaded!

"I will say this once and only once: I am in love with you, Romeo Payet, but I am not going to keep apologizing for the mistakes I made. So. I will be spending Christmas Eve at the association, and I hope you will be too and that you will have gotten over what happened so that we can pick things up where we left off. If you can't, too bad. But know that you will have missed out on something truly special."

And I turn on my heels under the surprised expressions of the three boys and go back to the stand, with an air of calm dignity.

The next time I look up to catch Romeo's eyes, they have gone.

Totally downcast, I get home at 9 o'clock on the dot.

I had truly hoped I'd make him react, or question himself a little more, or maybe change his mind. But clearly none of those things happened.

I keep looking at my phone, but Romeo hasn't sent a single message.

I drop my bag in the entrance hall and slump onto the couch, ready to gobble down the four last bags of *papillotes* that I bought.

But Ines comes out of her room, followed by Serena, and joins me.

"Ah, there you are! How was it?"

"Christmassy. Children and happy people everywhere."

"Oh. You haven't heard from Romeo then?"

I shake my head. Serena gives me a little smile, since of course she knows about the two of us.

"He'll come round."

"I'm not so sure about that. I saw him at the Christmas market. He clearly wasn't interested."

"He's acting."

I sigh. "Well, then he's an excellent performer. I'm starting to think I'm imagining the fact that we feel the same way about each other."

Serena sits down next to me, her long black hair falling to her waist.

"You know, Romeo didn't have much money when he first got here. Going to mainland France wasn't the greatest idea in the world, his parents had told him that, but this is where he had decided to study so he had to go through with it. To get here he had to take out a loan that was just enough for him to buy his plane ticket, buy a computer, pay the security deposit on an apartment and the first six months' rent. It wasn't long before he found himself in a terrible situation. His apartment was miserable, and the heating sucked up all his money. The first electricity bills he received used up all his savings, and the money his parents sent him wasn't enough."

Serena pauses before continuing.

"The reality, Annie, is that he was so badly off during winter that he was only eating every second day, it was so cold in his apartment he got sick all the time, and he struggled to keep up with his classes. But no one knew anything about it. He never wanted me to come and visit, so I ended up figuring this out on my own. I'm lucky enough to have parents who can pay for my studies, so I wanted to help him. But that just made him angry. He thought I pitied him, but more than that, he feels that he alone is responsible for the situation he's in. So he got a job, but that wasn't enough."

"And the ASEL?"

"It took months before he agreed to go. It was hard for him to accept that he needed help. The association acted as a guarantor so that he could change apartment. In exchange and without them asking anything of him, he made himself available whenever Elise needed it, he worked extra hours and the only thing he would accept from me was help with his studies. Annie… Romeo is fiercely proud. He fights a continual battle to stay on the same footing as everyone else and not show how much he's struggling. When he found out about your parents' financial situation, that just took him back to his own experience, his own failure, supposing there even is one."

"But it doesn't change anything for me."

"But for him it does. Because once again he feels like he's at the bottom of the ladder. You've done nothing wrong. You weren't obliged to talk about your parents. I just think that Romeo is in denial and would rather make you the villain. It makes him less vulnerable."

I look down. Her words touch a chord within me and encourage me not to give up.

Romeo has never learned how to accept a helping hand.

Except that it's not just my hand I'm offering, it's my heart.

Serena leaves me alone with my thoughts, with a lump in my throat and my eyes filling with tears.

I want to write to him. I want to tell him. I want to feel better. I want us to be together…

I pick up my phone without thinking about it.

I know I shouldn't be sending you a message and that I should be waiting for you to contact me. But I've had a dead weight in my stomach ever since Gavin, ever since you said that you and I were not meant to be. And that weight is getting heavier.

Serena explained a lot of things to me so I'm not as angry anymore. I understand you a little better, but at the same time I don't understand you at all.

You have feelings for me so why do we have to go through all this pain? This is not what life is for. Life is for living and I want to live it with you. Who cares if I have money, who cares if you have less… I want to fight for both of us, but I can't do that on my own.

I love you, Romeo, it's a simple as that. And if you love me, well, then, the rest doesn't matter…

Send me a message and tell me I'm not the only one to feel this way.

Send me a message, please.

We deserve to be happy.

I reread my message ten times, a hundred times… but I can't bring myself to send it. My heart is beating so fast… I'm scared.

Scared he won't answer. Scared to feel even more pain.

I slide my finger over the screen.

I highlight the words.

I delete them.

This sucks.

22
December

Last night I inhaled the four bags of *papillotes* I had brought back. I ate them in one go, while wrapped up in my duvet in bed watching *Love Story*. I cried the whole way through. It's the best and worst love story in the history of the world. The film is so old my mom wasn't even born when it came out, but it's at least the tenth time I've seen it. And I always end up in tears. You've got to wonder why I put myself through it.

I stretch out in my bed and push back the duvet. I feel nauseous. That'll teach me to think I have an iron-clad stomach.

As I get up, making sure I don't step on the tissues scattered over the floor, I hear some muffled music coming from Ines's bedroom. While I was barely awake, I heard Serena leave at the crack of dawn for the hospital, and Ines probably didn't go back to bed.

I can't remember when I last saw her with so much energy. Unlike me, since she's been going out with Serena, doing exercises every day, shifting the furniture in her room into three different settings, and she even went on an incredible spring-cleaning spree of the entire apartment even though winter has only just started. She goes out almost every night.

But especially, and most importantly, she seems to have decided to forget about the pressure from her boss. Knowing that she's so happy gives me at least one reason to smile.

I get my stuff ready, go into the bathroom and take a quick shower. Elise has persuaded me to stay for Christmas, so I have plenty of time now to finish the snow globe that I should have done days ago. While Ines is still in her room, I go into the kitchen and lay out all my paraphernalia so that I can take stock of what I have: one crooked tree, one broken tree I haven't had time to stick back together, and that's about it. I've got a long way to go, a very long way…

As Ines is already awake, I put on a bit of music with my phone, repair my tamarind tree and start to make a new one.

Romeo is always on my mind. I have no idea how he's going to react when I give him his gift. Maybe he won't even want it.

If that's the case, well, too bad. At least I will have done what I set out to do, and to the best of my abilities.

I roll out the clay, I create details in the leaves and branches, I model tiny fruit and flowers knowing that they're not amazing, but that at least you can pretty much identify what they're meant to be.

After two hours, I put everything on a baking tray and into the oven.

"Hey, have you been up for long?" Ines asks as she comes out of her room, seeing me dressed while she's still in her pyjamas.

"A little while. And what were you up to locked in your room?"

"I was reading! And for my own pleasure, can you believe it? That's what life post-exams is for. But now I want to see your finished project! Let's see what we have so far."

She comes over and peers through the oven window. "Not bad!"

"For someone with extremely poor eyesight."

"You're too hard on yourself. What are you doing now?" she asks, watching me roll up little balls of Fimo.

"I'm going to try and make people to put in the globe, on the beach. Romeo's family."

Even without looking at her, I can feel Ines smile. "He's really gotten under your skin, hasn't he?"

"If only he hadn't. Everything would be far less complicated."

"True. But it would be less exciting too! Hey, don't worry about it. He's going to see your snow globe and go nuts for you."

"Hmmm… It'll probably snow in the Sahara before that happens. It's not that I want to be all gloom and doom, it's just that things are not looking great."

"I wouldn't be so sure if I were you…" says Ines, but I can't help the grey clouds hanging all over me.

One hour later, I've made all my pieces and baked them. I hope Romeo won't get mad at me for this relatively unfaithful portrait of his family. They look like deranged elves who have gone through an acid bath. It's hard to see exactly what they're meant to be, but never mind, I gave it my all.

And now all I have to do is put all these little elements together.

I open the globe and apply glue to the base so that I can draw the beach and its blue shoreline. I sprinkle blue glitter on top, remove the excess by tapping on the back of the base and then do the same thing with the gold glitter for the sand. I screw the upper glass part back on just so I can see what it looks like and… disaster! It slips out of my hands and smashes into a thousand pieces on the floor.

I'm completely speechless. It feels like ice is running through my veins.

Ines runs into the kitchen.

"What just happened? Oh… you broke your snow globe!"

I feel like crying, and I guess my face gives it away. The salesperson had told me it was the last base they had, and that they wouldn't be getting any more in.

"Let's not panic," says Ines. "I have an idea."

"Which is? You're going to stick it all back together? Forget about it. This actually solves my problems, now I don't need to go to the ASEL on the 24th. When the universe says no, it means no."

"What, and leave poor Romeo without a Secret Santa while everyone else gets a gift? Don't move, I'll be right back!"

She disappears into the hallway and returns with a glass candy jar full of bits and pieces.

"I originally bought this to put positive thoughts in. I saw the idea in a magazine once for when you're feeling sad, but I never did it. You can use it."

She grabs a plastic bag and pours the contents of the candy jar inside.

"Look! It's almost the same size as your snow globe. Just turn it over and… ta-dah!" she says, putting it upside-down on the table.

I get a sceptical look on my face. The top of the jar is flat, but it's better than nothing, I guess.

"Umm… thank you."

"No worries! There's nothing like having an Ines to call on when you're stuck!"

She disappears with a laugh, leaving me to my snow globe.

It takes me most of the day, but by 3 o'clock the tropical forest, the flowers and the exotic fruits are all glued in place, the little birds are perched on their branches, the sand and sea are sparkling, the Payet family are standing together on the beach, and the glittery snow has been poured into the jar. All I need to do is turn the base upside down, slide it into the jar, screw it shut and… cross my fingers that nothing moves.

Ines is next to me. She holds her breath and so do I.

The suspense is unbearable!

One… two… three… I turn over the base, I slide it in the jar, I screw it shut and…

"Oh wow, it works!" I cry as I turn the jar onto the table. "And look, there's snow everywhere! It's really pretty!"

I mean, if you ignore the wonky decorations I made.

"Congratulations! You should open your own store. Well, maybe not one that sells portraits," Ines says, as she notices the faces on the Payet family.

I start laughing too – they look like they've been crossed with an angry hippopotamus.

"Alright Miss Rodin, I'd better go. I've still got a few things I need to do before work. Not long before my Christmas vacations start!" she says as she leaves the kitchen.

Just as she does so, the doorbell rings, surprising both of us. Normally you need to ring the intercom downstairs before being able to enter the building.

Ines goes to open the door and the voice I hear paralyses me.

"Hi. The door downstairs was open, so I came up without ringing. Is Annie here?"

Ohhhh shit, it's Romeo!

I grab the snow globe and shove it in the first place I think of: the oven!

Then I realize that if Romeo is here, it's because he wants to speak to me. I take a deep breath, pat my hair idiotically and go out to see him, ready to listen to whatever he wants to say.

"Hello!"

My tone is a little too cheerful after all we've been through, but the snow globe has been quite effective at putting me in the Christmas mood. I've lost my bearings a little.

Romeo observes me without a smile. He doesn't look all together comfortable. As the two of us look at each other in silence, Ines clears her throat.

"Well, then, I'm off! I have to go to work!"

A good hour early…

She pulls on her sneakers, grabs her bag and coat, and disappears. All that in a fraction of a second.

"Come in," I say to Romeo, pointing to the living room. "Would you like something to drink?"

"No, thank you, I've just come to speak to you."

My heart is racing at a million miles an hour.

I sit down on the couch so he can sit next to me, but he chooses the armchair opposite, leaving a generous metre between us.

Breathe, Annette, breathe.

"I'm listening."

He nods, looking unsure about what to say before he begins speaking slowly. "I'm sorry I reacted so badly. Of course you didn't have to tell anyone about your parents' financial situation. Not even me. I overreacted and that was stupid."

My first reaction is to heave a great sigh of relief, but Romeo doesn't seem to have finished, so I remain calm and just nod my head.

"You did nothing wrong," he goes on, "and I think if I had been in your shoes, I would have done the same thing. I would have preferred you told me straightaway, but you made the right decision. And in case you're worried about the others, I think the students at the association feel the same way."

"Yes, Elise reassured me about that. I truly did not want to hurt anyone, even though Gavin had warned me I might. I just never thought he would be the person to tell everyone."

"He's an asshole."

"I didn't think he'd ever do something like that."

Once again we lapse into silence, but I want to clarify an important point.

"I'm sorry I didn't tell you right away. You thought it was a question of trust, but I was just afraid that people wouldn't understand why I wanted to volunteer. You and I don't know each other very well yet, and I didn't know how to go about it or how you would react."

"Yeah, I get that, it figures," says Romeo.

So why does he still seem so tense? Why does talking to me not take a weight off his mind?

"I hope you'll still keep working at the ASEL. We need people like you."

"And do you count yourself among the 'we'?"

"Yes, I'm a low-income student," he replies with a detached air.

This isn't looking good…

"Yes, but what about just the plain student, what does he think?"

Romeo's jaw tightens. And so does mine. I don't like this.

"You and I, we can't keep seeing each other," he says forcefully.

My heart misses a beat, but I try and keep control of myself.

"And why is that? What is there to stop us?"

"Everything, Annette. When I first met you, I wondered what you saw in a guy like Gavin. Now that I know, I wonder what you see in a guy like me."

"A guy like you?"

"You're a multimillionaire."

"My parents are, not me."

"OK, your parents are multimillionaires, and I have absolutely no money. Imagine what that would look like.

You want to go out, do an activity, go away for a weekend, anything, and I can't. I can't afford things, so you pay. I'm struggling, so you'd want to help me, you wouldn't want to leave me in the lurch. But I have a sense of dignity, Annie, I just can't do it."

I swallow.

"I understand, you have a sense of dignity, and I respect that, but do you have feelings for me? Yes or no?"

He doesn't answer.

"You know, all you have to do is say that you don't feel the same way as I do, and we can stop right there."

"But that's the problem…" he whispers.

My heart is going to explode. Why is he doing this to us?

"I have feelings for you, but I want you to forget about me. We're not compatible, it would never work."

I leap up, disgusted by what I'm hearing.

"Says who? Who decided that people in love have to be exactly the same and have the same background? Shall we do a remake of *Love Story*? I call my parents and tell them I don't want to inherit anything, that I'd rather manage on my own because I fell in love with a guy who can't accept that I come from a wealthy family? If I do that, then will we be compatible?"

He gets up in turn. "You're refusing to understand."

"Because it's crazy, Romeo! You and I are a perfect match. You want us to avoid situations where people could tell I have money? OK. That I make sure we're on an even footing in that respect? OK. Anything is possible."

He shakes his head.

"You can try all you want, but you could never renounce who you are or where you come from."

"So what does that mean? We say good-bye and we meet up again in twenty or thirty years when you have a great job and you're not ashamed of your bank account? I've never heard anything so ridiculous in my life. You're falling victim to your own foolish pride, and you don't even realize it. If we love each other, nothing else matters. And I love you, that's for sure, and all the money in the world has nothing to do with it."

"For now. But one day you'd be sad you didn't have the same lifestyle as before or that you were with someone who has be careful with money. Because I'll never be rich, Annie, and I do not want to be dependent on anyone. Ever."

"I understand that, but we can work at it! And can I also say it's a bit soon to be thinking about our future life together as a couple? You have no idea what the future holds or what it might bring, for you or for me. So why don't we start by trusting one another?"

He gives me a humourless smile. "You're such an optimist."

I shake my head. "Optimism has nothing to do with it." Not knowing what else to do, I take his hand. "Romeo…"

He doesn't give an inch. He's not going to change his mind; I can read it in his eyes.

I'm so bewildered by the situation that I'm this close to crying. But there's no way I'm going to do that.

He's proud? Well, I am too.

I unlace my fingers from his. I have to bring this conversation to an end. It's too painful.

"OK. I'm not going to fight anymore. But don't count on me to forget what we had between us."

"I won't be forgetting anything…" he murmurs.

And that's worst of all. I would rather he didn't care. It would be so much easier.

There is a long moment of an all-consuming silence during which we both seem to be waiting for something from the other – a word, a gesture.

But although our bodies and hearts are crying out for the other, neither of us takes a step.

Romeo looks at the door. "I should go. My shift starts at 4:30."

"OK. I guess we'll still see each other on the 24th?"

To give you a gift into which I poured all my feelings. And that is so ugly that no one would ever suspect a multimillionaire heiress had made it, so you should be happy about that.

He nods.

"Yup, see you on Saturday. And once again, I'm really sorry."

"Not as much as me. See you on Saturday."

My voice is brusque. I want to cry, and I think Romeo can tell. He lifts his hand as if to touch my cheek, then changes his mind.

My breath comes faster, I want to hold him back; I don't want him to leave.

But I close the door quietly behind him and lean against the frame.

I thought I would burst into tears, but I can't even do that.

Why not? Because apart from holding my head high, I don't know what else to do.

I think of my mother and all she has accomplished. Of my father and his unwavering support. Of where they both are today and of all the energy they have expended to get there. I imagine telling them what has happened and them replying that mountains are rarely steep on all sides; you just have to find out which side you should start from in order to scale them.

Unfortunately, for the time being, all the access points seem blocked. And knowing that Romeo has feelings for me too makes it even worse.

I would rather he hadn't told me.

I go and collect the fake snow globe from the oven and stare at it as if studying the heavens in the hopes of seeing a shooting star and making a wish.

If only it could do something to change the way things are.

23
December

Going to bed early and getting up early can sometimes be a good thing. Last night I shut myself in my room with Netflix, a TV dinner, and the desire to forget that everything is falling apart right now. And it worked. I binge-watched a series, emptied my mind and fell asleep so quickly that I didn't even hear Ines get back.

Wrapped up in my duvet, I look at my phone automatically and frown when I see there's no message from Romeo. Not that I was expecting him to send one, but I was still holding onto a glimmer of hope.

Never mind. I refuse to mope around any longer. It's time to forge ahead!

I leave my room reluctantly. Walking along the long hall, I come to a sudden halt at the opening into the living room.

Ines is up too and is sitting on the couch in her panda pyjamas ripping up dozens of pieces of paper and making a pile out of them on the coffee table.

"What are you doing?"

"I'm trying to calm down."

Despite her explanation, I still don't understand what she's doing.

"Did you have a bad night?"

"Bad night, bad evening. But the time has come to take back control!"

"Do you want to talk about it?"

"First things first, I need coffee!"

I follow her into the kitchen gladly. There's nothing like a good breakfast when you're feeling down in the dumps first thing in the morning.

Ines looks after the coffee machine, and I toast some slices of bread. Then we sit at the table.

"So?" I ask, just as she has her mouth full.

Her reply is barely comprehensible.

"Pished ush off sho much!"

"Um, OK, who was that?"

"My boss! I dunno if it's the Christmas vacation coming up that put him in such a state, but he was unbearable! Yesterday he said that we must have got our child-care certificates off the back of a Bonux packet. I don't even know what Bonux is."

"It's a really old brand of laundry detergent that dates from like pre-historic times."

"Oh, that figures. He's only one step removed from a caveman himself. Anyway, we wanted to make Christmas flowers out of crepe paper and so we went online to look for photos of real poinsettia to show the children. And he arrived at exactly the same time and went totally berserk. We shouldn't be showing them how to access the internet, blah blah blah, there might be X-rated pop-ups, blah blah blah, their parents might file a complaint. Honestly it was such a drama, even worse than those Korean television shows!"

"Really? At least it sounds like this time he wasn't just laying into you."

"Yeah, he yelled at all of us! So we stopped that and decided to make Christmas-themed fans. And then he says it's too gendered and that the fathers might get upset. What the actual…?!"

When Ines gets into a mood like this I almost want to laugh, but I don't because I can see she's really upset.

"So, what did you end up making?"

She wrinkles her nose. "Christmas cards. The guy was born a lamebrain and will die a lamebrain, that's for sure."

"And so that's why you're tearing up bits of paper?"

"Yeah, otherwise I'm going to go berserk too. Today's the last day before the vacation, and I can just tell he's going to be even more infuriating than usual. So I'm thinking I'd better exorcize all my rage now, before I go back there."

Exorcize her rage with pieces of paper? Really?

"You wanna know what else?" she continues. "The more time I spend with girls, the more I realize how useless guys are."

I smile. Ines loves to generalize.

"Anyway, tell me about you and Romeo. What did he want last night? To get back together?"

"Um, no, not exactly."

I tell her everything, and the more I explain, the greater her look of surprise.

"I mean, sorry, I really like Romeo, but what the hell is he thinking? What was it about yesterday? Was it Jackass Day or something?"

I giggle. Talking with Ines always makes me feel better.

"You know what," she goes on. "Let's exorcize together!"

"By ripping up bits of paper? That's nice of you, but I don't think it's going to solve any of my problems."

"It's not meant to solve them. It allows you to confront them. Come on, let's try!"

She gets up and charges into the living room. I follow her, curious but also baffled.

"Sit here next to me. You'll see, it's so liberating!"

On her left there is a metal trash can with little flower-shaped holes around the upper edge. She picks it up and puts it on the coffee table.

"What are you up to?"

"We're going to cast a spell on everyone who's pissed us off, you'll see!"

"Cast a spell?"

I wonder if she's starting to lose it…

Next, she picks up a torn piece of paper and writes something down on it.

"Your turn!"

"Um, what am I supposed to write?"

"How come you don't know about this, Annette Reynaud?! You write down something that annoys you about Romeo! For example: 'I hate it when Romeo asks Serena to hang out at his house, when actually my friend Ines wanted her to come here.'"

I laugh again, but I'm still kind of confused. Wherever does she find these outlandish rituals?

"And don't forget to write down things about Gavin too! We'll be able to get three birds with one stone!"

I have no idea where this is going, but I play along and write down whatever pops into my head.

Ines gets up, goes into the kitchen and comes back with a box of matches.

"Right, time to get down to business."

"Are we going to burn them?"

"You got it!"

"Shouldn't we get rid of what's already in there first?" I suggest, noticing that the trash can is far from empty.

Setting the apartment on fire, that's just what we need.

"Nah, don't worry! The spell only works if you hold the paper for as long as you can between your fingers. By the time you drop it, there are no flames left! I'll start. My boss has the IQ of a steamed mussel!"

Then she lights a match and burns her first piece of paper.

"You don't think it'd be safer if we did this over the bathtub?"

"Naaaaah! The trash can is a symbol. You throw whatever you want to get rid of inside it. Get it?"

I take a bit of paper and read it aloud before setting it on fire.

"Romeo is stupid!"

The paper burns, I let it go, and the ash falls into the trash can.

Ines starts again.

"My boss is an *aghyul*!"

"A what?"

"It means 'donkey' in Kabyle. Right, your turn, keep it moving, go go go!"

"Gavin has a tiny…"

I mark a brief pause and watch as Ines gets an astonished look on her face.

"… brain!" I finish with a laugh.

The paper burns up.

"My boss thinks he's a Ferrari, but really he's a plastic tricycle!" continues Ines.

I'm snorting with laughter!

"Gavin is a self-centred jerk."

"My boss's breath stinks!"

"My turn! Romeo threw all the chestnut skins from his bag on people!"

I say it with conviction while burning the paper, but Ines stops and looks at me with a raised eyebrow.

"What was that pathetic one?"

"The truth."

"And that's the worst thing you can think of to say about him? At least try and come up with a good insult if you don't know what to say!"

I shrug my shoulders. Yeah, that one was kind of average.

"You're far too nice. Wait, I'll show you how it's done."

She picks up a piece of paper, writes something down and reads it out loud before burning it.

"Romeo, you're an ignoramus, and your mom drinks water out of puddles! Your turn!"

I'm so taken by surprise I nearly choke on my saliva as I laugh.

I write down the first thing that comes to mind and read it out.

"Um… Romeo, I want to dunk your head in the sink!"

Ines raises an eyebrow.

"You really can't do any better than that? Go on, make an effort."

I think quickly and scribble down something else. And then another. Great, I have two up my sleeve!

"Gavin, your ears are like giant slippers!"

This time it's Ines that cracks up. It feels like the stupider the things we write down, the more we let off pressure. So much so that Ines, who has just lit a match, doesn't have time to fully burn her paper before dropping it into the trash can. I don't know exactly what was in there, but an enormous flame shoots into the air, making us jump back.

"Oh, shit!" I cry, as I try and put it out with the first thing to hand: a scarf Ines uses to tie back her hair, which is lying on the back of the couch.

Extremely bad idea: the material goes up in flames instantly, and the fire gets even bigger. There is so much smoke that the detectors in the apartment start to go off.

"Open the window," I yell at Ines.

Another bad idea: the draught fans the flame in the trash can. We're going to burn the whole apartment down!

I run into the kitchen, fill up a glass of water, wet a dish towel and throw it in the burning trash can. The fire goes out, leaving only thick black smoke. The living room is enveloped in a dense cloud, the fire alarm is screeching non-stop, and our neighbour is knocking at the door as hard as he can.

"Open up, it's Mr. Duriez! I can see smoke coming out your window, is everything OK? Open up!"

Ines and I look at each other in shock, then dissolve into laughter and can't seem to stop. We didn't even burn half of our pieces of paper, and we nearly set fire to our apartment, but I don't think we've ever laughed so much in our lives. And I bet that right now she's forgotten all about her boss, just like I've managed to forget that Romeo is an *aghyul.*

"I'm calling the fire department!" shouts Mr. Duriez.

We open the door in our pyjamas, tears running down our cheeks and our hair in a mess. I'm practically hiccupping as I see Mr. Duriez, frozen in shock in the stairwell, as well as our two downstairs neighbours standing there in slippers and bathrobes. I wouldn't have thought it possible, but they almost look worse than us.

"Everything is fine," I reassure them. "We just had a tiny issue with a fire in a trash can that we've managed to put out."

They look at each other, unconvinced.

"Are you sure?" asks one of the neighbours.

"I just put the trash can in the bathtub," says Ines.

"Sorry we disturbed you! Have a nice day!"

I close the door behind me, and of course, we immediately start laughing again. Except that the sight of the apartment quickly brings us back down to earth. The ceiling is black with soot, the metal bucket has left a big ring on the wood of the coffee table, and ash has settled over the whole living room.

Ines and I look at each other, crestfallen.

I guess we should start cleaning.

"Your parents will never believe this," says Ines, looking up at the ceiling covered in black soot. "Do you think your insurance will cover it?"

"No, I don't think so. But I can get someone in to paint over it and we won't tell anyone."

"That'll cost a fortune."

She gives me a sideways look and then understands.

"Oh no, you're not paying for this on your own! It's my fault too!"

"OK, then we'll do it ourselves. But I'm warning you, it might not be such a great idea to entrust me with a paint brush."

She giggles.

"It can't be any worse than you and Fimo clay!"

"Hey, take that back, you brat!"

Ines drops onto the couch and closes her eyes. "You know what? This is going to be the best of all my university years, I can tell."

"No way, for you they've only just started."

She opens her eyes and narrows them at me.

"But not for you? That's it, you've decided to drop out?"

I sigh. The kind of sigh that means everything and nothing.

"No… No, I'm not going to stop."

"Woohoo!" yells Ines.

I can't help laughing again. "Don't get too excited, I might have to do extra classes to make up my credits, and I'm scared I'll get so discouraged that I'll change my mind again!"

"No, I don't think so. If you fail an exam, you can just redo it."

"I've been thinking. Sociology isn't necessarily for me, you know, but I'm sure that social development and improving the well-being of each and every person is. Because I want to take care of others and help people get through tough times. You were right about the association."

Ines smiles. "I'm always right! So, what are you going to do?"

"Change my classes and pick a new major as soon as I can."

"I'm really glad to hear that. And I believe in you, you doofus, so come and give me a hug." She opens her arms, and I open mine.

We give each other a good, long hug, then Ines starts giving me little pats on the back like you do when you're consoling a child.

"How are you feeling about the whole Romeo thing?"

I pout. "Like a strawberry tart."

Ines steps back to better look at me.

"Pardon me?"

"Yeah, a strawberry tart that's so expensive that even though you really want it, you leave it in the store, because you don't have the money to buy it."

Ines huffs out a breath of air. "He'll never keep this up. Tomorrow, he'll give in, you'll see."

I shrug, desperately wanting to change the subject. "Why don't you tell me about Serena and you? I've been so focused on myself, I haven't even asked you how happy you are."

Ines smiles. "OK, but first of all, I'd just like to say that you're an incredible strawberry tart, and if I wasn't already in love, well… I'd buy you!"

I give a snort of laughter. “Liar! You’ve never been interested in me!”

“True, but I’m saying it anyway.”

I smile. “Go on, tell me all about the two of you.”

Ines pretends to swoon. “I just adore her! We get on so well. It’s as if I’ve finally found the person I’ve always been looking for. She makes me laugh, she’s generous, she’s patient.”

“One in a million.”

“Yup. It’s weird, the first time we… you know what I mean!”

“Yes, I know!”

Ines closes her eyes. It’s as if she’s been transported back again. “It’s weird because I’ve only ever been with guys, but with her it was so natural that I thought ‘Wow, I’m so lucky to have met her.’ I’ve never felt so free, Annie. It feels like she and I were destined to meet, that we could have been doing anything or living anywhere, and we still would have ended up meeting.”

“Oh, that’s true love… It sounds like a dream.”

She reaches out a hand and strokes my cheek with the tips of her fingers.

“I know you’re hurting, but I’m hoping that things work out in the same way for you.”

“Thank you.”

“You know what?” Ines says suddenly in a cheerful voice. “We’re planning on going to Réunion together!”

“Really?”

“Yes! Serena wants to introduce me to her family.”

I try to suppress a sigh. Obviously I'm excited for her, but I still feel a little pang. I would really like to be in her shoes.

"I'm so happy for you."

"And I'm happy for you too!" she replies.

"Um… and why is that?"

"Because we're all going to go to Réunion together, the four of us, of course!"

I laugh out loud. That'll be the day…

"Things would have to change quite a bit for that to happen, and I'm not sure they will. But I would love to."

"So think positive thoughts. PO-SI-TIVE! Should we start another trash can fire?"

I throw my arms in the air. "No way!"

"Not even just a tiny one?"

I shake my head, but I'm smiling. "And are you going to talk to your parents about Serena? Will you tell them you're in love with her?"

A shadow falls over her beautiful face. "Would you believe me if I said I was worried about their reaction? And about my brother's reaction?"

"They wouldn't be happy for you?"

"I don't know, we've never talked about it. I guess it's up to me to reassure them."

"Your parents have always supported you one hundred percent. And your brother adores you. No one has ever tried to make things difficult for you, quite the opposite. I'm sure the day you decide you want to tell them, they won't judge you. They'll be happy for you."

"And if they aren't?"

"PO-SI-TIVE," I mimic her. "Think positive thoughts! Should we start another trash can fire?"

I make her laugh at least, and right now, that's the most important thing.

"Another hug?" she asks, opening her arms wide.

I grab her tightly without hesitating.

In some ways I don't feel as lost as I did three weeks ago, but in others I feel a thousand times more lost. But despite the uncertainty and the sombre moments, there is one thing I know for sure: my friendship with Ines will last a lifetime.

In only a short time, she has become the best friend I've ever had. And even though in the past few days I've spent so much time thinking my brain has nearly turned to mush, my soul has been crushed by heartbreak, and today my ceiling nearly went up in flames, I know we will always be able to count on each other.

Apparently everything eventually falls into place if you have good friends, and you place your trust in the world.

Ines has faith in my future, and I have faith in her.

24
December

"Ready for your first Christmas without us?" asks Mom.

She's being a touch dramatic, but I smile. "I am. And what about you? Are you ready for your first Christmas in a freezing cold hotel room in Lapland?"

Because that's where my parents have ended up: an igloo hotel right in the heart of Swedish Lapland, which is where she's calling me from. To be honest, I'm quite happy to be here and not there!

"It's glacial!" she tells me, as if it were some big surprise. I can see that she's bundled up in a three-layer puffer jacket. "Actually, your father's in a natural hot spring as we speak. I refused point blank to get in because I would have had to get undressed. What on earth possessed me to come here…"

I start to laugh. "Bring me back some icicles as a souvenir!"

"Ha ha! Very funny. Anyway, how is your Christmas Eve among strangers shaping up? Are you dressed already?"

I sit my phone on my desk, get up and step back a little to show her my outfit. I'm actually very proud of it, but I didn't consider the fact that Mom might not like it. She widens her eyes, a little horrified.

"Umm… what in the name is that?"

"This evening's dress code!"

"Ah. It's… original."

It sure is! My red wool-knit dress, with its delicate stitches and thick rollneck, falls to mid-thigh, the perfect length for the sparkly green opaque tights I chose. But the showstopper is elsewhere… right between my breasts: an adorable plushie dog's head that looks as if it's emerging from my chest. A brown-and-white chihuahua wearing diamante green Christmas glasses, a reindeer headband topped with two Santa Claus mittens, a bell that tinkles when I walk and a white sweater with candy canes on it.

The height of simplicity!

Mom is appalled, but I love it.

"Well, if you think you know what you're doing…"

"I sure do!"

Could she be any more dubious? I almost laugh.

"Will Gavin be there?" she finally says.

I sigh. I haven't even talked about our break-up with my parents. Mom has no idea of the troubles I've had these past few weeks.

"We broke up," I say, taking a seat. "It was my idea."

"I see. Well, I'm not surprised, to be honest. I thought something was up. Is there another boy on the scene?"

My mother, with her insight and direct questions! But I don't want to lie to her, especially because even though yesterday I was totally euphoric, today I have a leaden feeling in my stomach. I'm worried about how the evening will go and scared that Romeo won't change his mind about us. So I let it all out and tell Mom what I've been through lately. Although she said she wasn't surprised by my break-up with

Gavin, I can see she's a still bit taken aback, but she listens without interrupting. When I finish, she smiles, and despite the telephone screen between us, I can still feel her love. It does me a world of good.

"You're going to go out this evening with your snow globe, your courage and the knowledge that Romeo is going to fall right into your arms."

"Are you going to put a spell on him?" I joke.

"No, I don't even need to, because you are the most intelligent, most interesting, most beautiful and most stubborn girl he's ever met. Ah! It looks like your father is done with his turn. He's as red as a lobster! He wants to quickly say hello. Have a wonderful Christmas Eve, darling."

My mother's face gives way to that of my father, dressed in a bathrobe. He does look as if he's gotten some colour!

"Merry Christmas, sweetie. I can't talk for long, my toes are already frozen! Don't forget to go and get your Christmas present on Monday, your mom and I have sent you a little something."

"Thank you, Dad, and Merry Christmas to you too. I love you both so much."

"And we love you too," calls out Mom from her frozen room.

I hang up, my heart full of love for my caring and supportive parents.

"It's almost 9, are you ready?" asks Ines, poking her head into my room.

I'm dressed and wearing a little make-up with my hair in a messy bun. My heart feels full enough to burst, and the snow globe is all wrapped up – in ten or so sheets of white paper, seeing as how I didn't have any proper wrapping paper – and enclosed inside a hideously ugly paper pouch with Christmas trees on it that I found somewhere.

Everything is pretty much ready, so, yes, we can go.

When we get to the association, extra Christmas decorations have been added to the window and main entrance, with lots of little multicoloured lights flashing as if inviting us to come inside to a safe place. As least, that's how I choose to interpret it. It reassures me.

Serena is supposed to be coming with Romeo. They might already be here. My heartbeat speeds up as we climb the stairs to the common room, but the first thing I notice when we go in is the warm and welcoming Christmas atmosphere. Everyone is smiling, having a drink and wearing such an ugly sweater I can't decide whose is the worst.

"Now I'm jealous of your dress," whispers Ines in my ear. "I'm the one who stands out."

"But only a bit!" I tease her.

She had only been brave enough to wear the reindeer headband I brought back from the association, even though I had told her about the theme!

"Wait, I have an idea," I say. "Don't move!"

On the wall there are fake holly wreaths with lots of tiny elves and snowman figurines amongst them. I pinch a few and eye up the little nest formed by Ines's hair gathered up in a bun. She sees me coming and backs off.

"Hey, hey, hey. I'm not a Christmas cake, you know."

"Let me work my magic, I'm going to make you ugly. Although, I would have had to start a while ago for that!"

But in the end, it looks really cute. I take a little string of coloured lights and drape it around her neck.

"There we go, now you look perfect."

And, of course, I have to get out my phone and take a selfie to immortalize the two of us in our outrageous outfits. With me poking my tongue out and Ines doing a bratty pout face.

"Look at the two of you!" laughs Anthony as he comes in. "Go and grab a drink and have something to eat."

I quickly cast my eye around the room: no sign of Serena and Romeo. Phew, I still have a few moments' respite. Argh, I'm such a scaredy-cat.

But I have only just picked up my glass of sparkling wine when Ines nudges me with her elbow. Romeo is here. As soon as I see him, I get totally flustered and realize that I haven't even put his gift under the tree. It's still in my tote bag.

"Ah, now I don't feel so alone," says Ines. "Romeo's not wearing an ugly sweater either."

Or just barely… On his black sweater I make out a tiny Santa Claus next to his heart.

Romeo looks at me from head to toe and smiles at me. Meanwhile my legs are like jelly. Then he turns his back on me intentionally, and my eyes widen.

Right in the middle on his back are the words:

I'm Santa Claus and you know it.
Make a wish.

"Huh!" says Ines, "If that doesn't tell you all you need to know!"

"You think that's for me?"

"No, it's for your mother!" she hoots. "Who else would it be for? I'll let you reflect on that for a bit. I'm going to see Serena."

Fine. Do I get excited or not?

I want to believe he's wearing this sweater just for me, so I can make a wish hoping that everything will work out between us and my wish will be granted... but I'm going to play it safe, just in case.

"Now that everyone is here," announces Elise, walking to the centre of the room, "we can start the Secret Santa. This wine is so good, if we wait too long the presents might get mixed up!"

Laughter rings out among the students.

Just then, Romeo heads towards me, gives me a wink and puts a tiny gift beneath the tree. Then he goes back to where he was, as cool as can be.

I swallow.

"As Annie was the one to come up with this excellent idea, I think she should be the one to tell us what to do next. Annie, over to you!"

I join Elise in the middle of the room, feeling a little intimidated as I haven't seen any of the students since the Gavin debacle. But despite being worried stiff, I can see that not a single person seems to be looking at me funny. They're even smiling, which makes me feel slightly more relaxed.

"Um… hi, everyone. And first of all, thank you for having played the game. It's really cool to see all these gifts. And by the look of the wrapping paper, I'm not the only one to have two left hands!"

A ripple of laughter runs around the room.

"If it's OK with you, I'd like to start with the girls. In theory, each gift should have the name of the person it's for and who it's from. Let's go!"

Thanks to my carefully calculated approach, whereby the girls open their gifts while the boys look for theirs, no one will notice me giving mine to Romeo and then dropping dead in anticipation while I wait for him to react.

I go with the girls to look for my gift. It's a large envelope from Radana's housemate Thea, who's studying fine arts. She looks at me expectantly, so I open it right then and there.

I rip open the envelope and pull out a sheet of art paper with a portrait of me. I gape at it and then at her. We haven't spent that much time together and yet the way she's captured me is incredible.

I thank her from the bottom of my heart, and tell her how touched I am and that I can't wait to get it framed.

Radana receives a recycled candle and Thea some potpourri made with cinnamon sticks, cloves and star anise. But it's Elise who hits the jackpot: Romeo's gift. He has made a strange, unidentifiable animal out of a painted matchbox with matches for feet that he has baptized the 'best-ever ring box.' It's pretty hideous, but I refrain from commenting as it's about the same level as my snow globe.

I glance over at Serena and Ines and guess that they must have given each other their gifts privately, out of sight of prying eyes. They seem so in love.

I smile and get back to the subject at hand. The boys are waiting.

I look over at Romeo when I announce that it's their turn. I can't make out what he's thinking or what will happen once he opens his gift. All I know is that a malevolent being has taken over my insides and is delighting in setting them alight. I have never been so stressed in all my life.

I grab his gift and retreat to the stairs I fell down with Radana. Leaning against the wall, I can see everything that's going on.

Anthony, Romeo, Ionut and Kowè all go to the Christmas tree, and of course there are only three gifts left. Obviously Romeo draws a blank, so he looks around to check who hasn't done their job properly, only to settle on me. I'm holding the present in my hands, inside that awful green pouch with the trees on it. He shakes his head with a smile, only half-surprised.

He comes over slowly, without having the slightest notion of what he's doing to my heart rate. Unless, of course, he knows exactly what he's doing.

I move back to the landing between the two floors, just out of sight. Romeo joins me and in this cramped little space, it feels like he's taking up all the room.

"So… you're my Secret Santa."

"You didn't guess?"

He shakes his head.

"Not at all."

I try to run my hands through my hair, then realize I have a bun and shift a little awkwardly on the spot, not sure how to handle the nervousness inside me.

"So, here it is. Merry Christmas."

As he takes it, our fingers touch. Instead of removing his hand, Romeo leans forward and places a light kiss on my cheek. I have to tamp down a shiver of pleasure.

"Thank you."

"I'm not very good at crafts, so…"

He pulls the package out of the pouch, unwraps the layers of paper protecting it and looks at the snow globe, totally dumbstruck.

"Because you miss your island and you love the snow, I wanted to put both of them into a jar so they can always be near you."

He doesn't say a word, but inspects every detail carefully, until finally, he tips it upside down and watches the white flakes fall gently inside.

"Did… did you make it?"

"Yes. That's why it's a little ramshackle."

"No, it's amazing, Annie. I'm really touched."

Romeo places the globe on the stairs and reaches his hand out to caress my face. A slow caress that crosses my cheek, my jaw and the corner of my mouth. I close my lips, on the brink of an explosion.

"I'm not going to be able to do it, you know…" he says.

"Do what?"

His gaze is so tender.

"Go without you."

"Well, no one is forcing you to, especially not me."

"Especially not you."

Then he leans down towards me, making my heart race. He's about to kiss me…

But suddenly, he stops and stands up straight again.

"I do have one problem with this wonderful Christmas snow globe."

"Oh?"

"Someone is missing."

I try to understand and say the first thing that pops into my head. "Oh… A dog? Do you have a dog?"

He bursts out laughing. "No, I don't have a dog."

He pauses a second. "It's you. Because when I go back to Réunion, you will be with me, and I'm going to introduce you to my family."

"Oh, Romeo…"

He smiles at me, leans over again and finally places his lips on mine. Gently at first, then with a kiss that devours the both of us, like a promise to never let ourselves be separated again.

With our foreheads touching, we catch our breath.

Romeo pulls back, digs into his pocket and pulls out something wrapped in a piece of white tissue paper.

"What is it?"

"A gift for you."

I smile, happier than I have ever been.

I unwrap the tissue carefully and discover the sweetest shell you could imagine. It is white, dotted with pink and in the shape of a heart.

"It's a heart cockle I found washed up on Manapany Beach."

"It's gorgeous."

"We can go looking for them together."

I think my smile speaks louder than words.

Manapany Beach, Lille, it doesn't matter where: as long as it's with him.

I hold him tightly, and he wraps his arms around me. I close my eyes.

"OK, lovers, how long is this going to last?" Ines interrupts us. "We're waiting for you before we start eating!"

Romeo and I look at each and laugh, then go back into the common room, hand in hand. The table is laid. It looks simple and welcoming. Candles are lit and gold stars are sprinkled across the tablecloth. Everyone is sitting around the table, talking, laughing and clinking glasses. It's as if for a brief moment in time, all the troubles in the world have been forgotten. The food market no longer exists, and day-to-day needs no longer bother us. All that remains is our shared friendship.

I don't sit down immediately. I pull Romeo over to the Christmas tree standing proudly in front of the window, while outside it starts to snow, with huge, fat flakes falling and blanketing the city.

We exchange glances and look down onto the street. As I lay my head against his shoulder, I think back over all I've experienced in the past twenty-four days.

The best days leading up to Christmas I've ever experienced.

No matter what the future holds, whether I'm rich or poor, I know that everything I've been looking for is right here, right now.

That's the magic of Christmas.

Oh, I almost forgot the most important thing…

All I want for Christmas is youhhhouuuuuuuuuu!

To you, my dear readers,

There is one thing I've been wondering ever since *A Heart for Christmas*… Are you really able to only read "one chapter a day" until December 24?

Because there is no way that I could! Well, I guess if… no, I definitely couldn't. Especially after what happens at the end of Chapter 19, just saying…

And I can hear you from here: those in Team "Yeeeeess!" and those in Team "Noooooo!" But do you know what? It doesn't even matter. What matters for me is that you enjoy every moment of Romeo and Annette's romance, in every way possible, and that the magic of Christmas can be felt on every line.

As you read, I'll be accompanying you on your journey, never too far away. I can't wait until you are all reading the same story, at the same time, wherever you might be.

Because that is also magical.

So, a little ahead of time, I wish you a moment of pure reading pleasure, a Merry Christmas and (pretty much) all your heart desires.

Much love,

Sophie Jomain

An Advent novel for every age group!

My first
ADVENT NOVEL

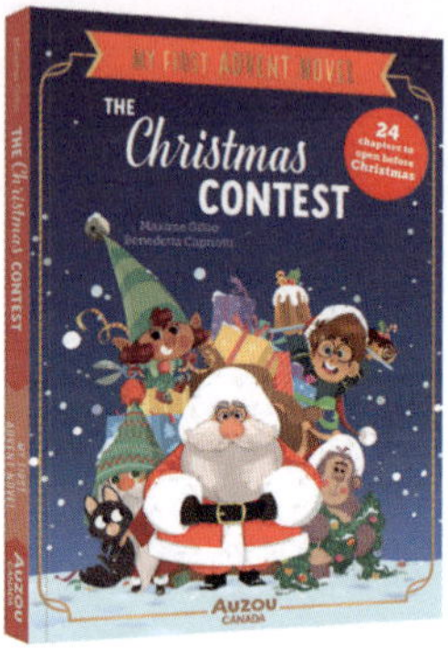

ADVENT NOVEL

ADVENT MYSTERY

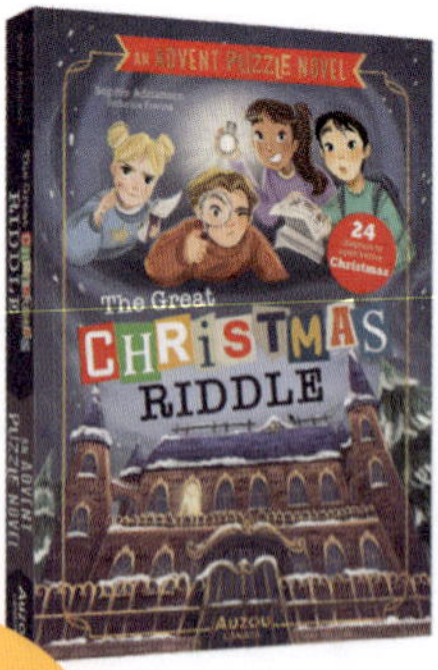

Includes riddles to solve!

ADVENT ROMANCE

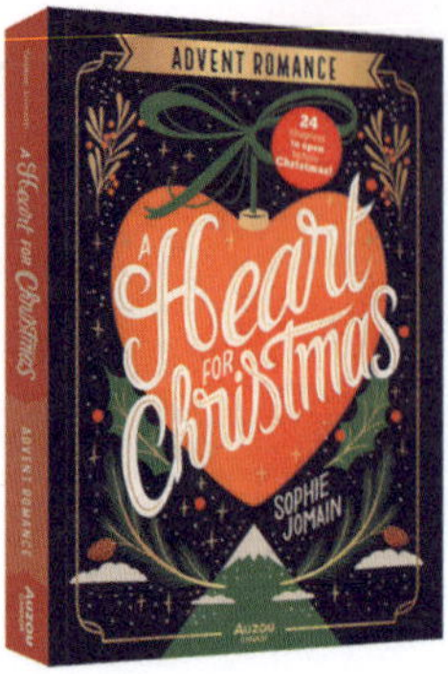